Little Eden

Book Two

A Magic Book opens the heart and expands the mind.

For my sister

KT King lives in England & has suffered with Chronic Fatigue Syndrome (CFS/ME) for over 25 years. A healer, psychic and ascension coach she has put her life experiences into fiction & created Little Eden as an escape place for the kind hearted & curious!

ISBN: 978-1-9164296-2-8
Little Eden - Another Magic Book

KT KING

Little Eden

Book Two

Another Magic Book

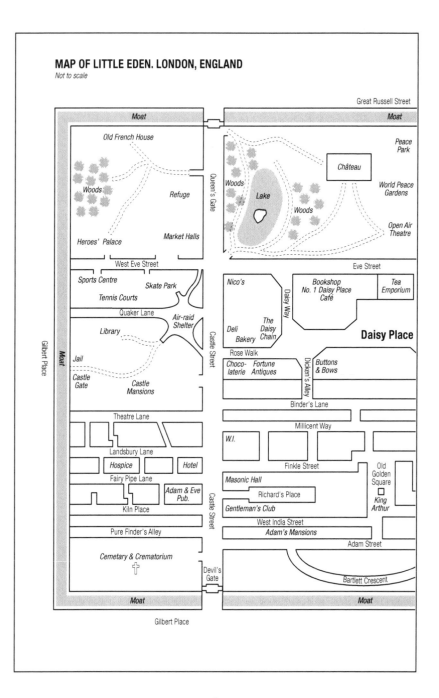

MAP OF LITTLE EDEN. LONDON, ENGLAND
Not to scale

Great Russell Street

Moat — Moat

Old French House

Peace Park

Château

Woods

Woods

Refuge

Lake

World Peace Gardens

Queen's Gate

Woods

Open Air Theatre

Heroes' Palace

Market Halls

West Eve Street

Eve Street

Sports Centre

Skate Park

Tennis Courts

Nico's

Bookshop No. 1 Daisy Place Café

Tea Emporium

Daisy Way

Quaker Lane

Air-raid Shelter

Library

Deli Bakery

The Daisy Chain

Daisy Place

Jail

Castle Street

Rose Walk

Choco-laterie

Fortune Antiques

Buttons & Bows

Gilbert Place

Moat

Castle Gate

Castle Mansions

Dicken's Alley

Binder's Lane

Theatre Lane

Millicent Way

Landsbury Lane

W.I.

Hospice

Hotel

Finkle Street

Old Golden Square

Fairy Pipe Lane

Masonic Hall

King Arthur

Adam & Eve Pub.

Richard's Place

Kiln Place

Castle Street

Gentleman's Club

West India Street

Pure Finder's Alley

Adam's Mansions

Adam Street

Cemetary & Crematorium
✝

Devil's Gate

Bartlett Crescent

Moat

Moat

Gilbert Place

4

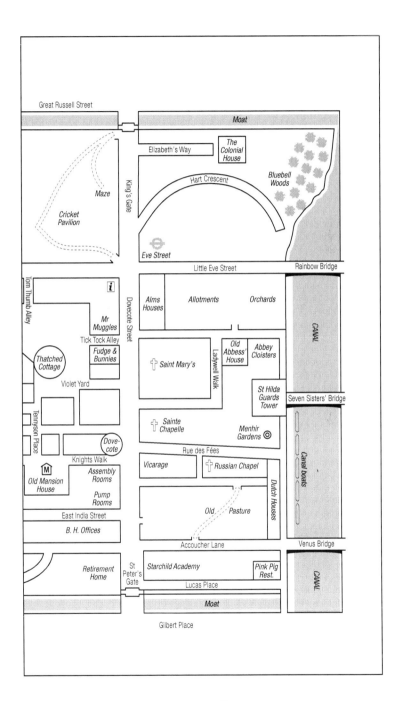

Great Russell Street

Moat

Elizabeth's Way

The Colonial House

Hart Crescent

Bluebell Woods

Maze

Cricket Pavilion

King's Gate

Eve Street

Little Eve Street

Rainbow Bridge

Tom Thumb Alley

Alms Houses

Allotments

Orchards

Mr Muggles

Tick Tock Alley

Fudge & Bunnies

Thatched Cottage

Violet Yard

Dovecote Street

Saint Mary's

Ladywell Walk

Old Abbess' House

Abbey Cloisters

St Hilda Guards Tower

Seven Sisters' Bridge

CANAL

Tennyson Place

Sainte Chapelle

Menhir Gardens

Dove-cote

Knights Walk

Rue des Fées

Canal boats

Old Mansion House

Assembly Rooms

Vicarage

Russian Chapel

Pump Rooms

Dutch Houses

East India Street

Old Pasture

B. H. Offices

Accoucher Lane

Venus Bridge

Retirement Home

St Peter's Gate

Starchild Academy

Pink Pig Rest.

Lucas Place

Moat

CANAL

Gilbert Place

The story so far...
~ * ~

At the end of 2011 Lilly D'Or died leaving her two nieces, Lucy and Sophie Lawrence, in charge of No.1 Daisy Place Café-Bookshop. She also left a gap on the board of the Little Eden Trust.

Taking advantage of being down to three trustees, Robert's mother persuaded her younger son Collins and great nephew Lucas to vote to sell the town (worth over eight billion pounds in real estate) but Robert was determined (or at least he was in the end) to save his ancestral home and by doing so continue to protect the spiritual dragon portal beneath the Abbey.

After some hard ball negotiations (or blackmail depending on how you look at it) Robert's on and off girlfriend, Shilty Cunningham, persuaded Collins to agree to take a pay off of two billion pounds in cash and leave Little Eden in the capable hands of Robert. Cousin Lucas agreed to take the same amount on the understanding that he would only have to wait two years to be paid.

In order to save the town from demolition, Robert and his friends are seeking any source of income they can find; so far they have not yet raised even a quarter of the four billion pounds they need.

To add to their troubles, the dragon portals around the world are now open for business, and the 2012 ascension of the Earth and mankind is well underway. The old guardians of the Earth, the Atlanteans, have to hand over control of human incarnation to the Pleiades Council. The transition can go smoothly, or it can lead to Armageddon - no one yet knows which it will be.

In order to prevent the new galactic regime from destroying their belief system and hierarchy, some of the Atlanteans have taken to using dark forces to create mayhem and fear amongst the guardians and Star Children, in the hope that they will leave the dragon portals just as they are - full of corrupted cultural beliefs, religious dogma and patriarchal dominance.

Evil is easily harnessed and Linnet Finch's ex-husband Marcus, recently out of prison, kidnapped their young daughter and portal guardian, Alice, in a bid to take her away from Little Eden. Luckily, Robert saved the day; unfortunately (or perhaps fortunately) Marcus drowned in the lake near the chateau. If Robert is found guilty of murder, Collins and Lucas would have full control of the Trust and Little Eden is doomed.

Linnet's old fears from years of domestic violence were whipped up too, and she took her dark side out on her girlfriend Minnie, who had to sadly walk away from the relationship. Minnie at least found a new best friend in the form of the new Star Child Academy's headmistress, Adela Huggins, who came to live in the town with her son, and Star Child, Joshua. Adela proved popular with all the residents - Lancelot especially seems to be quite besotted with her and so far she seems to prefer him to all his rivals.

The spirit of the original founder of Little Eden, Alienor Bartholemew, along with Aunt Lilly and some of the true saints, try to guide the friends and teach them that there is much more to Little Eden than it first seems. As the battle between the Atlanteans and the Pleiades for the hearts and minds of mankind escalates it's time for sleeping light workers to wake up and face their own fears…

Chapter 1
~ * ~

Hovering far above the Abbey, Sophie slowly descended from her vantage point, like a feather floating gently on the morning mist. As she was enveloped by the eerie stillness of the silent convent, she felt the coolness of the short, dewy grass welcome her bare feet. From the patchwork of mellow flagstones up to the dignified carvings above, rays of golden sunlight glowed through the majestic archways, illuminating the cloisters which framed the Abbey courtyard on all sides.

Sophie found herself standing in the very centre of this sacred, slumbering garden. Beside her the fountain sparkled in the hazy dawn, and luminous, yellow petals of early primroses and the bejewelled, violet buds of rising crocuses twinkled into view.

What am I doing here? She thought to herself. Before she could wonder about it further, she was beguiled by the mellifluous melody of Kyrie Eleison[1] whispering through the sheltering stones.

From amongst the hushed cloisters, invisible footsteps could be heard approaching.

Sophie tried to focus her thoughts, but they were like notes playing on the air and they would not stay with her. She knew that she was lucid dreaming yet the vision was so substantial that the stones seemed tangible.

Something shimmered in the cloisters. The flutter of a cobalt cape passed by an open archway. Then, she caught a glimpse of another, and then another, then another, dancing through the mist.

At length, she could make out the silhouettes of five nuns.

The women were gliding down the pathway towards her. The holy sisters encircled the fountain, bowing their heads towards her in greeting. Sophie wasn't sure how they knew who she was. She looked down at her apparel and realised that she too was dressed in a soft, finely woven, habit and a delicate silk cowl.

Who are they? she wondered. *More to the point who am I?*

Sophie forced her third eye to make out the features of the nuns and she smiled with relief when she recognised their wise and familiar faces.

Before her stood her Aunt Lilly, Alienor, St Katherine, St Hilda and St Therese.

"Who do you think I am?" Sophie asked them.

---

1 Kyrie Eleison, Hidergard of Bingen, 12th Century

"You are Queen Bertha, my darling," Aunt Lilly replied as if she recognised both Sophie and Queen Bertha as one and the same.

Sophie put her head to one side, trying to think. "You do know I'm Sophie though, don't you?" she asked her aunt.

Lilly just patted her arm and winked. "You're always Sophie to me," she reassured her.

Sophie was getting used to travelling in and out of different timeframes now. Past lives had become almost as important to her as her present lifetime. Since moving back to Little Eden, visions like this one had become common place, and even more so since the threat of eviction and demolition.

"Little Eden is not yet safe," Alienor told the sisters. "Robert must not go to prison. Without a true king the ring site will be lost to the darkness. Collins will take control of the Trust and the dragon portal will be left unguarded. The dark forces will take London for themselves."

Aunt Lilly nodded sadly. "And if London is lost - the whole world is lost."

Sophie felt a pang of fear as the idea of Armageddon seemed close at hand again. She wondered why such holy beings were not in control of everything already. There were many who believed that God's plan was preordained and immovable. But she wondered more and more if the element of freewill really existed.

Perhaps life on Earth was a bit of both - fate plus a hell of a lot of stupid mistakes!

"Hasn't the end of the world been decided already?" Sophie asked. "I mean, what can we do about the outcome? The human race will become extinct at some point like every animal species must, so I suppose the end is going to be nigh at some point isn't it?"

"We are entering the end times," Alienor agreed. "It can end with the destruction of mankind and planet Earth or it can be the transition from one species to another. The old ones can leave peaceably or wage war. They may leave the planet a hospitable place for the future or they may wreck it beyond recognition. The decision has not yet been made."

"We promised to stay 'til the end of human existence to help souls in human bodies make good choices - compassionate choices - but we cannot force their choices upon them," St Katherine explained.

St Hilda nodded in agreement. "As holy ones it is our duty to stay until the end - whatever the outcome may be. But the outcome is not our choice to make."

"What are we doing here right now?" Sophie asked, a little overwhelmed by the conversation. "Why am I channelling Queen Bertha?"

"You will see. All will become clear in time," Alienor replied.

Sophie scrunched up her face in frustration. She hated the cryptic messages from spirit.

"We are here to support you in your task," Aunt Lilly told her.

"My task? As in Sophie's task? Or as in Queen Bertha's task?" Sophie asked.

"Both!" said all the women in unison.

"Firstly, you must save Robert from prison," Alienor told her.

Sophie shook her head in amazement. "Er...and how exactly do I do that?" she asked.

"You will hold the inquest here in Little Eden and find him innocent of the crime," Alienor explained.

Sophie was bewildered. "I don't have the power to do that," she told them.

"Sophie," Aunt Lilly said, "You must form a jury of five holy women. This has always been the law in Little Eden. There were five nuns here who have the keys to help save Little Eden. You must find them again in this lifetime and form the jury."

Sophie just gazed at the sisters in stupefaction. "There hasn't been an inquest held by nuns in Little Eden since before the Reformation," she said aghast.

The sisters looked at her in astonishment. "Are you a light worker or are you not?" St Therese asked her.

Sophie was taken aback. "I, I don't know!" she stuttered. "Am I?"

"A true light worker will do whatever is required," Alienor told her.

Sophie wrinkled her nose: she really wanted to wake up and go home. "I don't remember volunteering to channel Queen Bertha or to work for the Light, and what are the keys?"

"You have told us many times that all you want is to be compassionate and to help others," St Katherine replied. "We have heard your prayers."

"Well, yes," Sophie admitted. "But I meant more like inheriting lots of money and helping the poor or planting millions of trees. Helping someone across the road or, I don't know, signing a petition for Amnesty International, things like that. Not this kind of crazy stuff!"

"We cannot work on Earth unless humans allow us to guide their voices, their hands, their thoughts and their actions," St Hilda explained.

"What can we do without a physical body?" St Katherine added. "We have no hands to work with, no voices to speak with."

"We remained in the spirit world to help mankind, but we can do nothing without human beings to work with us," St Hilda continued.

"I honestly think you're asking the wrong person," Sophie told them. "I don't have any power to do anything. I am not this Queen Bertha. I'm just Sophie Lawrence."

Sophie desperately wanted to ask more questions but the vision was fading, and as the sisters placed their hands in prayer position, a glorious beam of rose-gold light began to glisten all around them and sparkle through the fountain. The water began to pop and fizz with iridescent bubbles. Sophie hoped they were sending divine help, but to her dismay the sparkling liquid suddenly transmuted into a thick inky black tar.

The hideous oily slick spun itself into a tornado and swirled upwards into the sky. It loomed higher than the Abbey walls, blocking out the morning sun and plunging the cloisters into darkness. She watched in horror as the jet black tower of spinning doom transformed into a colossal, beady eyed crow.

Sophie felt evil run through her veins. She begged herself to wake up, but she did not. The unctuous crow plunged back into the water and the Abbey garden was filled with the deepest shade of lapis blue she had ever seen.

As the rich blue light faded, Sophie was shocked to find she was no longer in the cloisters but in a sunny graveyard - which at first she did not recognise.

A shimmering mirage of a small, red brick and grey cobbled stone church, with a stocky tower and three small adjoining tiled sheds, materialised in her path. She could smell the faint hint of the rosemary bushes which flanked the pathway and she could just make out the tiny, white bells of lily of the valley peeking out from beneath the sorrowful low hanging trees. Long grass hid many of the falling, neglected gravestones which were so weather-beaten that their inscriptions were barely visible.

As she stood, transfixed by the vividness of the scene, a sense of familiarity crept over her.

This is not the church I built, she thought. She ran her fingers over the rough grey stones and mused on when she had seen it before. *This is the site. I remember being here, but this is not how it is meant to look*, she thought.

An anger rose inside her so vehemently that it felt as if it had come from her soul. *They plugged it!* She thought. *They plugged my dragon portal with their fake religion, their stone churches and their spells.*

Whoa! Sophie thought. *Where did those thoughts come from? How do I know this place?*

She pondered for a few moments and it became clearer to her. *Oh, I get it*, she said to herself. *I'm not Sophie right now. I'm Queen Bertha. And as Queen Bertha I know this place. This is my sacred site - my dragon portal.*

Sophie's anger subsided and was replaced by an overwhelming feeling that her heart was breaking. It was not just her heart which she could feel crumbling away, but the heart of every man, woman and child in the world. *They put spells over my beautiful rose site*, she thought. *I planted the seed of the love of Mother Mary beneath a little wooden chapel. I put the key in there so that everyone in England could find her. But now her consciousness - her love - it's been stopped like putting a cork in a bottle and she can't get out. Everyone's heart is blocked too. Everyone is struggling to find compassion within themselves. Those dirty, rotten, so called 'religious' men, who have nothing but power and greed in their hearts - they've taken over the dragon portals and corrupted the keys. How dare they!*

Sophie (and Queen Bertha) made a pledge right there and then. *I'm going to get it flowing again if it's the last thing I do. I'm taking it back! I'm waking up the goddess within everyone!*

Suddenly, Sophie awoke to find Lucy standing over her bed holding out a cup of tea.

Chapter 2
~ * ~

"Lancelot and Adela are coming over in an hour," Lucy told Sophie as she placed the hot drink on the bedside table and perched on the end of the bed. "Robert's bringing Shilty, unfortunately," she added.

Both sisters rolled their eyes. "Are you well enough to come through?" Lucy asked.

Sophie sighed. She had taken a shower and washed her hair that morning for the first time in a week and it had exhausted her. But she was sick and tired of being sick and tired and of being alone. She wanted so desperately to be part of life again. "I'll come through for a bit," she said, "But I'm not sure how long I'll be able to stay."

Lucy smiled sadly. "I'll help you get dressed," she offered. She went to the chest of drawers and pulled out a comfy pair of jeans and a cosy jumper. "Here," she said, "Put these on. You'll be as snug as a bug in a rug on the sofa." She helped Sophie out of bed. "Your hair's gone all funny! You slept on it wet didn't you?" Lucy giggled.

"I was too tired to dry it," Sophie admitted.

Lucy put the radio on and the song Crazy[2] spilled into the room. She put the hair straighteners on to heat up and found some mascara for Sophie to use.

"Next time, tell me when you need some help," Lucy scolded her softly.

"You're busy with the café and with Tambo and Alice," Sophie replied. "I can't ask you to help me every time I need help, that's just not possible." Sophie recalled the vision dream she'd just had. "I've been asked to do something that might be impossible though," she added.

"What do you mean?" Lucy enquired as she began to straighten Sophie's hair.

"Aunt Lilly has asked me to set up a jury of five women to run Robert's inquest," Sophie explained.

"Is Aunt Lilly with us now?" Lucy asked, looking around. She had been feeling Lilly's presence every day in the café-bookshop but wished she could hold conversations with her as Sophie seemed able to do.

"I had a vision in my dream just now," Sophie explained. "Aunt Lil', Alienor, St Hilda, St Katherine and St Therese were all there and they seemed to think I was Queen Bertha - you know - the one who gifted

2 Crazy, Gnarls Barkley, 2006, Downtown/Warner

Alienor with the land for Little Eden over a thousand years ago? They told me we had to hold Robert's inquest here, and I have to find five women, who used to be nuns here at the Abbey in a past life, to serve on the jury."

"Well, you'd better do it then," was Lucy's reply.

"But, I don't know how to do it?" Sophie admitted. "I mean, where do I even start?"

"Tell Lancelot when he comes," Lucy suggested. "He'll know the legal ins and outs and I suppose you could ask Aunt Lilly to guide you to the women you need. I hope one of them isn't me!" She stepped back to admire her handy work on Sophie's hair and ran some moisturising oil through the ends.

"You believe me then?" Sophie asked her.

"Of course!" Lucy replied.

"I'm so glad you always believe me when I tell you about spirit guides and such," Sophie said. The song on the radio came to an end and Sophie laughed. "You don't think I'm crazy then?"

Lucy shrugged. "You're the most honest person I know - sometimes too honest! If you say it happened, then in my book it happened."

Sophie sighed. "Millions wouldn't!" she replied.

"Yeah well, sod them!" Lucy laughed. "In my heart I know Aunt Lilly is with us in spirit, and Alienor too. Look up. There!" she said, screwing the top back on the mascara. "You look very pretty and no one would guess you were ill."

"I think that's half the problem," Sophie sighed. "When I do go out in public everyone thinks I'm fine because I don't look like I'm at death's door. Chronic Fatigue Syndrome is an invisible disability that's for sure."

"Drink your tea," Lucy told her, not wanting Sophie to dwell on her illness. "Noddy has nearly finished your new bedroom. He's having trouble moving the big wardrobe though. I don't know how Aunt Lil' got it up the stairs in the first place all those years ago. I reckon it must come apart somehow. I've taken all her things out of it but it still weighs a ton."

"Did Jack value those things we set aside?" Sophie asked her.

"Yes, but they are not worth much, only about two hundred pounds for the lot. He said the only things worth anything are Aunt Lil's pearls and great grandma's diamond brooch, but I told him we were keeping those, and besides, even they're not worth much more. I'm sorry there's not more to sell to keep you going financially."

"It's okay," Sophie said. "I never expected we'd inherit anything really. Unless Aunt Lilly's got some hidden treasure under the floor boards, we were never going to be millionaires."

Lucy shrugged. "The legacy she left us with was love and the guardianship of the café-bookshop. I'll take both of those over money any day. Come and see the bedroom," Lucy suggested.

The sisters went into Lilly's old room which was sans carpet and furniture save for the wardrobe and a bed. A step ladder, covered in multi-coloured paint splashes, was leaning up against the wall, and there was the distinctive whiff of white spirit mingled with the smell of damp wallpaper. "Noddy wanted to paper behind the wardrobe but even with Jack's help he can't shift it. It's like it's nailed to the floor or something!" Lucy explained.

Sophie looked at the huge white Louis XV style wardrobe and wondered why it was so immovable. She opened the doors and peered inside. "I've not noticed this before," she said. "Do you think the base on the outside doesn't match the inside?"

"It just looks normal to me," Lucy replied.

"Where's a tape measure?" Sophie asked her.

Lucy looked in the tool box. "Here," she said and offered it to Sophie.

Sophie bent down and measured the outside of the wardrobe, base to the floor, and then the inside. "There, see!" she exclaimed. "The inside suggests there might be a false bottom!"

Lucy went to fetch a torch and started to investigate. Sophie lay on the bed to rest again whilst her sister knocked and pressed on the wooden boards inside the wardrobe. Then, just as Lucy was about to give up, she caught sight of a little brass latch in the far left corner. She flipped it upwards but nothing happened. However, when she pressed it down again, lo and behold, the floor of the wardrobe had come loose.

"There's a secret compartment!" Lucy exclaimed in delight.

"Wow!" Sophie said and got up off the bed to see.

Lucy lifted out several of the small floor planks. "Good grief!" she exclaimed as a deep concealed hiding place was revealed. "You're right, Aunt Lil' does have some hidden treasure after all!"

"What's down there?" Sophie asked, full of excitement and desperate to see.

Lucy shone the torch inside the obscured cavity and they both peered in.

In the dark space were three small metal containers - a tobacco tin, a 1950's Quality Street tin and a much larger rusty box. The first two were easy to remove but the third one was so heavy Lucy couldn't even get hold of it to lift it up.

"It weighs a ton!" she said. "No wonder the wardrobe wouldn't move. It feels like it's welded to the floor!"

Sophie went to help her and after much manoeuvring and some leverage they managed to get the box out; but it was too heavy for them to hold and they had to let it fall straight onto the floor. It hit the ground with a heavy thud!

"Oh my god, this is so exciting!" Sophie said. "I love a mystery."

"Should we look in them?" Lucy asked.

"Why not?" Sophie replied.

"I don't know. I just got a funny feeling all of a sudden," Lucy admitted, "As if they're not for us."

Sophie paused a moment and thought. "I think we should look inside them anyway," she concluded.

Lucy didn't dare touch them. She felt a prickly heat on the back of her neck and a shiver down her spine. She held her breath and waited as Sophie tentatively opened the first one.

The small tobacco tin contained a tiny key, a passport photo of someone they did not recognise, and a rubber band.

The girls looked decidedly disappointed.

The chocolate tin was stuffed to the top with old photos - a little more exciting but hardly the crown jewels.

Sophie turned her attention to the last box. "It's locked!" she exclaimed disgruntled.

"Is this the key?" Lucy asked, holding out the one from the tobacco tin.

Sophie tried it but it wasn't.

"Is there anything else in the hole?" Sophie asked.

Lucy went back with the torch and searched around the best she could in the clandestine cavity. "Nope, not a thing," she replied.

Sophie sighed. Then, she had an idea. She went over to Noddy's tool box and pulled out a hammer.

"You're not going to smash it are you?" Lucy asked her.

"Why not? The box itself isn't worth anything I shouldn't imagine. Well, I hope not anyway!" Sophie giggled.

Lucy still felt uneasy as if she was trespassing into the past. She got a flash in her mind of opening a mummy's tomb. "What if there's a curse on it?" Lucy suddenly blurted out.

Sophie paused for a moment. *It is possible*, she thought. "Maybe we can risk it?" Sophie said, holding up the mallet. Her curiosity was stronger than her fear.

"Go on then," Lucy reluctantly agreed.

With one almighty whack, Sophie smashed open the lock, and the top of the box flew sideways exposing the contents.

The girls gasped with delight.

Chapter 3
~ * ~

"I think we've just found something worth selling!" Sophie giggled. To their astonishment, the girls could see, gleaming in the blush of the sunset which was now streaming through the voile curtains, a dozen gold ingots.

They stared at them for a few moments in awe. It was so surreal to find real treasure in a wardrobe!

They carefully took them out, one at a time, and laid them on the bed. Hidden beneath them was a large leather pouch. Sophie tipped out the contents and hundreds of thin, roughly hewn, gold coins glittered like confetti onto the mattress.

"Good grief!" Lucy said in wonderment. "Is there anything else left to find?"

"Looks like there's one more thing," Sophie said, as she took out an antique wooden box which was inlaid with squares of jasper and mother of pearl. From inside it she produced a small scroll which was wrapped in, what looked like, Clingfilm.

"That box alone must be worth a bit!" Lucy declared. As she picked it up she could sense it was very old indeed and the scent of myrrh lent it a mystical quality. She noticed the top layer inside came out; and under it Lucy found a large velvet bag tied with gold braid. It felt heavy and uneven to the touch. The sisters looked at each other, unable to imagine what might be inside. As Lucy opened it exquisite jewellery cascaded out.

Some of the most precious gems on Earth glinted in the sunset as if awakening from deep hibernation.

They both gasped at the radiance of the opulent stones. A collection of elaborate golden crosses, of differing sizes, all adorned with a myriad of luxuriant crystals, tumbled out amongst the coins and ingots onto bed.

"Oh my god, we're rich!" Lucy squealed.

"Oh my god, it's like pirate treasure!" Sophie exclaimed.

They jumped up and down and hugged each other with glee.

"I can't believe it!" Lucy said again.

"It's all so beautiful," Sophie added.

The sisters picked up each precious piece in turn and began to feel a deep sense of reverence rising within them as if they were holding holy relics. It was clear that this was no ordinary hoard. The glorious items were clearly hundreds of years old and in some cases maybe even thousands. Some crosses were attached to chains and others to rosaries. Some had been made into brooches, belt buckles and even hair pins. A Canterbury cross with a pearl dove set in the middle was particularly dazzling. A splendid Catherine Wheel had topaz tear drops set around it which twinkled as if they were alive with light. One piece, which Lucy especially admired, was a solid gold cross which was rather plain except for a charming ruby rose at its heart. There were many more wondrous and magnificently crafted pieces carved with bearded faces, stylised birds and other strange animals. The piece de resistance however, was a large St Cuthbert's cross, which was bejewelled with hundreds of scintillating fire opals.

"It's like winning the jewellery lottery!" Lucy giggled.

But all of a sudden, Sophie didn't feel quite the same elation as she had done initially. "If only we'd found this years ago," she sighed, "Before Collins decided to destroy Little Eden. We could have sold this and we'd never have had to worry about money ever again."

Lucy grimaced and felt herself drop back down to earth with a bump. "Yeah, you're right. I knew it wasn't for us before we even opened the first box. I suppose we'll have to give it to the Save Little Eden fund, won't we?" she said in dismay.

"It looks as if it belongs to the Abbey or at least to some holy place," Sophie said. "I wonder why it's been collected together in this way?" She mused over the sacred pieces. "They all seem so different from each other. They can't have all been made in the same place or at the same time."

"I wonder why Aunt Lil' had them in the wardrobe?" Lucy pondered. "If she knew about these things why did she never tell us? There has to be some reason why she was sitting on a fortune and keeping it a secret. Maybe she didn't even know they were there?"

"Why didn't she ever mention these things even when she was dying? She must have known about them," Sophie said.

"She'd have given them to you when you lost everything if she could have," Lucy nodded. "If she didn't tell us about them or leave them to us in her Will, then they are certainly not for us." Her heart sank a little further as she realised the truth of the matter.

Sophie agreed. "No, they are not for us."

Sophie had begun to put some of the crosses back into their bag when she suddenly noticed a small ring which seemed out of place within the collection of such rich and bewitching crosses. It was thin and plain, with a simple amethyst cabochon set within a dull, silver coloured band. "Funny," she said as she showed it to her sister. "This one doesn't fit with the rest."

Lucy tried it on. "Maybe we could keep this one? As a keepsake maybe?"

Sophie laughed. "Like a finder's fee!"

They had almost forgotten about the scroll as the spectacular cache had taken so much of their attention. As Sophie picked it up she started to shake. "I'm burning up," she exclaimed. "My hands are burning!" She quickly dropped the scroll on the bed.

Lucy fanned her with a paint sample brochure.

Before they could pick it up again, Tambo called out to them from the landing, and Alice followed close behind. They peered around the door and asked to come in. They were both more subdued than usual and not in the mood for homework. For some reason, which she couldn't explain, Lucy quickly threw a dust cover over the jewels and gold bullion to hide them from the children.

"What have you got there?" Tambo asked, seeing the two smaller tins.

"Nothing, really," Lucy told him. "Just some old photographs we found in the bottom of the wardrobe. Here, you can look through them if you like - see if you recognise anyone or if they are of Little Eden."

Lucy and Sophie agreed to keep quiet about the rest of the discovery - for now at least.

When they went into the living room there were photos already strewn all over the coffee table. Lucy brought out some rhubarb muffins and glasses of milk for them all and they sat browsing through the old images together.

Some of the photographs were of Little Eden. "That's Mr Muggle's Clock Shop!" Alice laughed. "It hasn't changed a bit. Look! He even has the same clock in the window - the one with the cherubs on the top."

"This must be Peony's when it was a barbers shop," Tambo said and showed everyone. A heavily whiskered chap sporting a leather apron stood proudly outside the bow fronted window which had the words *Hairdressers by Appointment* in large lettering above it.

"He even looks like Vincent!" Lucy laughed.

Then, without warning, Alice screamed and threw a photograph over the back of the sofa in fright.

They all just looked at her in surprise.

"There was a ghost in that one!" Alice cried. She shivered and wiped her hands as if some of the ghost might have gotten onto her fingers.

Tambo quickly retrieved it from the floor and they all rushed to look more closely at the spooky image. Outside the walls of what looked like Little Eden Abbey was a group of five nuns. There was nothing remarkable about the image at first, but on closer inspection they realised that through the bottom of one of their habits you could see the curb stone of the street!

"Good grief!" Lucy asserted. "It is as well. You can see right through her skirt. She's a ghost! I've got to show this to Jimmy when he gets back from America."

"Can I take it to school tomorrow?" Tambo begged. "The lads will go ape over this!"

"Oh, don't!" Alice pleaded, wanting nothing more than to get as far away from the photograph as she could. Tambo waved it at her, and she screamed again as he chased her around the room.

Alice hid behind Lucy, almost in tears.

Sophie took the photograph off Tambo and smiled. "I hate to put the kybosh on your ghost hunting but this often happened in old photographs. Don't be scared Alice - it's just a trick of the light - it isn't supernatural."

"Are you sure?" Lucy asked, hugging Alice who was still clinging to her.

Sophie had to admit that she didn't know the exact science of it. "It's a fairly common phenomenon in Victorian photographs," she explained. "I think it's to do with using double exposure or is it a very long exposure? I don't know. But I do know you can recreate it quite easily and it's not at all magical or paranormal."

Alice sighed with relief and felt brave enough to go back to her muffin and milk.

Sophie looked closer at the image. *I wonder if these are the five nuns I'm looking for?* she thought.

She showed the photograph to Lucy who had started to prepare some food in the kitchen; the children continued to look through the other photos.

"Do you think any of these nuns look familiar?" she asked her sister.

"I'm not sure," Lucy replied. "Let's see. That one, the one with the see-through skirt, she reminds me of Minnie, and to be fair this one, at the end, she has a look of Iris Sprott about her don't you think."

"That's what I thought," Sophie agreed. "And this one, in the middle, the

21

tall one, she could be Adela if you put her in modern dress."

Lucy looked again. "I suppose she could be. I think they're all familiar in one way or another, but this photo must be a hundred years old - we can't possibly know them."

"People often reincarnate over and over in the same place, and even do the same things lifetime after lifetime - even more so with earth angels. Once a nun most likely always a nun," Sophie laughed. "'Til nowadays that is. There are no nunneries left for us to live in now."

Alice called over from the sofa. "Look! I've found one of The Daisy Chain but it's not a florist's."

Lucy smiled as she looked at it. "Yes, it used to be a Drapers. Look at all the old fashioned coats hanging up outside, and those look like baby clothes in the window."

Alice suddenly became melancholy. "Is mummy coming home soon?" she asked (as she had done every day for a week now).

"Not yet, sweetie," Lucy replied. "Maybe in a few weeks she'll be well enough to come home."

Linnet had become so fearful of Marcus, even though he was dead, that she had had a nervous breakdown and was now perpetually drunk and unable to care for Alice or her shop. She had finally agreed to go into the rehabilitation centre at the Refuge and was trying to get herself sober. Cheri and Bob Tackle, her shop assistants, were trying their best to take the reins, and Alice had come to stay permanently with Lucy.

Alice prayed for her mum every night and was missing her so much. Her comfort was living with Lucy, Sophie, Tambo and Aunt Lilly (in spirit of course). She seemed quite comfortable with Aunt Lilly's spirit around, but other ghosts - not so much.

"This one's of the café," Tambo said. "Look that's Aunt Lil'." The photograph showed a gang of friends who were gathered together near the counter of Daisy Place Café. Their clothing and hairstyles suggested it had been taken in the 1960's.

"I'm sure that's Robert's dad, Melbourne," Lucy said. "And these two look like Ace and Maggie Fortune don't you think?"

Sophie agreed. "They're younger than when we knew them, but I remember Maggie always had that way of smiling which made you think she was up to something mischievous!"

"Is that Stella?" Tambo asked. "

Yes, I think it must be," Lucy replied. "Could she have a higher beehive? I don't know who that other waitress is but she looks familiar too."

"They look cool!" Alice said, admiring Stella's outfit and hair.

Suddenly, Tambo got very angry and pushed the photographs off the table. "What are you doing?" Lucy exclaimed.

Tambo burst into tears! "I want Aunt Lilly to come back," he sobbed.

"You know Lilly is still here don't you?" Sophie asked him. "In spirit, maybe not in person, but she can hear you and see you and you can talk to her. She can't play the piano with you but she can sit next to you and listen to you play and sing."

Alice nodded. "She's always here."

"I feel bad for feeling happy and playing music when everyone else is so sad," Tambo admitted.

"Lilly would never ever be cross about anyone being happy," Lucy told him. "All she ever wanted was everyone in the whole world to be happy!"

"You know she would sing to cheer people up. That was her way of 'spreading the happy' and now you have to keep doing it for her," Sophie reassured him.

"You think she's still singing in the spirit world?" Tambo asked.

"I know it!" Sophie replied. "And if you are lucky, and if the wind is blowing from the east, you just might hear her!"

"Let's sing to her now," Lucy suggested. "She might join in." She took up Aunt Lilly's guitar from the stand in the corner and gave it to Tambo.

A bit reluctantly at first Tambo started to strum the strings. He looked at his mum for encouragement and she nodded and smiled. Alice began to hum and they both began to sing their own version of, God Gave Me You[3] .

Lucy was in tears and Sophie couldn't hold hers back any longer either when Tambo sang the line, 'We are stitched together…I pray we never undo'.

Tambo stopped singing. "It's not making you happy!" he said.

"It's cathartic to have a good to cry," Sophie sobbed, reaching for the tissues. "You're helping us heal. If we don't cry we'll burst with anger instead. We don't want to hold the sadness inside forever. It's best to let it out. Keep singing! Keep singing!"

By the end of the song they could all sense that Aunt Lilly was singing with them and a white feather floated out from under one of the photographs - which they all swore had not been there before!

3 God Gave Me You, Dave Barnes, 2010, Razor & Tie

Chapter 4
~ * ~

When the children had eaten their dinner, Alice wanted to keep looking through the photographs until bedtime. When she got to the bottom of the tin she pulled out a folded piece of paper.

"What's this?" she asked.

"It's just a list of names," Tambo said, looking at it as she unfolded it.

This is the list which Alice found:

1195 Admeta Babette
1231 Sympatico White
1270 Netti White
1307 Angelica Montagne
1356 Luna Honeydew
1390 Malamay Valoise
1412 Delice Drake
1444 Tulip Dancer
1505 Theresa Sunshine
1535 Tara Armagh
1564 Suzanna Portia
1697 Inganta Glenn
1610 Brodie Glenn
1631 Loretta Garrison-Pipes/
Humph'Lockington
1666 Sarah Barton

1672 Madeline Lyoness
1690 Jacqueline Gide
1702 ? believed to be Marie d'Youville
1725 Dove Franklin
1760 Genevieve Dumas
1791 Paradise Brightwater
1820 Easter Dudley
1866 Temperance Shadow
1880 Emily, Ophelia & Miranda Christie
1899 Jin Keung
1920 Moon Baker
1943 Trinity & Andara Tsfira
1956 Savanna
19- Lillianna D'Or

"Who are all these people?" Alice asked. "It's the family tree of the café-bookshop!" Lucy declared. "This is amazing! Aunt Lilly used to tell me about some of these women but I didn't know she'd made a list like this. I don't recall all these names but I remember Aunt Lilly saying that the Christie sisters were radicals and Temperance Shadow was a suffragist. This one," she pointed to the name Theresa Sunshine, "She was supposed to have come here for sanctuary after being accused of witchcraft, and Loretta Garrison-Pipes - she had to pretend that a man owned the place after the civil war because women were not supposed to run public houses."

"Why not?" Alice asked.

"Oliver Cromwell didn't believe in others having fun, especially women - although I believe he had plenty of fun himself in secret," Sophie giggled. "Women had to dress in black and could even be arrested for wearing bright colours."

"Is he the one who had the King's head cut off?" Tambo asked.

"Yes," Sophie nodded. "And, he banned Christmas."

"Banned Christmas?" Alice exclaimed, appalled by the very idea!

"Tulip Dancer was said to have escaped from the court of Margaret D'Angou because they wanted her to marry a Lancastrian. And look, there's Genevieve Dumas, we all know about her…"

"…She's the highwaywoman!" Tambo interrupted. "The one who's always looking for her lost booty."

Alice looked down the list again. "I like that name," Alice said, "Jin Keung. Who was she?"

"Ah, Jin! She came over from China to escape the Boxer rebellion," Lucy told her.

"What are Boxers?" Alice asked.

"They were called Boxers by the British because they could fight using martial arts. I don't think Jin was one of them, but they do say that she founded the Little Eden Kung Fu Society, and that she trained at the famous Shaolin Temple in China."

"Legend has it that all martial arts under heaven originated at Shaolin," Sophie added. "High up in the mountains amongst the mist and the pine trees she learnt the secrets of the great masters and brought them here to our little corner of England. They say she could jump over the roof tops like a tiger and would disappear into the shadows like a ninja. They say she could hear someone approaching over a mile away and kill a man just by looking at him."

Suddenly, a voice from behind them made them jump!

It was Jack.

"What's all this then?" he asked as he took off his sneakers.

"You scared me half to death!" Lucy said, putting her hand on her heart. She whacked him on the arm.

"Ow!" Jack said with a smile. "Where did all these photographs come from?"

The whole table and half the sofa were now scattered with black and white images.

"They're all of Little Eden!" Alice told him and started to show him her favourite ones. "And, we found a list of all the women who have ever owned the café. One of them was a kick ass boxer called Jin."

"Really?" Jack laughed. "I'm sure most of these women would have been kick ass gals if the current owners are anything to go by." He looked down the list. "I like the sound of her." He pointed to Luna Honeydew. "If she was anything like her name, I wouldn't have minded…"

…"Drink?" Lucy interrupted. "I've got some of Cubby's nettle and dandelion wine - he brought it over especially this morning."

"Just a cheeky one then," Jack smiled (Cubby's wine was almost lethal). "It'd be rude not to."

When Lucy and Sophie could catch Jack's eye, they beckoned him to follow them into the bedroom.

"It's not finished!" he said as he looked around, thinking that the girls had taken him in there to show him the new decorations.

"That's not what we want to show you," Sophie told him.

"Ta dah!" Lucy said as she whisked away the cover on the bed.

"F**k!" Jack exclaimed. "What the…? What did Cubby put in that wine? I think I'm hallucinating!"

"Shhh," Lucy scolded him. "We don't want the kids to find out about it yet. We found all this in the wardrobe along with the photos."

Jack was astounded by the glittering hoard. He examined each piece carefully, sorting as went. "Some of these are 12th Century," he said. "I wouldn't be surprised if these are much older. I mean much, much, older. The knot work on this one suggests it might be Anglo-Saxon."

"How much do you think they're worth?" Lucy asked eagerly.

Jack shrugged. "It's hard to say off-hand. If these gems are real, then it'll be a pretty penny. But, they will need to be declared as treasure trove."

"Surely not?" Sophie responded. "We didn't find them in a field. We found them in our own wardrobe. They're ours aren't they?"

"You might get away with it, but they should go to a museum," Jack said. He couldn't take his eyes of the magnificent pieces and he shook his head in wonder. "I've never seen anything like this in one place before. It reminds me of the Cheapside hoard only a million times more impressive. This one," he held up a box-bezel golden cross, "This one looks as if it's sapphires and emeralds. It's an early piece. I wouldn't be surprised if some of these are not holy relics. If they can be identified and linked to a saint or a particular church their value would sky rocket."

Lucy pointed to the gold ingots. "These must be worth a lot too?" she asked.

He nodded. "These are pretty old as well." He tried to gauge the weight in his hand. "These must be at least 1kg each, but if they are old, they won't be more than eighty per cent pure. Still, there are plenty there."

"What about the coins?" Sophie asked him.

He scrutinized the slightly wonky impressions. "These are from the 5th Century," he said. "They look like King Eadbald coins. They've all got his name on, see?"

Jack then looked inside the ornate box. "What's this?" he asked the girls.

He pressed the sides together and a hidden compartment shot out.

"How did you know that that would be there?" Lucy asked him, dumbstruck.

Jack smiled. "I have my supernatural ways just like you two," he laughed.

There was a letter and a postcard inside the secret drawer.

The postcard was of a church and when Jack turned it over written on the back was:

*"St Martins. Earliest Christian site in England.
Founded by Queen Bertha of Kent. Circa 580."*

"That's the church I went to in my vision!" Sophie exclaimed.

"King Eabald was married to Queen Bertha," Jack told them. "She was known as Aldeberge back then."

Lucy stepped away from the hallowed hoard. She had gone cold and felt a spooky sensation shiver through her bones. "Okay," she said. "I'm getting seriously scared now. This is weird. I don't like it anymore. It's giving me the creeps."

Sophie sat down on the bed. "I feel funny too," she admitted. "I feel as if we haven't just opened a box but also a time portal. I can feel it here in the room. These jewels and coins - they represent something from a past life. It feels dark and sinister now. The room feels like a dungeon."

Lucy shivered again. "I told you there was a curse on them."

"Don't be silly," Jack laughed, but he had to admit to himself that it had gone suddenly very chilly in the room.

"I can smell something icky like decaying flesh," Lucy said. She felt decidedly queasy.

"How do you even know what that would smell like?" Jack teased her. "What's in the envelope?"

Neither of the girls wanted to open it, afraid it might set off more evil energy.

Jack rolled his eyes at them. "Don't be so melodramatic," he laughed. He took out a letter. It was in French. He handed it to Sophie for her to read out loud which she did - very reluctantly I might add:

Le 11 Octobre 1789 a 4h ½ du matin

Chère Genevieve,

J'espère que cette lettre vous trouve bien. Je rends ces bijoux à la demande du père Clovis. Ils sont en sécurité chez nous depuis des centaines d'années ici à l'abbaye de Chartres mais nous ne pouvons plus garantir leur sécurité. Le royaume est perdu. Le mal est déchaîné. Nous vous souhaitons bonne chance pour l'avenir et espérons que ces pièces trouveront leur raison d'être à Little Eden.
Que la grâce de notre-dame soit avec vous et tout le monde

Soeur Marie

"Well?" Jack asked. "What does it say?"
Sophie translated it:

"Dear Genevieve,
I hope this letter finds you well. I am returning the jewels at the request of Father Clovis. They have been safe with us in the Abbey at Chartres for hundreds of years but now we cannot guarantee their safety any longer. The kingdom is lost. The evil is unleashed. Wishing you good luck for the future and hope that these pieces find their true purpose in Little Eden.
May the grace of Mother Mary be with you and with the world.
Sister Maria."

"Do you think the letter is addressed to our Genevieve Dumas? Is this the highway loot that Genevieve stole?" Lucy asked.
"It can't be," Sophie reminded her. "This letter says it was in France for hundreds of years before it was sent to Genevieve. But, I wonder if this is

28

the treasure the urban myth says she is looking for? Perhaps she never was a highwaywoman after all?" Sophie mused. "Maybe that part of the story was added later."

"But why were they sent to France in the first place and then sent back again? What are they for?" Lucy asked.

"Maybe this might explain more about them?" Jack suggested. He took the Clingfilm off the scroll. "It's made of vellum," he said as he opened it. "We need to get this to Mr T for safe keeping once we've read it. It'll start to deteriorate in no time out in the air." Jack knew a little Latin from his school days and tried to make out the medieval text. He did his best to translate it.

"I think it says something like...

...I, Queen of England, Princess of Paris, Mother of Canterbury, bequeath these jewels to Little Eden. Guard them well until the day of judgement is upon us. I dare to hope that we will not live to see the day that Little Eden crumbles to dust and the Light of the world is extinguished forever. When these jewels are needed let them be used against the darkness. I pray that we will be delivered into the new age with grace and sanctity.

Aldeberge Regina"

Chapter 5
~ * ~

"It's all very mysterious!" Lucy admitted, still a little bit freaked out.
"We need to get this lot authenticated," Jack said. "A friend of mine at the British Museum, Tobias Gilbert, he'll take a look. Why don't you take them to him tomorrow?"

He looked at Sophie.

"Me?" Sophie asked.

"I'll be busy. There's a new shipment coming into the shop. I'll text him. I'm sure he'll be there," Jack told her.

"I might be too ill," Sophie explained.

"If you can't walk all the way to the museum just take Hendrick's rickshaw and I'll pay for it both ways," Jack said. He winked at Lucy and she realised that Jack was trying to introduce Sophie to this Tobias Gilbert and the valuation of treasure was just an excuse.

"It'll be good for you to get out and you love the museum so much," Lucy encouraged her. "It's ages since you've been there."

Sophie wasn't sure. She really wanted to go but was afraid of feeling too fatigued. However, she wanted to pull her weight as much as she could. "Okay, I'll go," she agreed.

"I'll take the letters down to Mr T and get him to translate and authenticate them in the morning," Lucy offered.

"And I'll take the coins and bullion to Brindisi Thistle - see what he has to say about them," Jack added.

Sophie made sure the time portal was closed and the creepy cold feeling of death faded away. She started to feel a wave of fatigue coming over her and Lucy could sense her sister's energy dropping. "You go lie down," she told Sophie, "I'll let you know when dinner's ready."

Lucy began to make some fresh pasta and whizzed up some pumpkin seed pesto whilst Jack put Tambo and Alice to bed. He came back to find Lucy lying on the sofa looking very pale. "You okay, old girl?" he asked her.

"I don't know," Lucy replied. "I'm not sure if it's grief or the stress of taking over the café but I keep getting dizzy and nauseous. The other day I swear I felt sea sick. For just a few moments it was as if the whole building was moving."

"Sounds like an inner ear infection to me," Jack replied. "Better get that checked out."

He helped Lucy stand up.

"I'm okay now," she said. "It comes and goes. It's very strange."

Jack was about to say something when they were interrupted by a knock at the conservatory window.

Jack rolled his eyes as he saw who it was.

Slinking sensually through the doors, draped in her white mink coat and carrying two bottles of Louis Roederer Cristal Champagne, Shilty Cunningham entered the room followed by Robert. Her presence was always magnetic, alluring and slightly arousing. Jack felt a little uncomfortable in her presence. Whilst he didn't like Shilty as a person there was no denying that she was dangerously tempting.

"What are we celebrating?" Lucy enquired.

"Let me tell them! Let me!" Shilty begged Robert as he took her coat from her.

"Tell us! Tell us!" Jack mimicked her.

"We can hold the inquest here in Little Eden. How about that?" Shilty told them triumphantly.

Lucy couldn't help recalling Sophie's dream from earlier that afternoon and felt a little ripple of excitement run through her.

Shilty handed the champagne to Jack for him to open and perched herself on one of the breakfast bar stools. He couldn't help noticing her long, smooth, tanned legs and how divine she smelt.

"Lancelot asked me to help so I asked Clive to work his magic and it's done," Shilty laughed. "It seems you can't do without me here in Little Eden."

"That's wonderful news!" Lucy said and kissed Robert on the cheek as she accepted a bunch of daffodils from him. She excused herself on the pretext of finding a vase, and slipped out to see Sophie.

"Wake up!" Lucy said softly.

"I'm awake already," Sophie replied from under the covers. "I could hear Shilty's entrance from here!"

"Did you hear what she said?" Lucy asked her.

"Not exactly," Sophie admitted, coming out from her nest of covers.

"Well, this day just gets curiouser and curiouser!" Lucy declared. "You'll never guess what's happened now?"

Sophie sat up sleepily. "What? Robert is engaged to Shilty?"

"Bloody hell!" Lucy exclaimed. "I hope not!"

"Then what? Collins has had a change of heart? They've found Uncle Frith? Jennifer has been killed in a freak boating accident?"

"No, no!" Lucy giggled. "Shilty just announced that Robert's inquest can take place here in Little Eden after all. Clive arranged it apparently. The Home Office have agreed and now Robert can't possibly be found guilty. It's just like Alienor wanted it to be - just like in your dream."

Sophie couldn't believe her ears. "So, Alienor has pulled a few strings from the other side has she?" she said.

"Well, Shilty and Clive did the string pulling really," Lucy corrected her.

"We definitely need to find a jury of five women now," Sophie mused. "I don't know who would want to sit in judgement on Robert though, would you?"

"No, I wouldn't want the job, but Iris Sprott is a qualified magistrate so she might preside. Do they have to be women?" Lucy asked.

Sophie nodded. "Don't you remember Melanie? She was tried by a jury of five nuns."

"Yes, I remember. They used psychic sight to tell if she was guilty or not. That means you'll definitely need to be on the jury," Lucy told her. "Although, do the women all have to be Catholic?"

Sophie thought for a moment. "No. I don't think religion matters anymore."

"It's all a bit spooky. It's all happening so quickly since you had that dream," Lucy said.

"It is strange that when something needs to happen - like having the inquest here or finding more money towards saving Little Eden - spirit seems to pull out all the stops: but when I ask for a cure for the Chronic Fatigue Syndrome, nope, nada, nothing happens," Sophie sighed.

"I've often wondered that myself," Lucy admitted. "How some things happen so easily and others just get worse. I prayed and prayed for the angels to save Aunt Lilly. No one could have prayed harder than I did. They didn't help us then."

"Beats me!" Sophie shrugged. "I suppose that's the eternal mystery of the universe."

"Are you going to join us?" Lucy asked her sister. "Dinner's almost ready."

Sophie shook her head. She was too fatigued to eat.

"Well, wish me luck," Lucy smiled. "Lancelot will be drooling over Adela and Shilty will be draped all over Robert and Jack doesn't know where to put himself."

"What do you mean?" Sophie asked.

"Let's just say if Shilty's boobs get any bigger I'll have to set another place at the table!" Lucy laughed.

Returning to the others, Lucy found Lancelot and Adela had arrived. She smiled to herself as she saw Shilty give Adela a look that made her think of how one cat would stare at another who was wandering into its territory.

They all sat down to dinner and Lucy filled them in on Sophie's idea of having a jury of five women at the inquest. (She didn't mention the treasure trove as she wasn't sure she wanted Shilty to know about it).

"It's rather an unusual idea," Lancelot said.

"It's what Alienor wants," Lucy insisted.

"Well, we can't disappoint a dead woman, now can we?" Jack teased her.

"If we are holding it here there doesn't seem any reason why we shouldn't follow the ancient protocol," Robert suggested. "If we are seen to be following our own rules, at least it might look as if we are attempting to have a fair hearing."

"We all know you are innocent, old chap," Jack told him. "There's no question about that."

"I know," Robert said. "It was all a ghastly accident, but we need to be seen to be just and fair."

Lancelot agreed to let Sophie organise a jury of five women - if she could find them.

"I could be on the jury," Shilty offered. "I'll have to set the example if I'm to be the next Mrs Bartlett-Hart."

Lucy nearly choked on her pudding and Jack's champagne went down the wrong way!

"It's a shame we can't go back and live in the chateau. I wonder if I could get the monks to move out?" Shilty wondered.

It was Robert's turn to nearly choke on his pavlova. He looked at the amazed faces of his friends and felt more than a little bit guilty that he had not warned them about his impending nuptials.

Lucy quickly asked Lancelot to help her make some coffee in the kitchen area.

"What the hell is going on?" she whispered as she switched on the machine so the others couldn't hear her. "Why is Robert back with Shilty and why is she talking about being the next Mrs B.H?"

Lancelot pretended to know nothing.

"Don't play innocent with me!" Lucy scolded him. "You don't like Shilty any more than we do so why are you encouraging Robert to marry her?"

Lancelot didn't answer.

"OMG!" Lucy exclaimed. "You're pimping him out aren't you?"

"I don't know what you mean?" Lancelot replied as he gathered some espresso cups together.

"Yes you do! You knew you'd need Shilty to get to Clive and you've orchestrated the whole thing!" Lucy said.

"I wouldn't go that far," Lancelot said rather sheepishly. "Shilty helped convince Collins to take the cash pay off in the first place, and now she's saved Robert from possibly going to prison. You could at least be grateful for her help."

Lucy pursed her lips. "Well, if you put it that way. I suppose so. But, I still wouldn't trust her as far as I could throw her. You don't seriously think Robert will marry her do you?"

Lancelot leaned in and whispered seriously, "We need Shilty Cunningham - for all her faults - and to be honest we could do with her money too. The government want Little Eden to collapse. The council tax is worth millions per annum to London Council and the Major can't wait to get his hands on it. Shilty is like our political shield. Her father was Melbourne's friend and he is still very powerful in Westminster as are most of her friends. We need to capitalise on that. Don't ruin it."

Lucy nodded reluctantly. "Okay. I'll go along with it, but if he marries her I'm going to blame you!"

"How is Joshua finding Little Eden?" Lucy asked Adela when she brought over the coffees.

"Oh, he loves it," Adela replied. "He's never had so many slumber parties in his life and he's made so many new friends. Little Eden really is the friendliest place on Earth. He was bullied sometimes back in L.A. He's very sensitive, not just to food, but to emotions and other people. He's an empath as well as a Star Child. Here, in Little Eden, it's like he's found somewhere he belongs. He adores Tambo and Alice too. He's happier than he's ever been!"

"And you?" Lancelot asked her. "Are you happy here too?"

Adela smiled at him. "I'm happier than I have ever been too."

Lancelot wanted so badly to tell Adela how he felt about her, but he was not one for romantic speeches and he wanted to be sure of his regard for her before he bared his soul. *Jack would have made love to her already, he thought. Even Robert would have kissed her by now! What's wrong with me? Maybe I just don't do relationships. India says women like to make the first move these days. Do I wait for her to say something first? She's so beautiful and smart and kind and easy to talk to. Maybe I'll just wait a little longer before I say anything.* Lancelot talked himself into delaying owning up to his emotions. Yes, he decided, *I'll wait a bit longer.*

~ * ~

<jameshollywood@hauntedornot.com>
to Lucy

Not got much to report about Frith. The energy on the letters and the watch Faberge sent isn't opening up. The trail stops the day he walked out of his bedroom. Some PI's think he was in India, Africa and even South Am' years ago so that narrows the field - not! Been to Emp' State and Statue of Lib' today with the crew - got you a little something in Bloomingdales. Carrie has some friends in Lily Dale so going to chill with them tomorrow. Jazz club tonight, already started on the Jacky D! Can you ask Lancelot to give us more expenses? He's being a tight arse.

Love ya babe
J

<lucylawerence@daisyplacecafebookshop.com>
to Jimmy

Hi honey

Missing you so much. It sounds like you're having fun. Sorry to hear it's not going well with tracing Uncle Frith. Stella says one PI thought they had found him in India in 1989 but when they got there it wasn't him and there was no record of him at the ashram. Stella says Elizabeth tried looking for him again in 1991 after her husband and daughter died but that PI thought he'd never left the US. But you'll know all this anyway from the files I guess. I wish I was there with you, it sounds amazing and I'd love Tambo to see New York. Things are okay here. Busy as usual. Can you pick up a Yankees baseball cap for Tambo and an I love NY mug for Alice? I'll pay you for them when you get back. I'll try to talk to Lancelot but I can't promise anything. We're trying to save every penny towards saving Little Eden.

Love you so much
Lucy

<LBHsec@littleeden.co.uk>
to Jimmy

Dear Mr Pratt - Hollywood,

Thank you for your email.
Mr Bartlett-Hart wishes to convey to you his sincerest thanks for your update and looks forward to daily reports from you regarding the situation.

Mr Van Ike mentioned to us about providing you with extra expenses but we must advise that alcoholic drinks, mini bars, room service, use of the spa facilities, entry to tourist attractions and the purchase of souvenirs or clothing along with entry to nightclubs cannot be covered.

A budget of $30 a day for food for each crew member had been sanctioned in the contract and I can confirm that your hotel, flights, car hire and insurances will be covered as agreed.

Yours sincerely

Birgitta Jensen
Secretary to Mr Lancelot Bartlett-Hart

<jameshollywood@hauntedornot.com>
to Van Ike

Just as I thought! Lancelot's being a right dick. Can't get anything but food on expenses! Your negotiating skills suck man! There's no way we are finding this bloke. This is such a fucking waste of time! Wherever he went he's so well cloaked the devil himself ain't finding him.

Jimmy

\<vanike@hauntedornottv.com\>
to Jimmy

Just film stuff and I'll edit it to make something out of nothing. I always do. Just make the best of it. Fake it.

Ike

\<vanike@hauntedornottv.com\>
to Carrie

Carrie, darling. Jimmy's kicking off. Do whatever you need to do okay? Take plenty of shots of alleys, stop signs, barriers, places that look derelict - you know the score. I want some shots of down and outs as well so we can suggest Frith could be one of them. I also want some hippy dippys to suggest he went into a sect. Go to Lily Dale and get some footage. Take some shots of the grand hotels as well then we can suggest he's a tycoon or even a senator who doesn't want his past to come out - think men in suits and limos. Make sure we've got plenty of the tourist NY as well. Get St Pauls church and Woodlawn Cemetery - day and night. Interview someone in a bar, one of those milkshake places, and in the Plaza lobby. Don't let Jimmy wear that bolo tie or a Stetson, he's not Clint Eastwood for fucks sake. Oh, get some images of guns. Text me any problems.

Ike

\<carrie@hauntedornottv.com\>
to Van Ike

I'll do what I can. Jimmy is still a prat even with the name change! I'm not working with him again - this is the LAST time!!!!

You're going to have to fake it. There are no leads. This guy just fell off the planet. If you ask me - he's probably tied to a concrete slab at the bottom of the Hudson River.

Carrie

\<lucylawerence@daisyplacecafebookshop.com\>
to Jimmy

Hi honey, not heard from you in days, hope you are all okay. Thought maybe you didn't have a phone signal or internet where you are? We have found something that'll blow your mind here. Can't wait to show you when you get back. I'm still having funny dizzy do's and nausea. Jack thinks it might be an inner ear infection but Silvi Swan says it could be something called ascension symptoms? Apparently some people are getting them due to 2012 energies. Have you heard of them? I wondered if Carrie or one of the others were getting them? They can include dizziness, nausea, memory loss, insomnia, panic attacks, palpitations, anxiety for no reason and migraines/headaches. Anyway, missing you lots and can't wait for you to get back. I hope you've got a lead on Frith for us, we're all counting on you.
Love Lucy

\<jameshollywood@hauntedornot.com\>
to Lucy

Sorry been off line babes, really busy. Talk when I get back.
J

~ * ~

Chapter 6
~ * ~

The next day Sophie took a rickshaw from outside the cornucopia to the gates of the British Museum. The monumental classical façade towered above her as she walked up the wide, crowded path towards the long flight of steps.

She felt a flurry of excitement race through her.

She never knew why this place gave her a thrill, but it always did. Passing through the grand pillars and into the vestibule, which seemed uncommonly dark after the bright sunshine outside, she found a guide and asked to be shown to Tobias Gilbert's room.

As she entered the great court, she was overwhelmed by the intensity of the light as it flooded through the glass vaulted ceiling and reflected off the white marble floor and walls, making the grand space glimmer and gleam. The vast atrium was full of visitors chattering and looking at maps, turning them one way up then another, trying to decide which exhibition to visit first. She felt butterflies fluttering in her stomach but also a sense of inner peace - the museum was a welcoming place. The guide led her through her favourite exhibition hall - the Egyptian sculpture gallery - where the grand busts of famous pharaohs stood amongst finely carved figurines of animal gods: from cats to crocodiles and jackals to flacons. Wondrous and ancient objects d'art in glass cases seemed to whisper to her as she walked by. She wished she could awaken the spirits within them. They seemed so familiar to her - like family of old.

She was ushered through a locked door which had a sign saying, 'No entry,' upon it.

"Up the stairs, to the right and it's the third room on the left," the guide told her.

Sophie thanked her, and leaving the crowds behind, she walked down the empty corridor which echoed with her footsteps. She felt privileged to go where the public were usually forbidden. She couldn't help but peep through every window just to catch a glimpse of what lay behind the scenes. Finally she reached the office belonging to:

Tobias Gilbert
Senior Curator of Antiquities

Her excitement turned to anxiety. Since a massive relapse of chronic fatigue last year had made her jobless, homeless and ninety percent house bound, meeting new people, which had once been no trouble to her at all, had started to fill her with dread. She prayed to Aunt Lilly to give her courage and knocked on the door.

"Come in," a friendly voice called from the other side.

Sophie tentatively opened the door and stepped inside.

The small office was in semi-darkness. Venetian blinds were partly closed creating shafts of dust filled light across the room. The scholarly space was filled with book shelves and an array of small statues, funeral vases and carved scarab beetles. The scent of fresh wood shavings filled the air as they cascaded from a cluster of partly opened packing crates.

Tobias Gilbert looked up from his laptop and smiled.

He took her breath away.

Wow, she thought. *I didn't expect him to be so good looking!*

Tobias held out his hand as he stood up to greet Sophie. His dark eyes caught the half-light and they seemed to take her far down deep into his soul. He did not attempt to take his hand from hers very quickly. She finally let go of his, afraid he may think she had lingered too long (or had he lingered too long - she wasn't entirely sure?).

He came around the desk and took a stack of books off a wooden Captain's chair so she could sit down.

Tobias's voice was mellifluous and confident. He was smartly dressed and carried himself with a polite yet affable air. Sophie was afraid that she might come across as tired and pathetic when she spoke (the fatigue sometimes made her voice seem weak and she often struggled to find her words or follow a conversation for long. She knew her eyes lacked sparkle these days and she rarely had the energy to put on make-up or do her hair). As she listened to him talk she couldn't stay focused on what he was saying; today though it had nothing to do with the fatigue. She was actually distracted by her own thoughts which were wandering off in another direction…

Pull yourself together! I might not look too pale and haggard in this dim light. She tried to get a grip on herself. *Don't be silly! It doesn't matter what you look like, he'd never fancy you in a million years anyway, and besides he's so gorgeous he's probably gay. Are those pecs under that jumper? Nice knitwear and I like those jeans. He looks as if he works out. I wonder what he looks like naked? Stop it! Good job he's not a mind reader.*

But, dear readers, Tobias Gilbert wasn't gay and this is what he was thinking…

Wow! So this is Sophie Lawrence. Jack said she was pretty. I've wanted to meet her for so long. God, I hope my breath doesn't smell. She's got the most beautiful eyes. I don't have something in my teeth do I? He thought of the tuna and rocket sandwich he had had for lunch and began to regret not having looked in the mirror since. *I'm such a geek. Just act natural! Find an excuse to get her phone number. I wonder what she looks like naked? God, I hope she can't read minds.*

Suffice to say, Sophie showed the jewelled crosses to Tobias, who tried to stay interested in them and not keep wondering what it would be like kiss her and take her right there on the desk.

He typed up an inventory, took some photographs, and signed off each item. Sorry not to find an excuse to keep her there any longer he walked her out, down the stairs, wondering when he should ask for her out on a date. As they came back into the Egyptian exhibit she seemed interested in the sculptures and he took the opportunity to linger, trying to impress her with his knowledge whilst he gathered his courage to ask her out.

I hope I don't have love-karma with him, Sophie thought as she let him explain the Rosetta Stone to her. *He'll break my heart, I just know it. This better be just a frisson - nothing more. I bet he has lots of pretty students or curators throwing themselves at him. I bet he's a right player - probably got a new woman every month.*

With that, an attractive young woman, with a museum badge dangling around her neck, came up to Tobias and spoke to him like a good friend.

Oh yes, see, I was right! Sophie pretended to be fixated on a case of funerary statuettes, but she couldn't help noticing that the woman's tight white blouse was open a little too far down and the top of her pink lacy bra was peeking out from beneath the soft cotton.

He'll fancy her no doubt. Sophie thought: and wished she had put something nicer on instead of just a baggy jumper and jeans. *I wonder if he's a good kisser? He has such a lovely smile. I could so kiss that smile. Damn it! If I don't leave soon I'll fall in love with him and I'll obsess about him for weeks on end and drive myself crazy. I should just go home.*

Sophie wanted to stay and yet simultaneously wanted to escape so she made an excuse to leave and hurried away. She regretted it as soon as she was back in the atrium but she had no excuse to go back now.

Tobias was a little startled by her quick exit. *Damn it!* he thought, *I didn't ask her out.*

Back outside, Sophie took a deep breath and looked up at the turquoise sky. Peach ribbons laced the white clouds - it was a fine spring evening. She wondered whether to hail another rickshaw or to attempt the walk back into Little Eden: she decided a crash the next day might be worth it. She missed drinking in the heady scents of the lilacs and bathing in the luminous lime green of the trees. A busker, singing near the entrance to the Queen's Gate, was playing, Fallin' For You[4] , and she smiled at the synchronicity of the lyrics, hoping it was a good sign.

Passing the park she spotted Robert who was just coming out of the Refuge. She called to him and he crossed the road to meet her.

"It's good to see you out and about," he told her.

"I haven't left the flat in over a week," Sophie replied. "It's lovely to see the flowers - everything changes so quickly in the spring."

"Speaking of flowers, I've just been to visit Linnet," Robert told her.

"How is she?" Sophie enquired.

Robert shrugged. "They say she hasn't touched a drop in nearly two weeks now. But, there's still a long way to go. She looked as if she'd not been sleeping well. She said she hoped to be back home in less than a month."

"Do you think she will be?" Sophie asked.

Robert sighed. "I don't know. Time will tell I suppose. She might need a lot longer than that to fully recover herself." He gave Sophie his arm. "I was headed to the café. Come on, you look pale. You need a cup of tea and a sit down."

When they reached the café-bookshop it was deserted, everyone having just gone home for the day, but they found Alice sitting on the stairs cuddling Cedric.

"Are you okay?" Sophie asked her.

Alice shook her head and kissed Cedric's soft fur. "Cedric's frightened to go upstairs," she replied.

"Okay," Sophie said, glancing sideways at Robert. "And can Cedric tell us why he's so scared?"

---

4 Fallin' For You, Cobie Caillat, 2009, Universal Republic

"Can't you see them?" Alice asked her.

Sophie and Robert looked at each other, unsure what Alice meant. Sophie sat on the stair and tickled Cedric under the chin. "We can't see whatever it is you can see so you'll have to tell us about it," she said kindly.

"All the women!" Alice replied as if Sophie should know what she meant.

"Women in spirit you mean?" Sophie asked. "Are they nuns?"

Alice shook her head again. "No, they're the ones on the list - the ones who used to work here in the café. There look! Can't you see them?" Alice pointed up the stairs.

Sophie closed her eyes and engaged her second sight.

"What is it Sophie?" Robert asked.

"Alice is right. There are women on the stairs and the landing. They seem to be milling about as if gathering for a meeting that hasn't started yet. I don't think they're scary though," Sophie explained.

"I didn't think they were scary but Cedric wasn't sure," Alice replied with relief.

Sophie smiled. "I don't think they mean us or Cedric any harm. They belong here just as much as we do, I suppose. They owned the café once upon a time. Why they're all showing up here now I'm not sure. I've never seen or felt them before, have you?"

"I only ever saw Lilly before," Alice admitted.

"We'll come up the stairs with you," Robert reassured her.

"I don't like walking through them," Alice admitted. "It feels funny when you walk through a ghost."

Sophie laughed. "I suppose we could ask them to move?"

"That's if they can see and hear us," Robert said. "I can't see them."

"Well, I guess we'll have to give it a go," Sophie suggested, and was about to try to communicate with the spirits when they vanished into thin air and were gone. "Oh!" Sophie said. "I don't know if they heard us or not but they've disappeared."

Alice checked all around. "They've gone, Cedric!" she told him and he jumped out of her arms and pootled (I say pootled as he is too old to run) up the stairs without a care.

Chapter 7
~ * ~

Up in the apartment, Sophie told Lucy and Robert about her meeting with Tobias Gilbert (minus a few of the more personal details which she saved to tell Lucy about later).

"Why didn't you tell me you'd found some treasure?" Robert said aghast.

"We didn't have chance," Lucy told him. "We didn't want to say anything in front of Shilty."

"You could have taken me aside," Robert replied.

"When you're with Shilty, it's like you're stuck together with some kind of magic sex glue," Lucy laughed.

"Don't worry, it's in safe hands," Sophie told him. (She couldn't help thinking about Tobias's hands for a moment…).

"But, is it worth anything?" Robert asked.

"Jack's taken the gold to Brindisi Thistle for valuation and Tobias will get back to Jack when he's authenticated and dated all the crosses," Sophie explained. "He thinks the pieces have been gathered from holy places around the world over thousands of years. One was a genuine Egyptian Ankh, apparently, which could be over three thousand years old. "

"Gathered, or stolen, from around the world?" Robert laughed.

"I guess we'll never know if we are handling stolen goods or not, but Tobias said they come from as far away as Russia. He said one of the crosses might have been made for St Hilda of Whitby in the 7th Century and might be one of the Lindesfarne crosses. If we can prove it, it might be worth up to one hundred million pounds at auction."

Robert looked stunned and amazed. "What makes that one so special?" he asked.

"Apparently, a cross just like that one was buried with St Cuthbert in about 686. He's the patron saint of Northumberland. There's a rumour that there were three of them made and the other two have never found. One of them may have belonged to St Hilda who founded Whitby Abbey down the coast from there. We might have just discovered it in the middle of London, in our wardrobe of all places," Sophie said.

"Couldn't you use some psychometry and feel who it belonged to?" Robert asked her.

"I suppose I could, but now I know it might have been St Hilda's, I won't be sure if I am making it up or not, and besides, no one is going to pay millions of pounds for something just because I had a vision that it's the genuine article," Sophie replied.

"I suppose we could ask Jimmy when he gets back from America," Lucy suggested. "As long as he doesn't know the details beforehand he can't make it up."

"That's true," Sophie agreed.

Robert sighed. "You should keep some of the money from this treasure for yourselves and Tambo," he suggested.

Lucy shook her head. "It's not for us. It's for Little Eden."

"You need it as much as Little Eden does," Robert replied.

"You can't seriously think we would steal from Little Eden and from the people who gathered this treasure together over all those centuries?" Sophie said astonished.

"It's only stealing off Collins and Lucas," Robert said. "They are the ones who want the money. You owe Little Eden nothing. You mustn't sacrifice yourselves for everyone else."

"You are prepared to sacrifice yourself for Little Eden," Lucy told him.

"Am I?" Robert replied.

"If you're really thinking of marrying Shilty Cunningham," Sophie said, "Then yes! I would say that's a massive sacrifice."

Robert grimaced. "How did you know that? I hate it when you're a mind reader."

Sophie laughed. "I didn't read your mind. Lucy told me last night that Lancelot was trying to pimp you out to help save Little Eden."

Robert sighed. "I wouldn't quite put it like that. But Lance does have a point. Shilty is very useful to us right now."

"That doesn't mean you have to marry her, surely?" Lucy exclaimed. "Unless of course you do love her?" she added tentively - hoping to god he did not!

"What's love got to do with it?" Robert replied.

"Well, it is a second hand emotion!" Sophie giggled.

"What does it matter who I marry anyway?" he asked and turning to Sophie he added, "You don't believe in love. It's just love-karma. That's what you always say."

"I do say that," Sophie admitted. "Love-karma makes us feel as if we are in love. But, if you don't even feel you love her, then it's just regular karma. At least if you marry because of love-karma you stand some chance of being happy."

"You are still a romantic at heart!" Robert laughed. "I don't want to marry Shilty but I will if I have to. She's got political connections. Her family gatherings are like being at an embassy party. She has her own money, and when she inherits from her father she'll have even more. She has billionaire friends who might just be generous enough to help us. I know you and Lucy have never liked her, but…"

"…no one but Shilty Cunningham likes Shilty Cunningham," Lucy interrupted. "Don't worry, we'll be polite to her and welcome her as your wife if we have to. Although, I'm not sure I could ever trust her."

Suddenly, they heard a commotion down in Daisy Place.

They all went out onto the roof to take a look and could see a large group of truculent residents jeering and shouting at someone they had encircled. Robert couldn't see who it was that they had imprisoned within a wall of savage sound. He was afraid someone maybe hurt.

"Stop!" Robert shouted down and quickly descended to the square via Sumona's balcony and the wooden steps from the old coaching inn. "Stop!"

Robert broke into the centre of the hostile crowd to find his mother, Jennifer, clinging to the Victorian water pump for dear life. Astonished and appalled to find the elderly woman being brutally harassed in such a way, Robert commanded everyone to stand back and be quiet. They did as he ordered. He put his arm around his mother who was shaking with terror. "How dare you!" Robert reprimanded the crowd, which he could see was a mixture of all ages, men and women and even a few children. "You should be ashamed of yourselves!"

A woman, holding her baby, bluntly replied, "She's trying to destroy us! She wants to take our homes, our businesses, our lives. She's the one who ought to be ashamed."

"Banish her!" someone shouted.

Robert caught sight of Derren Cox who was trying to sneak away from the brutal throng. Before he could skulk into Tom Thumb Alley and back to his Tobacconist shop, Robert called him out. "You!" he shouted. "This is your doing isn't it?"

Everyone looked at Derren and their expressions reassured Robert that he was right.

Derren turned and faced Robert. "This is what we all think, not just me," he said rudely. "She should be banished like your brother."

"Collins is not banished," Robert replied angrily. "He can return any time he chooses. My mother's home is still Little Eden. This is not the middle ages!"

"You can banish people when they hurt one of us," one young lady said angrily. "You sent my brother away."

Robert recalled who the woman meant and replied, "Your brother beat his wife and put her in hospital. She asked to be kept safe from him. This is hardly the same thing!"

But, as he heard his words out loud, he wasn't so sure that his mother was any less guilty of abuse than anyone else. Mentally, emotionally, materially, physically - bullying, violence and manipulation are equal no matter how they are manifested. He felt as if he didn't want to explore the philosophy of it right now and simply said, "You should have come to me in a rational, sensible way. Not attacked my mother like this. If you feel this strongly you know what to do. Get up a petition with enough signatures and we will discuss it at the next residents meeting."

He flashed an angry look at Derren but said no more, and led a weeping Jennifer off towards the café.

The mortified crowd began to disperse in disgrace.

Lucy opened the café door and ushered them inside. "Take her upstairs," she told Robert.

"What the hell?" Robert asked his mother when he had sat her down on the sofa, and Lucy had made some hot sweet tea. "What were you thinking? I told you it wasn't safe for you here but you insisted on staying. You should have stayed indoors at Stella's."

He handed her his handkerchief.

Jennifer sniffed and looked in her compact mirror. She wiped the streaks of mascara off her face. "I got bored. It's like being under house arrest," she grumbled and reapplied her lipstick.

"Why don't you go and join Collins in the Caribbean until this all gets sorted out?" Robert suggested.

Jennifer shook her head. "I want to stay here," she replied in a huff.

"But why?" Sophie asked. "You don't want Little Eden to exist anyway so why on earth do you want to live here?"

Jennifer sniffed again and sipped her tea. "I didn't really want to destroy Little Eden," she admitted. "I just…" she couldn't finish her sentence and broke down in tears again. She looked so frail all of a sudden, and older than her plastic face and layers of make-up made her appear at first glance.

Sophie felt her heart swell with compassion for Jennifer but she also wanted to bash her to death with the nearest heavy object.

As Jennifer calmed down she noticed the tin of photographs on the coffee table, and the one of the café, which they had found the day before, was on the top of the pile. She picked it up and looked intently at it.

"Do you know who all these people are?" Lucy asked her.

Jennifer nodded and pointed to one of the waitresses. "That's Lana Lansbury."

"The actress?" Lucy asked, astonished. She looked closer at the image. "Crikey, she's Hollywood famous! I'd never have recognised her in a million years."

"She used to come in here all the time as a young actress," Jennifer said boastfully.

Robert took a peek at the photograph and exclaimed, "Isn't that you, this other waitress, standing next to her, and that's Lilly?"

Jennifer reluctantly nodded.

"You once worked in the café?" Sophie asked, astonished by the idea.

"I worked as a waitress here for a few years. I…" she began to sob again and they had to wait (a little impatiently) for her to calm down again so that she could continue with her story…"I was a model in those days. I could have been the most famous model in the world had I not met your father and had you boys."

"You never told me you had worked here with Lilly!" Robert gasped.

"Savanna ran it back then." Jennifer half laughed and half cried. "It was quite the place to be for artists and actors. You'd call it hippy now I suppose, but then…then it was somewhere we could all be ourselves. There was such a buzz! Music and singing all the time. I met your father there. Lilly and I…" she stopped again.

"Were you and Lilly friends?" Sophie asked her.

Jennifer nodded. "We were…"

"Best friends?" Sophie guessed.

Jennifer nodded.

Lucy and Sophie both took an involuntary step back from her but they were not sure why.

"We lived in a flat in Castle Mansions with three other girls." Jennifer admitted. "It was crowded but we had so much fun!" She seemed to be seeing pictures of the past running through her mind. "Lana, she was called Jessica then; she went to Hollywood; made quite a name for herself and married a famous director. I don't know what happened to Ffion and Hadiya. We lost touch."

"How did you meet my father?" Robert asked her.

Jennifer sighed. "Melbourne loved the 'lovvies'. He made Little Eden into an artists' paradise. He came to the café nearly every evening to see them all."

"Why did he marry you?" Sophie enquired, without disguising her surprise.

Jennifer's countenance suddenly changed from pathetic to panther. She threw the photograph back onto the table in a fury. "Lilly wanted him but I got him! I got him!!" she snarled.

"Is that why you fell out?" Sophie asked her. "Is that why you hated her?"

Jennifer was seething with anger. "She never forgave me! She was always jealous of me!"

Lucy couldn't imagine Aunt Lilly being jealous of anyone. She had always taught them that forgiveness was the key to happiness. It seemed an unlikely tale.

Robert saw through her too. "Is that why father wanted Lilly buried in the crypt with the family - because he married you instead of her?"

"What do you mean?" Jennifer snapped

"Did he want to marry Lilly?" Sophie asked her.

"You're saying I trapped him?" Jennifer screamed. "Melbourne was in love with me! Not her!"

Jennifer was visibly shaking now and stood up to leave.

Sophie was still curious and wasn't prepared to let Jennifer go without more of an explanation. "Melbourne and Lilly were always good friends. We used to say he liked her more than he should. He was always in love with her wasn't he?"

Jennifer spat her words out with pure venom. "Lilly couldn't bear that I married Melbourne. She wanted to run away to America because she couldn't stand to see us together."

"So, why did he marry Christabelle and not Lilly when he'd had enough of you?" Sophie asked.

Lucy shook her head at Sophie - she thought her sister was going too far and Jennifer was about to blow.

"Take me back to Stella's!" Jennifer screamed at Robert. "This little girl thinks I'm a liar. How dare you? Who do you think you are?" she yelled at Sophie. "I know what you think! You think I got pregnant to trap Melbourne into marriage. Well! I won't have such slander against me! I'll sue you and your sister if you ever say anything about me in public!"

When Robert had taken his mother away, Sophie picked up the photograph. She had a wicked twinkle in her eye, "I think we should get this blown up, really big, and put up in the café where everyone can see it. And then, everyone will know her ladyship used to be a waitress here!"

"You are awful," Lucy giggled. "But I like it!"

Chapter 8
~ * ~

Thunder rumbled over the Sainte Chappelle. As she became aware of her surroundings, Sophie was overwhelmed by the scent of damp earth and fresh roses.

Oh crap, she thought. *I'm in another time portal. Wake up before something horrible happens!*

But Sophie didn't wake up…

Five nuns stood, like sentinels, gazing into the stone font in silent prayer. An ivory talisman, carved with the scene of the crucifixion, shimmered beneath the holy waters.

In the shadows Sophie couldn't quite make out the faces of the sisters. She wondered if they were the ones in the photograph, or perhaps they were the saints from her vision dream, but she had a strong feeling this was a different time in history.

A bolt of lightning flashed through the cobalt blue windows illuminating the hallowed scene with an unearthly aura.

The nuns were unsettled and on edge. Sophie had an uneasy feeling that there was something clandestine about their gathering.

"There will come a time when Little Eden is under threat of being raised to the ground," Mother Superior said softly to the others. "Not from plague, not from fire and not even from the Kings men, but from the Devil himself."

A deafening thunder clap rumbled directly overhead and a flare of lightening was hard on its heels, flashing midnight blue, wildly through the Chappelle.

The nuns crossed themselves.

"The true faith is lost here in England," Mother Superior continued. "Jesus Christ has replaced the protection of the Holy Mother. The spells of the crucifixion are used to perpetuate the evil men do. They build a false Heaven in the astral realms and it will be too late for those who follow the counterfeit God - they will find themselves trapped in an alternate spirit world instead of released into the arms of the Angels."

The other nuns tried not to appear frightened, but as another thunderous roar rolled ominously overhead, a sharp fork of lighting pierced the gloom, and the fresco above them was thrown into sharp relief. The face of Jesus loomed down upon them from his cross - watching them with an evil eye.

"One sacrifice to end all sacrifices," one of the nuns muttered.

"If we deny our own sacrifices and follow blindly the King's priests, we will never find our own way. The responsibility for our soul remains in our own hands, now and forever," Mother Superior said as she rolled up the wide sleeve of her habit and plunged her hand into the icy water. She pushed aside the ivory plaque and delved deeper into the font. Pulling a leather bag out from the concealed central hole, she shook the water from it and placed it on the stone rim. "Even in our own church, if we do not have the courage to look the Devil in the eye, we will never see the truth," she said.

Thunder boomed as if it were in the room with them - rattling the towering glass and shaking the pillars. The full force of the following lightening fired up the Chappelle with an incandescent blue flame.

They all gasped in fright, including Sophie!

Mother Superior tried to remain calm for the sake of her sisters but Sophie could feel the presence of Satan creeping silently amongst the stones. She wanted to warn the sisters but she could not speak. Dark spectres of shadowy dust whispered around her. She was desperate to wake up but she could not - she was trapped inside the portal and surrounded by evil.

Mother Superior emptied the leather pouch, spilling out some highly jewelled crosses.

Sophie recognised them immediately as the ones they had found in the wardrobe.

"These jewels have been gathered over the centuries and have been in our care for hundreds of years," Mother Superior told her sisters. "His Highness King Richard III gave them to the Abbess before his last battle. We will take them for safe keeping to our sisters in Chartres. They have promised to place them in the shrine of Saint Bathild until they are needed."

"How will we escape without being searched?" one of the sisters asked her. "The King's men are outside the walls waiting for us."

Mother Superior reassured them all. "Lady Bartlett has arranged safe passage for us all to Calais. They will not dare search those who travel under her livery. And, in case they do halt us, we will each stitch something into the hem of our habit so they cannot be found. We shall go by boat from Dover as arranged. May the Holy Mother have mercy upon us for we are in the hands of God."

Each of the sisters took some jewels and crossed themselves again.

"Sister Mildred, do you have the ring?" Mother Superior asked.

Sister Mildred took a delicate amethyst ring from her habit pocket. "I took it from the shrine at Glastonbury when the soldiers came to murder the Abbot."

"You were brave Sister," Mother Superior praised her. "God will not forget your courage. This shall be the key. Whosoever wears this ring shall wield the power of the Virgin and the power of all of the women who hold the Holy Spirit in their hearts. When we are called from spirit we shall return time and time again to fight the evil and wake the Holy Mother from her sleep."

A direful roll of thunder rumbled throughout the Abbey again, but this time it was distant, and the lightening came without intensity, gently lighting up the Chappelle from the other side. The faces of the nuns were finally illuminated and Sophie recognised them instantly. They were previous incarnations of Minnie, Stella, Iris and Adela; and the Mother Superior was Aunt Lilly.

"We must leave our sacred places unguarded until we can return," Mother Superior sighed. Her heart was breaking as she looked around the beautiful Chappelle.

Sophie now noticed how highly decorated it was. Every carving, every pillar, every alcove was painted with vibrant, joyful colours. *This must be the mid-fifteen hundreds*, Sophie thought. *Just before the Reformation.*

"Our sacred places will be taken by those who worship Jesus alone and the Holy Virgin will walk here no more. Our prayers must always be that she gives us the strength to carry her compassion in our hearts, wherever we may find our earthly bodies," Mother Superior told them.

Suddenly, a violent and deafening rattling resounded throughout the Abbey as the heavens opened and torrential rain came hurtling down upon the Chappelle roof.

"It feels like the end of the world," one of the sisters whispered.

Mother Superior nodded. "It is the end of our world. The hospitals, the poor houses, the schools - they will be no more. The old ways of sisterhood will be lost." She prayed to St Margaret to give her courage. "Fear not, my dear sisters," she told them. "Religions may divide us but religions are passing fancies. Our Holy Mother is eternal."

Mother Superior kissed her rosary and added, "Let us pray."

The sisters bowed their heads as they spoke these words…

Holy Spirit, be my shepherd and my guide, leading me amongst the green pastures and to the holy waters.
My cup runs over with your healing light and I am restored by your love and your blessings.
Let your holy golden staff be my guide and my protection, upon the path of righteousness.
Even though I walk through the valley of the shadow of death,
I shall fear no evil,
For in your holy footsteps, goodness and loving kindness shall follow me all the days of my life and I shall dwell forever in the heart of the Goddess and in your holy embrace.[5]

"We leave in one hour," Mother Superior told them. "There must be no delay. The tide will not wait for us."

Sophie awoke gently from her vision with peace in her heart and surrounded by the gently wafting breeze of the Holy Spirit. She felt as if the bed was made of feathers and she was floating, suspended on a cloud in a place with no pain. She didn't want this rare sensation to end, but as she glanced at the time she realised that it was four o'clock in the afternoon. She had asked Minnie, Stella, Iris and Adela to come with her to the old Abbess's house for a meeting about the inquest at a quarter past - she had to get up and get dressed.

At least now I know I asked the right women, she thought as she put on her jeans and jumper.

It was raining and cold as she walked over to the Abbey. She was glad to find that Iris and Stella were already there, and that they had put the electric heater and the kettle on.

Minnie and Adela arrived a few moments later and came in shaking their umbrellas.

The five women sat around the table in the Abbess's study which smelt of candle wax and piano polish. Sophie thanked them all for coming and explained again, as she had done on the phone, about the inquest, and the need to find a jury of five women from Little Eden.

---

5 Holy Spirit Prayer, KT King Prayers, Book Three, 2019

"I understand the concept," Stella said. "My only concern is that Iris is the only Catholic amongst us."

"I'm a lapsed Catholic," Iris reminded them. "I left the Church many years ago."

"It's fine," Sophie reassured them all. "I looked up the word nun in the dictionary and it means 'nonna' or 'grandmother' in Latin, and it's not exclusive to any religion. And actually, Nun is thought to be the oldest deity - it means the primordial or holy waters - and was used for healing and to invoke compassion. I believe it's the energy of the divine feminine which goes by many sacred names: Nun is just one of those names."

"Is Nun a pagan deity?" Adela asked.

"It's not really to do with any particular belief system," Sophie replied. "That's the point. Nun is just a word for a stream of consciousness and a portal through which all humans are born, and through which we all return at death. It is the etheric womb of incarnation, and at that stage, before our soul goes into the embryo, there is only love and compassion. I believe it is the last point at which we feel no fear, just before the human nervous system begins to develop.

"So, it's sort of a universal womb which doesn't belong to any one race or culture?" Minnie asked.

"Yes, I believe so," Sophie replied. "I believe if someone says they are a nun, it simply means they are trying to live a compassionate life and to embody the Holy Spirit. They are trying to be an earth angel. When humans have fallen into fear, and are in danger of being stuck in the wheel of karma, the pure energy of Nun will open their hearts and help them on their journey to compassion and enlightenment."

"I'm not sure I'm one of those," Minnie said. "Although, I'd like to be."

"Kindness and unconditional love is what it's all about really," Sophie said. "If you carry both in your heart, and always let them guide you, then you carry the energy of Nun."

"You always help those in need and protect them from harm," Adela told Minnie. "By Sophie's definition that sounds like you are a nun, if you ask me!"

"I have a question," Stella said. "The nuns here at the Abbey used second sight to find out what really happened during their trials - none of us can do that except you, Sophie,"

"Iris can see and speak with spirit," Sophie replied.

Iris wasn't sure if she was psychic exactly. "Back home we used to call it the shining, so we did. I can talk with the spirit of some of the saints, so I can, but whether I could see what happened that night by the lake with Robert and Marcus Finch, I very much doubt I could."

"I just know it has to be us five women," Sophie told them. "Trust me. I know. Besides, we all represent something of the divine feminine which makes us a formidable team. Minnie has truth, Adela has knowledge, Stella you bring strength and Iris you bring faith."

Stella laughed. "And, as Sophie means 'wisdom', I presume you are the wise one of the group?"

Sophie frowned. "Mmm, I'm not sure about that. I think I might just be a stand in for Aunt Lilly - she is the wise one. But together, we embody the 'Nun' that is potentially in every human. I have a feeling that the divine feminine is about to explode all over Little Eden anytime soon!"

"I have to admit that I feel uncomfortable sitting in judgement on Robert," Adela said.

"I'm not keen on the idea either," Minnie responded. "I feel as if we couldn't find him guilty even if he was guilty."

"We have all known Robert for a long time, so we have, and he'd never harm anyone intentionally, so he wouldn't. I have faith in him and his innocence," Iris said. "With or without evidence or second sight, I know he wouldn't harm anyone."

"If we save Robert we save Little Eden," Stella told them. "He's clearly innocent of any wrong doing. It was all in self-defence. Marcus would have killed him, and possibly Alice as well, if he had not drowned. Robert would never murder anyone. He's a born protector not a killer."

"So, will you all do it?" Sophie asked them.

The women all looked at each other and nodded.

"We will."

Chapter 9
~ * ~

The spring equinox was ushered in by a stormy night and the inquest began in the pouring rain. Around midday, many residents and the newly formed jury of five women gathered in the Pump Rooms, where wooden folding chairs had been laid out in rows. Iris took her place as magistrate behind a temporary trestle table, with Sophie and Stella to her left and Minnie and Adela to her right.

Sophie prayed silently to Alienor, Aunt Lilly and the saints to join and guide them. As she looked at her friends, she smiled to herself. With her third eye she could see that they were all wearing habits and looked like the nuns she had seen in the Chappelle.

Robert sat on the front row with Lancelot, India and Shilty. Lucy, who had Alice and Tambo with her, sat just behind. The many residents and journalists who had gathered in the hall were a little nervous, wondering if Robert would be found guilty of murder or manslaughter.

The chairs made for plenty of scraping noises against the sprung parquet floor, and umbrellas were leaving little puddles down the aisles. Once everyone was quiet, the proceedings began. Iris went through the legal motions. Witnesses were called, including Alice and Tambo (and I think, dear readers, that Cedric might have liked to have joined in as well - had he not been a dog).

Alice wasn't the least bit afraid of being questioned because, as she looked across the room, she could see the spirits of the café women all gathered at the back of the hall. The ghostly ladies couldn't see everyone in Little Eden but they had the ability to see Alice, Joshua, Elijah and Tambo in particular. Alice had become quite a favourite amongst them and was no longer afraid. Jin Keung and Dove Franklin waved to her from the back of the room. The only time it bothered Alice that she was surrounded by a constant flow of incorporeal beings was when she was in the bathroom. Yesterday, she had had to ask Temperance Shadow and Tulip Dancer to leave when she needed the loo!

After two hours the inquest was adjourned and the five jurors left the hall, gathering together in a side room which was usually used as a crèche. Amongst the piles of oversized Lego, a plastic Wendy house, toy railway and a few tiny chairs, they went through the evidence and ticked every box.

Mrs B popped in with tea and fresh scones for them, and she was a little sorry she couldn't stay.

All of a sudden Sophie felt a fizzy feeling travel up her legs which she recognised as energy coming up through the dragon portal. Then she began to tremble.

"Are you alright, my dear?" Iris asked her. "Have a scone - perhaps you're having a hypo? Your blood sugar has probably dropped," she suggested.

"It's okay, Iris, thank you," Sophie replied. "I think someone in spirit is trying to get my attention. Can you excuse me a moment whilst I try to see what's going on?"

Sophie walked towards the window. She stood looking out over East India Street. The rain had stopped, and in contrast to the heavy foreboding clouds which had darkened the town from day break, a patch of blue sky was now opening out just beyond the law offices. She felt the presence of spirit all around her and closed her eyes to focus her second sight more clearly.

Alienor was standing beside her. She was dressed in a leather suit of armour and the bejewelled hilt of her sword twinkled in the sunlight.

What do you want me to know? Sophie asked her.

Alienor took Sophie's hand and without warning, Sophie found herself standing by the lake near the Chateau: it was shrouded in swirling mist just as it had been that fateful night when Marcus had died. Sophie shivered as she felt the cold night air envelope her. She stood motionless in anticipation.

A wisp of mist cleared for a moment and she could see Robert, lying unconscious, on the wet grass and herself kneeling beside him as they waited for the ambulance to arrive. She could hear a siren in the distance and became aware of Lucy talking on her mobile phone.

Her visionary body involuntarily hovered down towards the dark lake. Poised just above the icy water she could make out someone moving in the shadows. Obscured in the blackness, something rustled amongst the bulrushes. Marcus's head shot up towards her from the inky water. His bloated body floated before her in the freezing lake.

From behind her, a dark figure shuddered through the water and loomed over Marcus.

It was Jack.

Sophie watched in horror, as instead of spinning Marcus around to see if he was still alive, Jack calmly pushed Marcus's head downwards and held him mercilessly under the murky water.

Shocked to the core, Sophie realised that Jack was making sure Marcus would not make it out of the lake alive!

Shaking with disbelief, Sophie was jolted back into the present and into the crèche again. She opened her eyes to the bright sunlight, and for a few moments she was blinded by its clarity.

Sophie wasn't sure what to do or say.

Iris called her over, and she walked like a zombie towards them and sat down again. She could hardly make out what they were telling her - her mind was so full of what she had just witnessed. It can't be true, she thought. *Why did Alienor show me that? What am I supposed to do with that information? Do I tell Iris?*

She had not expected that her second sight would come into play for the inquest as it was an open and shut case. Sophie felt overwhelmed and afraid. *I can't tell them about this*, she thought. *We don't convict people based on psychic visions anymore. Besides, I have no proof. It could all be nonsense. Jack wouldn't do such a thing. Or would he?*

As Iris led them back into the main hall, Sophie still felt cold from the astral visit to the lake - her feet were freezing. She felt nauseous and uneasy but decided to say nothing for now.

Iris happily told a relieved Robert and expectant courtroom that a verdict of accidental death by drowning would be formally recorded. The residents applauded and stood up to congratulate Robert. He had never shaken so many people's hands so quickly in his life. Shilty was proud to be part of it all and introduced herself to everyone as Robert's fiancé - which he did nothing to deny.

Lancelot and India were perhaps more relieved than anyone. Now, at least, they had a clear chance of saving Little Eden.

In fact, everyone in the room was over the moon - except for Sophie.

Chapter 10
~ * ~

Sophie escaped outside before anyone else. As she leant back against the wall of Knights Walk her head was spinning. She felt afraid of what she had just seen. The vision swirled and flashed through her mind like a virus. The more she tried to tell herself it wasn't true, the stronger the images became. She knew she had to find Jack - the urge to speak to him was overwhelming.

Luckily, she caught sight of him as he passed by the end of the alleyway with Johnathon.

Sophie accosted him. "Can I have a word?" she asked.

Jack looked surprised at her serious face. "Okay, old girl. What's up?"

"Privately?" she whispered. "Come in here."

Jack followed her into the old dovecote, which was open to the public at all times but right now was deserted.

"What is it, old girl?" Jack asked, intrigued by her secrecy.

Sophie thought it best to just get straight to the point. "The night Marcus died," she began to say, but stopped, as she was suddenly anxious about hearing the words spoken out loud. She plucked up her courage and continued…"The night Marcus died. You were in the lake, yes?"

"Yes, you know that. Johnathon and I dragged him out," Jack admitted.

"Was Marcus dead when you found him?" she asked.

Jack frowned. "Of course, old girl - what are you getting at?"

Sophie shrugged. "I know you don't really believe in psychic visions and all that mumbo jumbo, but I had a vision just now, and it seemed to me that Marcus wasn't quite 'gone' when you got to him - if you know what I mean?"

Jack didn't even flinch.

Sophie had expected him to at least look a bit guilty. His steadfast expression gave her hope that the vision had been wrong and she was mistaken after all.

Jack didn't speak for a few moments and started to make patterns on the dusty floor with his foot. He finally looked at her again saying, "Look, old girl, you might not want to ask me anymore about that."

Sophie's heart went cold.

"You'll get yourself into trouble with this second sight of yours. You're not going to mention this to anyone are you?" Jack asked her.

Sophie felt sick to the pit of her stomach. "Well, no. I mean, I don't know what to do," she stuttered.

Jack ran his fingers through his blond hair and his expression became pensive. A pair of white doves fluttered through one of the narrow open perches. They seemed to snap Jack out of his contemplation and he smiled. "Maybe they should hire you for espionage!" he laughed. "That's quite a trick you can do there. Do you know anything else you shouldn't?"

"I didn't ask to see what I saw - it just happened," Sophie explained. She paused for a moment. "Who are 'they' exactly?"

Jack looked preoccupied again.

Sophie could see he wasn't exactly joking about the espionage. Something dawned on her which she realised she had suspected for years but had never let herself believe. "Oh my god, you're a spy aren't you?" she exclaimed.

Jack turned away for a moment - not sure what to say.

"Those trips abroad aren't to find antiques for the shop are they?" Sophie asked.

Jack gathered his thoughts. "Look, old girl," he said, turning to face her again. "I don't know how you know what you know and I don't really want to know - if you know what I mean - but you can't tell anyone about this. Not even Robert, not Lucy…no one."

Sophie felt as if someone had physically punched her in her chest. "So, it is true then?" she asked, just to be sure. She was as close to Jack as she would be to a blood brother. This man, whom she had known all her life, was changing right in front of her into someone she didn't recognise. His features, his height, his body, his clothes, they looked the same, but a lie had been shattered and the energy between them could never be the same again.

Jack nodded. "Dad was MI6. So am I. The shop has always been a cover."

"Is that why your Dad was killed in the car bomb attack?" she asked him.

Jack's eyes were suddenly filled with sadness. "Maybe," he replied.

"And your mum? Did she know?"

Jack nodded.

"But when did you get involved in all that stuff?" Sophie wanted to know.

"They approached me when I turned eighteen," he explained. "Look, old girl, I can't say any more than I have already. If you blow my cover and anyone finds out about me, I'll be in danger, and perhaps the people close to me would be too."

He could see the look of disappointment on Sophie's face. "I'm sorry I've had to lie to you all," he admitted. "But you can understand why, can't you? This is something our family do. My ancestors - they've all done this kind of work."

Sophie tried to take it all in. "You don't have a license to kill, do you?" she dared to ask.

He realised what she meant. "I'm not James Bond if that's what you're thinking."

"But, Marcus?" Sophie said. "Would you have let Robert go to prison for something you did?"

Jack frowned. "He would never have gone to jail. I can promise you that." He could see she was struggling with the concept. "It wasn't Clive who arranged for the inquest to be held here in Little Eden, it was me. I told Lance to ask Shilty to ask Clive, but Clive and I had already arranged it."

"I don't understand - why did you kill Marcus when you could have saved him?" Sophie couldn't help saying.

Jack frowned. "Would you have dragged him out and given him mouth to mouth so he could live to see another day?"

Sophie wasn't sure what she would have done in his position.

Jack held her face gently in his hands as he might an innocent child. "This conversation never happened," he told her softly. "I'm just an antiques dealer, okay? Can you forget all about it - for your own safety and mine?"

Sophie wasn't sure if she would ever forget what she now knew. "I have to think," Sophie told him. "I'll speak to you later." She pulled herself away and left him standing in the Dovecote alone.

"Wait," Jack called after her - but she was gone.

The heavens opened again and Jack stood in the doorway watching the huge drops of water bouncing off the pavement. Suddenly, he heard voices. Lucy, Minnie, India and Lancelot, who had just been leaving the Pump Rooms, rushed into the cote looking for shelter. Thinking Jack was just keeping out of the rain, they commented on the weather and the inquest for a few minutes. Lucy looked out to see if it was still raining. The drops were lighter and the breaking sunlight cast a full rainbow against the deep grey sky. It shimmered above the allotments and seemed to end over in Bluebell Woods.

"I always wish Leprechauns were real," Lucy mused. "A Leprechaun could give us the pot of gold from the end of that rainbow and save

Little Eden in a flash."

Jack's phone rang and he took the call. When he had finished, he smiled at the others. "Good timing! I think we've just had a visit from your Leprechaun. Brindisi Thistle has had a valuation of those gold coins and ingots you found, and he has a buyer already lined up!"

"How much are they worth?" India asked.

"One million for the lot," Jack replied triumphantly.

"Is that all?" Lancelot frowned.

"That's a hell of a lot, old chap," Jack corrected him. "They're not worth that much for scrap. It's the fact they are 6th Century that's making them worth so much."

Lancelot sighed. "I just think this four billion we have to raise is impossible. We keep getting small amounts, which I grant you to most people are large amounts, but I think we might be fighting a losing battle."

"If only we could get to the bottom of that rainbow," Lucy sighed.

"You are nuts, you know that, don't you, old girl?" Jack teased her.

"I'm not nuts!" Lucy giggled. "Just whimsical."

"Is that right?" Jack smiled.

"If Jimmy can find Uncle Frith then we might only have to find half that amount. We wouldn't have to pay Lucas's share at all," India added.

"Speaking of Frith, is there any news from Jimmy?" Minnie asked Lucy.

Lucy shook her head. "I've not heard from him in days."

"He sent an email yesterday saying there might be a lead with an elderly relative who lives in Boston," Lancelot told them. "Only, there's a snag - she won't see anyone. She's a recluse and hasn't seen anyone except her doctor and maid for years. She won't even take a phone call from myself or Jimmy."

Just as he mentioned Jimmy's name Lucy's phone pinged.

"Talk of the devil!" Lucy laughed. They all waited to see what he had to say. Lucy looked at the txt but appeared unable to read it.

"What's he say, old girl?" Jack asked.

Lucy still seemed to be trying to make it out. She started to feel faint and the blood drained from her face. She handed the phone to Jack.

This, dear readers, is what the txt said…

<Can't wait to see you for our last night together babe. Call me>

"So sorry, old girl," Jack told her and kissed the top of her head.

India took the phone. "The bastard," she muttered under her breath.

"What is it?" Minnie asked. India gave it to her to read. "Maybe it was auto correct? Maybe it's a mistake," Minnie said hopefully.

But, as they all knew, and you all know dear readers, it wasn't a mistake! Another txt arrived.

Minnie, who now had the phone, nearly dropped it in surprise when it pinged...

<Can't stop thinking about last night. Send me a pic?>

Minnie didn't want to show it to Lucy. Even she couldn't put a positive spin on that one!

Then another txt popped up.

<Bring your toys tonight. I want to see you play!>

"Oh my god!" Minnie exclaimed and almost threw the phone back to Jack as if it was contaminated.

"When I get my hands on that bastard I'll..." Jack began to say but he stopped when he realised that Lucy was having a panic attack. "Breathe, old girl," he told her.

"I'll txt him back and tell him he'd better not come back to Britain if he wants to keep his bollocks!" India replied and reached for the phone.

"Wait!" Lancelot said. "Don't!"

"He's not treating Lucy like this and getting away with it!" Minnie agreed with India.

"We've got a lot riding on his documentary and his evidence. We can't afford to scare him off right now," Lancelot explained.

"I hate to say it but Lancelot is right," India reluctantly agreed. "We need to show the lawyers that Jimmy is close to finding Frith and that he may actually find him. We need to delay Lucas and Collins. We need longer to raise the money. Or, if we find Frith, see if we can stop the sale altogether."

"We need Jimmy on our side for a bit longer," Lancelot added.

Jack turned the phone off and put it in his pocket. He agreed too.

"Maybe they weren't from Jimmy?" Lucy suggested as she started to come round a bit. "Maybe he leant his phone to someone else?"

"Maybe someone stole his phone!" Minnie suggested. "It is New York after all, and maybe that's why he hasn't been txting you lately…"

…"Because he lost his phone!" Lucy said and felt a ripple of relief through her heart.

"Maybe I should txt whoever it is and say I know they've got my boyfriend's phone," Lucy suggested.

"Don't reply," Lancelot urged her. "I think we all know his phone hasn't been stolen. Just pretend you didn't get the txts - for now at least."

"You will, won't you, old girl?" Jack said. "For the sake of Little Eden?"

Lucy sniffed and wiped away her tears on Jack's shirt. She felt sick. "I suppose," she agreed half-heartedly.

"It's stopped raining at least," Minnie said. "Let's go home."

Jack was seething with anger as they left the dovecote. "If I ever set eyes on him again I'll kill him," he said under his breath.

Chapter 11
~ * ~

The next day, Sophie wandered into the kitchen in search of something to nibble and found Jimmy Hollywood lying with his feet up on the sofa, looking at his phone and enjoying a frothy cappuccino. He greeted her with a mumbled hello and then carried on txting whoever it was he was txting.

"Where's Luce?" Sophie asked him.

"In the café," he told her without looking up, "She'll be back up in a mo'."

Sophie didn't really want to talk to him: she actually wanted to slap him across the face then throw him off the balcony, but she thought she had better be polite and she wanted to know what he had found out about Uncle Frith. "Did you have a good time in New York?" Sophie asked as she opened and shut the cupboards several times, unable to decide what she wanted to eat.

Jimmy shrugged and continued to txt. "Was okay," he finally replied.

Lucy came in carrying a plate piled high with fruit cake. Sophie was about to go back to bed but the look on Lucy's face meant she wanted Sophie to stay with her. Lucy had been up half the night trying to come to terms with the fact that Jimmy was a liar and a cheat and that, for the time being at least, she had to pretend she didn't know.

Lucy was struggling to act naturally.

Sophie came to her rescue as much as she could.

"So did you find anything out about Frith which might help us get Lucas off the Trust?" Sophie asked him.

Jimmy shrugged again and sent another txt.

Sophie wanted to grab the phone out of his hand and throw it across the room.

"Who are you txting?" Lucy asked him. Her stomach was in knots at the thought it might be 'the other woman'.

"No one," he replied and took the plate of fruitcake from her. "We didn't find much out about the mysterious Frith but enough to put a decent programme together," he told them and tucked into the cake. "We made it look as if he's still alive somewhere. We just don't know where." Looking up at Lucy he added, "Didn't you bring any cheese to go with it?"

"Do *you* think he's still alive?" Sophie asked him as Lucy went to the fridge to find some Wensleydale.

"No, not really," Jimmy admitted. "The only lead we got was some old biddy in Boston who wouldn't meet with us anyway - batty as a box of frogs the solicitor said. I couldn't find any trace of him in the astral realms and if he is ten feet under he's not communicating with us from the other side. I think it's likely he was murdered 'cause that might explain why he's so cloaked and hidden. I wanted to take the angle that he'd been abducted by aliens but your Lancelot didn't fly with that. Shame really, aliens are big business, especially over the pond."

Lucy and Sophie sighed. Their hopes for finding Uncle Frith seemed dashed.

"And are you pleased to be back home?" Lucy asked him as she handed him some cheese.

Jimmy shrugged. "Yeah sure, glad to see you babe and to get some home cooking. Although, what I really want is…"

Lucy flashed a look of panic at her sister. She had been prepared to play along, staying friendly with Jimmy until the film was produced, but she couldn't bring herself to sleep with him as well. She was adept at faking orgasms but the thought of his hands and his sloppy kisses all over her made her flesh crawl.

"I think I'm going to throw up," Sophie suddenly said and grasped her stomach (to be fair, the thought of Jimmy having sex with her sister had made her feel a little queasy, so it was not exactly a lie).

Lucy played along with the charade. "I need to help Sophie," Lucy told Jimmy, knowing full well he wouldn't offer to help them and would leave straight away. He didn't like illness of any kind.

"Okay," he said and got up to leave without sympathy for Sophie or affection for Lucy. "I'll get going. See you later babes."

Lucy plonked herself down on the sofa with a sigh of relief. "Thank you!" she said to Sophie.

"How are you going to keep this up?" her sister asked her. "It could be weeks before the film's put together and scheduled for airing."

"I don't know!" Lucy replied and burst into tears. "I really love him," she admitted, "But, how can I forgive him for what he's done? I know I should be able to forgive him, but I hate him right now."

"There's a difference between forgiving someone and letting them treat you badly," Sophie replied. "And besides, you don't really love him do you? It's love-karma that makes you feel like you do."

"But I do love him," Lucy sniffed.

"It feels like love, I know," Sophie comforted her. "The thing is that without the love-karma clouding your rational judgement you'd not have given him the time of day. He might be flashy, with his psychic abilities and his slightly famous persona, but he's never been very nice to you, has he?"

Lucy pouted and wiped the snot from her nose with a tissue. "I hate it when you're right," she moaned. "I can't believe I love such a sh*t either, but I do."

After comforting her sister the best she could, Sophie went back to bed and Lucy dried her eyes. Mustering her courage, Lucy put her game face on and went back down to the café, which was just closing. She let the staff go home early and finished stacking the rest of the chairs on the tables. Putting on a CD of Lilly's recordings she began to mop the floor. The first song, Don't Dream It's Over[6], brought tears to her eyes and she just let them flow.

She wished and prayed for Aunt Lilly to come back to life and make everything alright.

Lucy's prayers were not answered in the way she had hoped but she did get a little more than she bargained for! Something miraculous happened - she began to see spirit. The café became filled with women of the past who were bustling about serving, cleaning, putting out cutlery and plates, carrying cakes and pouring tea. They were not all fully aware of each other, being from different eras, but they moved together in a kind of ballet - graceful and in perfect harmony. As Lucy watched them she realised she recognised some of them by their style of clothing. Even though she had never met them she realised one of them was Savanna, who was wearing a 1950's netted dress with cherries printed on it - her auburn hair was piled on top of her head and held in place with a can or two of hairspray. Lucy knew three of them had to be the Christie sisters as they were wearing green and purple sashes with the words Votes for Women printed on them. One of the ladies was stunningly beautiful and had ringlets in her hair which swayed and danced just above a plunging neck line and puffed sleeves. *That must be Madeline Lyoness*, Lucy thought. Netti White was distinguishable by her medieval dress and Tara Armagh had a look of Anne of Cleves about her. Lucy wanted to see Genevieve Dumas and she was not disappointed - a woman of tall and graceful stature wearing men's clothing, long, knee high, leather boots and sporting a ponytail was serving hot chocolate to a customer.

---

6 Don't Dream It's Over, Crowded House, 1986, Capitol

Aunt Lilly was there too. She was smiling and laughing as she served behind the counter - just as she always used to do.

Lucy dropped her mop and let it fall to the floor. Then she sat down sobbing her heart out.

Mrs B, who had her coat on ready to go home, came out of the kitchen, and when she found poor Lucy in such a state she quickly took her into the kitchen and put the kettle on.

"Lucy, my love," Mrs B said kindly. "What is it?"

Lucy just looked at her dear friend and couldn't even speak.

"What has happened?" Mrs B asked her.

Lucy shook her head. When she found her voice at last it was weak and almost a whisper. "Nothing," she replied. "Nothing more than usual."

Mrs B took off her coat and poured the tea. She didn't press Lucy to speak and just waited patiently until she was ready.

Lucy took the hot drink and sighed. "I want Aunt Lilly to come back," she admitted.

Mrs B nodded. She did too.

"I can't do this without her," Lucy sobbed. "Everything's falling apart."

Mrs B patted her arm and sat beside her. "You can do this! You're stronger than you imagine," she told her.

"I don't think I am," Lucy replied.

"I know you are!" Mrs B said emphatically. "You have proven yourself over and over. You can run this place. You're an independent woman with no one to tell you what to do or how to do it. You are free in ways that so many others are not. You can do anything you need to do - you know you can."

Lucy sniffed. "But, I also have to look after Sophie and Alice now too; and Little Eden might not even be here in two years' time; and we'll lose everything; and Linnet is falling into a pit of drink and despair and I don't know how to pull her out; and I'm so afraid Sophie will kill herself as there is no hope for her; and Robert is going to marry Shilty and we'll have to be her friend and I don't even like her; and…"

Mrs B handed Lucy some kitchen roll to wipe her eyes with. "You need St Margaret," she said.

Lucy blew her nose and looked at Mrs B in surprise. "Why St Margaret?"

"Because, my love, you need the energy of a queen with you. You need to spark your inner courage and St Margaret helps you to reconnect with your own strength."

"She does?" Lucy asked.

"She does, my love, she certainly does," Mrs B replied and she began to say a prayer. Before she had even finished it Lucy felt a lot brighter.

In case you should ever need it, dear readers, this is how it goes…

St Margaret, St Margaret, St Margaret,
Hear my call dear sister.
Your love is what I need for my heart is weak.
Your strength is what I seek to support my own.
Your wisdom is what I ask for to lead me forward.
Then together we will walk, hand in hand, dear sister, hear my call.[7]

"That actually worked!" Lucy admitted. "I do feel stronger somehow." She stood up and put down her teacup. "You know what, Mrs B, I won't let a stupid, ignorant, lying, cheating, rat of a man stop me. I'll show Jimmy Pratt I don't need him in my life to be happy." Lucy took off her apron and threw it onto the kitchen table. "I might have to pretend I don't know what a bastard he is, but I can do that for Little Eden if I have to, and I'll show him who can play games. I can have a better poker face than him, just you watch me!"

---

7 St Margaret Prayer, KT King Prayers, Book Three, 2019

Chapter 12
~ * ~

When Mothering Sunday arrived it was a day of mixed emotions for many. Robert was still not sure what to do about his mother, and Alice was missing hers. Those without mothers always felt the pang of loneliness, and some, cursed with the wrong mothers, felt the cruelty of fate.

Thankfully the weather was a little better. The air was damp but the sun was shining. In the early evening, a tree planting ceremony, in remembrance of Lilly, took place in the oak copse near the French House, where tree houses of higgledy piggledy designs perched amongst the heavy branches and wrapped themselves around the magnificent trunks. Many of the residents were squeezed onto the wooden balconies or leaning over the rope bridges to look down into the dell below, where the grass grows short and four leaf clovers are often to be found. This tiny, magical woodland twinkled with fairy lights strewn through the canopy and glowing lanterns which hung on the sides of green roofed gypsy caravans. The scent of wild garlic filled the air - its delicate flowers creating a carpet of white as far as the eye could see.

The oldest tree in Little Eden, believed to be over thousand years old, had been an ancient crooked oak whose branches became so lumbering that they had slowly bent down to touch the ground. An urban myth had grown up around this fabled tree - as folk tales are wont to do - and it was said that this enduring oak was the mother of all the other trees in Little Eden, and if she ever fell Little Eden would fall too. Much to the chagrin of the town, this dreaded time had come to pass when she had been struck by lightning in the summer of 2011, just a few months before Lilly's death. With the whole town now under threat of demolition it seemed as if the curse may have been real after all.

Since the grand old lady had had to be cut down the wood was taken for local craftsmen to use. Noddy had carved out the figures of Silky, Moonface and Saucepan Man[8] inside what was left of the stump, and had written these words within the bark:

Trees are our breath and our life. May we always find our soul in the woods.

---

8 The Faraway Tree, Enid Blyton, 1939-51, Newnes

A new sapling was now being planted only a few yards away, with a brass plaque at its feet dedicating it to Lilly. Robert used a ceremonial silver spade to throw soil into the hole and then he handed it to all the friends in turn, finishing with Lucy and Sophie, who patted the top soil down and hoped that their Aunt could see her new memorial from Heaven.

The day was supposed to be about the celebration of life rather than dwelling on loss, so the Little Eden Irish Band struck up and played folk songs well into the night, filling the air with foot tapping tunes and plenty of laughter. Fudge and Bunny brought one of their famous Hansel and Gretel Gingerbread Houses which stand 5ft tall and are big enough for the younger children to actually go inside. Everyone was invited to pull off the sweets and snap the biscuit window frames, tear away the marshmallows, smash open the brandy snap windows and munch on the candy stick flowers.

This wonderful woodland bacchanal was just what the residents needed to cheer them up!

To get away from the noise and crowds, Sophie lay down in one of the colourful caravans on a bed of knitted blankets and soft furs, and listened to the children's laughter which came tinkling through the trees, as songs were sung, games were played and dances danced. Gazing up at the bowed wooden roof of the caravan she felt her body and the bed begin to vibrate, and knew that she was about to have an out of body experience - over which she had little control.

Closing her eyes, she became aware of being inside the trunk of a humongous astral tree. The more she found her bearings, the more she realised that most of London could fit inside it. Wanting to see how big it really was she sent her mind up into its branches. They seemed to go on and on forever into the clear evening sky. At the very top, from her vantage point, she looked down upon the whole of England.

Suddenly, plummeting out of the sky at breath-taking speed, she crashed through curly bracken and into a wondrous underground world of burrows and roots. She traced the tree roots with her mind and to her surprise, her head popped out at Uluru, in the middle of the Australian desert. The sound of music changed from the prancing fiddle and flittering accordion to the deep reverberation of the didgeridoo. The rich booming notes worked their magic and opened her consciousness to new spiritual revelations. Although the information she was receiving felt like her own thoughts, she knew it was being downloaded from an ancient memory bank.

The thoughts in her head were these:

Each major dragon site also has an etheric tree growing from it. Out of London grows the biggest tree in the world. Humans pass their thoughts around the globe using trees, plants, rocks and animals. She suddenly saw the roots and branches as fibre-optic broadband. *All the trees on the planet keep us alive by transforming carbon dioxide into oxygen, but they also keep us connected to everyone and every living thing. Without the trees we lose our connection not only to the planet but to each other and to the spirit world. They make astral travel, psychic sight and telepathy possible. When other dimensional beings first began to explore the third dimension they used the trees to ground their spirits. Then they learnt how to ground into animals. When the Atlanteans wanted to experience full incarnation they downloaded their consciousness into mammals and eventually into specially designed human bodies. Few remember how to use this natural internet and the fewer trees there are, the harder it will be to remember. Do not mourn the loss of the old trees. The Star Children will plant the trees again. The new trees will be of a higher vibration and can be used to communicate within the New Matrix.*

Sophie awoke gently from her vision to find Alice sitting at the end of the bed crying. Linnet had come out of the Refuge to spend the day with her daughter, and Alice had given her mum a beautiful moonstone bracelet, which Silvi had said would help heal her emotional wounds. Alice had thought it the perfect gift for her mum but Linnet had refused to wear it. Alice had burst into floods of tears and come in search of Sophie.

Sophie hugged Alice and dried her tears.

"Let's go and find mummy," Sophie suggested. "We'll ask her to come back to the flat with us all and she can put you to bed herself. I'm sure she'll wear the bracelet soon enough. She doesn't like crystals or healing very much. She needs more time to wake up to her true self, that's all."

Back at the flat, Linnet had settled Alice to sleep and came into the kitchen where Lucy, Peony and India were tucking into some Late Night Cheesecake.

"Thank you for taking such good care of Alice," Linnet told Lucy.

Lucy handed her some cheesecake and a spoon. "We're all here for you and Alice - for as long as it takes," Lucy reassured her friend.

"Can you do one more thing for me?" Linnet asked.

"Anything," Lucy replied.

"Can you tell Minnie I'm sorry."

Lucy frowned. "I'm not sure I should do that," she replied as she licked her spoon.

"Why?" Linnet asked.

"Because you should tell her yourself," Lucy replied. "Why don't you go over there now, before you go back to the Refuge, and tell her how you feel."

"I can't," Linnet moaned.

"Why not?" Lucy asked.

"In case she hates me," Linnet admitted.

"Minnie doesn't hate you," Lucy replied. "You owe it to her to talk to her face to face, no matter how hard it might be for you or her."

Linnet nodded. "I suppose you're right." She looked out of the window and across the square to Buttons and Bows, where a light was on in the living room above the shop. She took a deep breath. "I'll go over now," she decided. "Wish me luck?"

When Linnet had gone, Lucy went to check on the kids, leaving India and Peony in the kitchen finishing off the cheesecake.

"What happened to Lucy and Sophie's mum?" Peony asked India, rather directly.

India wasn't sure whether to tell Peony anything or not and felt a little wary of talking about it.

"I mean," Peony continued to say when she realised India was pausing a little longer than normal, "They talk about their Aunt Lilly as if she was their mum but she's clearly not their biological mother."

"Are your parents still alive?" India asked her, hoping to change the subject.

Peony nodded and helped herself to another spoonful. "They live in Paris. We moved there when I was a young girl to be with my grandparents. I had wanted to set up a shop there but I couldn't afford the rents in the city. Daddy was a friend of Lilly's and she suggested I came here."

"And are you glad you came?" India asked her.

"Oh, yes," Peony replied.

India was a bit confused. She had imagined that Peony's debacle with Marcus Finch might have put her off Little Eden for life, but before she could say anymore Peony carried on...

..."Are your parents alive too?" she asked India.

India shook her head. "No, papa died when I was three and mum died when I was eighteen."

"Oh, I am sorry," Peony replied.

India shrugged. "It is what it is," she said.

"So, is Lucy and Sophie's mum dead too?" Peony asked.

India rolled her eyes - she knew she had to say something to appease Peony's curiosity. "No, she's alive. She lives in the South of France. She's an artist. The light is better for painting over there, apparently."

"So, why did Lucy and Sophie live here from being babies?" Peony asked.

"I think their mother thought painting was more important than motherhood," India replied.

"Oh, that's awful!" Peony exclaimed.

India went to put the kettle on. "I don't know if it's awful or not," she responded. "If their mother realised she was not a natural mother then maybe she was better off admitting it early on. Lilly couldn't have children of her own so it all worked out quite well in the end for everyone concerned. Lucy and Sophie have been happier here than they ever would have been with a neglectful mother."

"To abandon your own children," Peony shivered. "I could never do that."

India sighed. "I think it's better not to be a mother at all than to be a bad or a reluctant one," she said.

India, turning round to pass Peony her cup of tea, suddenly moved sideways for no reason as if dodging out of the way of someone. Peony looked at her quizzically. India wasn't sure why she had done it.

"Are you alright?" Peony asked her.

India shook her head. "That was really odd. I suddenly thought there was someone standing right here."

"Perhaps it's your mum come back in spirit for Mother's Day," Peony suggested.

India frowned and pulled a face. "Good god, I hope not!" she replied.

"Wouldn't you like your mum to visit you like Lilly visits Lucy and Sophie?" Peony asked, thinking she would love to be visited by a friendly spirit or two.

"No, I would not!" India replied emphatically. "My mother wasn't exactly fond of me when she was alive and I don't think being dead would change her opinion of me."

Peony was dying to ask more questions when Lucy came back into the room.

"I wonder how Linnet's getting on," Lucy said, and went to look out of the window.

"You don't mind looking after Alice for Linnet then?" Peony asked her.

"I don't mind at all," Lucy replied. "I love Alice like my own daughter. She spent most of her time around here before anyway."

"Being a single mum though, that must be hard," Peony said.

"It's harder now without Aunt Lilly but it's never been hard without a man," Lucy told her. "I don't have to ask anyone else's permission to do anything as far as Tambo is concerned."

"What happened to his dad?" Peony asked.

Lucy laughed at the look on India's face. She knew India didn't like people asking personal questions but she didn't mind so much. "Tambo's dad didn't want to know," Lucy explained. "I met him in Kenya when I was volunteering out there, and when I got pregnant he told me he was married, but it was too late by then."

Peony looked totally shocked. "That's awful!" she declared.

"You shouldn't be so shocked," India laughed. "After Marcus Finch's behaviour to you and Linnet you can't really think men can be trusted can you?"

"Not all men are liars," Peony said. "Robert and Jack seem very honest men."

India laughed again. "Robert and Jack have probably told as many lies as the next man to get women into bed. A good looking face doesn't mean a man is honest underneath."

"What about Lancelot?" Peony suggested. "He seems a perfect gentleman."

India had to concede that as far as she knew, Lancelot was a rare find, and would never lead a woman into trouble or down the garden path under any circumstances.

"I think parenthood should be taken more seriously in general," India said. "So many men think they can just ejaculate and walk away."

"Or, like Marcus, they think they have a right to steal the child from its mother when they want to," Lucy added. "The father turns up after years of not paying a penny in child care then takes them to court to get access - that they don't even really want. All they want is to get control. I've seen it so many times with friends and with women at the Refuge especially. With Marcus it went too far. He just thought he could take Alice as if she was his property not a person."

"I believe the biological parents should be allowed to see their children no matter what they've done," Peony protested.

"Even abusive parents?" India asked her.

"I think I would love my parents no matter what they did," Peony replied. "Even if my dad was in prison I'd still love him."

"Children never stop loving their parents no matter how abusive they are - they stop loving themselves instead," Lucy said. She looked out of the window again, and seeing Linnet leaving Minnie's shop she sighed. "Linnet needs help but she just won't accept it. Due to the years of domestic abuse she's stopped loving herself too."

~ * ~

<JBH@littleeden.com>
to Collins

Collins

You have probably heard about the outrageous attack on me in the street! If you were here none of this would have happened. Robert has done nothing to defend me. I feel I only have one loyal and loving son left. I shall be coming to live with you as soon as I can arrange everything here. Can you believe he has thrown me out of my own home? I am having to live with Stella which is very cramped as I only have one floor to myself. The wardrobe space is severely lacking and I cannot find anything when I need it. What I am to do with all my precious belongings I do not know! I expect Robert will sell them all from under me to raise money for his precious Little Eden.

Your loving mother,

Reply at once. I don't like having to wait. If you don't have a good internet connection then get one immediately.

<CBH@littleeden.com>
to Jennifer

Dear Mother
Varsity and I are having a grand time here in St Lucia. We would like you to come and live with us for a while but Varsity is feeling a little below par at the moment and due to her condition the doctor suggests she gets plenty of rest. Leaving London has upset her somewhat - she did rather like Little Eden apparently. Perhaps you could visit the Moppets as I believe they are in Antigua for the season and I hear they have a new villa which once belonged to actor Stewart James. They are issuing general invitations. We have been invited but due to Varsity's condition we won't be able to take them up on it.
Your affectionate son,
Collins

<JBH@littleeden.com>
to Collins

I can tell when I am not wanted and it is obvious that you and Varsity intend to keep yourselves to yourselves. I just hope she can cope better with motherhood than she can with your business affairs, which I might add, are none of her business! I can't stay here in Little Eden. As I told you before MY LIFE IS IN DANGER!!!! Not that my life seems important to you or Robert anymore. I shall find sanctuary somewhere else if I'm not welcome in St Lucia. I shall not force myself upon the Moppets as you suggest but I pray that someone is kind hearted and generous enough to offer me shelter far from here. I will have to rely on the kindness of strangers as both my sons have abandoned me. After all I have done for you both I cannot believe you could be so cruel and heartless towards me.

I will be coming next week regardless. I expect you to meet my flight.

<CBH@littleeden.com>
to Shilty

Shilty old thing, I hate to have to say this but I need your help. Mother wants to come and stay here in St Lucia and she won't take no for an answer. I'll pay you anything to keep her away from here. You owe me one. Get back to me asap - this is serious.

Collins

<ShiltyCunningham@Cunningham.com>
to Collins

Collins darling,

I don't owe you a fig but Robbie told me his mother was attacked in Little Eden and now the residents are calling for her to be banished so she has to go somewhere. I should just let her come to you, it's no less than you deserve, but I'll see what I can do. Luckily for you I have been asked to help Papa with something and your mother might be the solution. I don't want any money for myself but you'll have to reduce your demands on Robert and Little Eden. I'll be in touch when it's settled. Be prepared, it'll cost you.

Shilty

<CBH@littleeden.com>
to Shilty

I don't care how much it costs, just keep her away from here or Varsity will kill me!

Collins

<ShiltyCunningham@Cunningham.com>
to Collins

Collins darling,

You'll be pleased to know that I've sorted out your little problem. Your mother has changed her mind about coming to you and is going to Italy indefinitely. The Duca di Pitti, who is recently widowed for the ninth time, asked Papa to find him number ten. Your mother was more than willing, despite his age or perhaps because of it.

I've attached the terms for brokering the deal. If you don't agree, I'll call the whole thing off and she'll be on the plane to you next Monday instead. The ball's in your court, old thing.

Shilty

\<CBH@littleeden.com\>
to Shilty

Shilty, you're an absolute queen for arranging this even if the Duca is an ancient fossil. Last time we saw him at Naples he was on his last legs, although I hear the old chap is worth billions more since his last wife died.

Your terms are bloody ridiculous and you know it but Varsity has persuaded me to agree to them. She wants to return to have the baby at St Mary's and thinks Robbie will forgive us when he sees his new nephew. I've told her she's living in a dream world.

I need to know who the firm handling the marriage contract between Mother and the old coot is? If you know, let me know. I want to make sure mother stands to inherit at least what I am giving up!

Collins

\<ShiltyCunningham@Cunningham.com\>
to Collins

Collins darling,

Always happy to help Robbie and Papa and seeing as it has helped you as well, it was nice doing business with you. Why don't you change your mind about selling Little Eden? Once Robbie and I are married I'm sure I can persuade him to forgive you and seeing as the search for your great uncle Frith looks like it's going to delay things indefinitely I would advise you to rethink your position. From what you say it sounds as if Varsity would rather you didn't sell and would like to return. If not, you know the terms of our little arrangement.

Shilty

~ * ~

81

Chapter 13
~ * ~

The next major event in Little Eden was Good Friday, which blew in cold and windy. Joshua looked out of the window and began to fret as he tucked into his cornflakes.

"Momma, we can't play in the rain," he moaned.

Adela looked out the window hoping to see some blue sky, but grey clouds hung over the Bluebells Woods, threatening to shower them at any moment.

The annual Good Friday match between the Little Eden Lances and the Montgomery Chargers was scheduled for that afternoon. The long standing friendly rivalry had begun back in 1849 when 'Bobby' Bartlett-Hart had challenged his new brother-in-law, Geoffrey Montgomery, who had returned from India with a love of the game, to a match; and the tradition of playing polo on Good Friday had been upheld ever since.

Joshua had been learning to play polo for the last two months and this was his first outing in public.

"The sun might come out later," Adela tried to reassure him.

"I hate England!" Joshua grumbled. "It's always raining."

"You don't hate it," Adela laughed. "You love it here and you know it."

She did have to admit to herself that it rained far more than even she had expected it would, and some days she longed for clear azure skies and deep yellow sunsets over the Pacific Ocean. Sometimes she dreamt of walking on the beach, watching the sun go down; and her feet could still remember how the top layer of fine sand was cool against her toes, whilst the warmth of the day was held just beneath the surface. She'd not gone bare foot or worn flip flops since arriving in Little Eden, and she had had to buy a whole new wardrobe. Luckily, Minnie had knitted her a long, chunky, cable knit cardigan which she put on top of just about everything else. She pulled it round her now and shivered.

The polo match had become quite the pageant over the years. The residents had hijacked it, adding other displays, including show jumping, dressage and best in show. Melbourne had introduced riding for the disabled, and children as young as three were encouraged to parade around on Shetland ponies. The games always took place on the old pasture, which was not really 'old' as it was still used on a daily basis. The main stables, next to Queen's Gate, were classed as 'new' because they had been built in the 16th Century.

It was very confusing for a visitor to the town as nothing is ancient, modern, old or new in linear time. Little Eden is a strange mix of past and present, and some days one is never quite sure which century one is living in. For example, even though the motor car took over from the horse drawn carriage many decades ago, the sound of hooves on cobbles can still be heard every day. An open carriage takes tourists around the streets, and a horse drawn hearse, with glass sides and black plumes, is sadly an all too common sight. Horses are ridden and exercised nearly every day on the pasture, and when walking through the woods, hoof marks are imprinted in the mud all along the pathways.

Thankfully, by eleven o'clock, the clouds had begun to blow away and patches of warm sunshine peeked through. Unfortunately, the showers had made the grass on the pasture very slippery, and the grooms were desperately trying to dry it out with huge industrial dryers. Most of the spectators came wearing their raincoats and wellies. Many were carrying umbrellas as well - just in case. Horse boxes and Land Rovers lined Old Pasture Lane, and stalls selling tack, saddles, English riding apparel and horse supplies were laid out along the canal side. The tarpaulins flapped in the wind, and drips of water had to be avoided when browsing, but the overall atmosphere was a joyful one. Sissy and Ginger had brought their piano onto the tow path and, quite appropriately, the song which greeted Joshua and Adela as they walked through from Accoucher Lane was a ripping version of, I Can See Clearly Now![9]

The President of the Little Eden Equestrian Society, Phillipa Rider, was compering the event from a gazebo on a platform at one end of the field; and when she was announcing over the tannoy, her voice could be heard as far over as Adam Street. Jack, Lancelot, Robert and Devlin, with Johnathon as substitute, made up this year's team, with Tambo, Elijah, Harry Thistle and Corrigan Trip creating the junior team. Joshua was hoping to be substitute for them next year, but for now he was going to be in the beginners display team with Wiktor Dabrowski, Shilpa Agarwal and Alice. Alice had saved up her pocket, Christmas and birthday money to buy a pink, silk covered riding hat with a fake fur pompom on the top, especially for the occasion. She longed for her own horse, as did Tambo, but they were lucky to be able

9 I Can See Clearly Now, Johnny Nash, 1972, Epic

to ride at all - it was one of the perks of living in Little Eden. Dr G had allowed Blue to ride one of the Shetland ponies in the under seven's show class. Blue was very proud to be part of it all, and as he couldn't say the word Shetland very easily, he called his pony 'Shelar ta'.

Adela, Peony, Vincent, India, Minnie and Lucy were all there to watch the games. They found a dry spot under one of the horse chestnut trees, which were all in full flower; their pink and white candelabras heavy with flowers and their fresh lime green leaves shining in the sunlight. The edge of the pasture was sprinkled with daisies and dandelions, and the sweet scent of damp grass and horses floated on the air. Sitting on a picnic blanket, not far from the podium, they had a good view of not only the rosette presentations but also of where the players gathered before and after the matches.

The first match was a close run thing, but was finally won by the Little Eden Lances - much to delight of most of the crowd!

As they waited for the second match to commence India nudged Lucy and they giggled.

Peony turned to see what they were sniggering at and gasped in delight.

Adela's eyes nearly popped out of her head in surprise when she saw what the others could see...

...The men's polo teams were taking off their shirts to put on clean ones ready for the presentation.

"Hand me a diet coke!" Lucy laughed. "I'm about to have a moment!"

Adela smiled to herself. She liked Lancelot but she had not yet seen him 'sans clothing' and now she knew she definitely liked him - a lot! She had not expected him to be quite so toned and fit.

"Ooo la la, beaux gosses!" Peony joked.

Vincent laughed, "I think I got to get me a polo player or two!" he said, fanning himself with his napkin.

India rolled her eyes. "You're not even gay!" she and Lucy reminded him at the same time.

"I wouldn't kick Devlin out of bed for eating crackers that's for sure!" Minnie giggled. "What?" she exclaimed as they all looked at her too. "We can't go to bat for the other team now and again?"

After lunch the Little Eden juniors also won their match and the kids were over the moon with their first ever trophy.

Joshua got his chance to shine when the beginner's demonstration began. Adela and Lancelot watched with pride as he showed off his latest skills and he was, by far, the best.

"If he continues like this, he'll get a shot at Player Two in a few years' time," Lancelot told Adela. "He's a natural."

Adela beamed and put her arm through Lancelot's, now more aware of his strength and the feel of his hard, muscular body than she ever had been before. "Thank you for teaching him. He loves it..." Adela didn't get chance to finish her sentence before...

...she suddenly screamed!

The crowd gasped as they watched Joshua's pony slip on some wet grass, and he could not hold on! The horse slid down onto its knees and fell sideways, sending him flying over its head towards the podium. Adela watched helplessly - in what seemed to be slow motion - as Joshua cracked his head on the side of the platform and landed with a thud on the ground. Lancelot jumped over the rope and ran as fast as he could towards him. Robert grabbed the pony and helped it back up to its feet whilst Johnathon radioed for the St John's Ambulance.

Adela threw herself down by the side of her son willing him to move, but...

...Joshua lay motionless on the damp grass.

Chapter 14
~ * ~

After a few moments of pure horror, Joshua opened his eyes. Luckily, Dr Holmes had been down by the canal with his family, and was on the scene within minutes. The crowd watched, silent with shock, as Joshua was carefully lifted onto a stretcher, meticulously strapped up and carried into the waiting ambulance. It sped off, lights flashing and siren screaming, to the nearest A&E.

The rest of the day fell flat. The rain clouds gathered again, and a torrential downpour ensued, sending the subdued spectators home early. The traditional hog roast was called off and the stall holders and exhibitors packed up in dismay and went home wet and unhappy.

Around six o'clock Lancelot came to Daisy Place, looking tired and anxious. He had not had chance to change out of his polo gear and stood in Lucy's living room shedding dried mud from his jodhpurs all over her carpet. She made him stand on a piece of newspaper whilst Jack found him some jeans and a jumper to borrow.

He assured them all that Joshua had no spinal injuries, not even a sprained ankle or wrist, but that they were keeping him in overnight because of a slight concussion. "Just to be on the safe side," he said. He was in a hurry to get back to be with Adela and Josh. He wouldn't eat anything in spite of Lucy's nonstop attempts to feed him. Sophie gave him a Rose Gold Rainbow Rescuer and some Arnica to take to Adela and Josh, and he hurried away.

Alice was so relieved to hear that Joshua was alive and uninjured that she burst into tears. Neither Alice nor Tambo had felt like celebrating their wins, and they had just put their trophies on the window sill without ceremony. When Alice and Tambo went to bed, Alice asked Sophie if they could have a meditation to help them to sleep.

Here is the meditation Sophie chose:

Imagine you are inside the largest tree in all the world and the trunk is hollow, smooth and shiny on the inside and gnarly, craggy and protective on the outside. Being inside the trunk is like being in a round room which goes up and up forever into the branches above, which touch the clouds in the sky…and as you relax inside the safety and comfort of this round room, you start to feel your whole body releasing…your breath begins to slow down…your breath becomes a little deeper…and again, your breath becomes slower and deeper…and slower and deeper, and you can feel your arms…your shoulders…your neck and your head…relaxing down into the bed…….your spine and your hips are relaxing now and your whole body is feeling heavier and heavier……your legs feel heavier and heavier…… your feet feel heavier and heavier……you are safe and warm inside the magic tree…you are protected and at peace inside the magic tree……now, from the soles of your feet you can feel that you are growing roots…just like the tree has roots…you have your own roots which grow off the end of the bed, down through the ceiling, down through the rooms below…down into the ground beneath the house and then…down they go deeper and deeper into the earth……going deeper and deeper……going deeper and deeper through the soil and through the earth…through the crystal caves and through the underground streams…through the gold and the silver… through the bedrock……going all the way into the centre of the Earth…… they are fire proof and they grow deeper and deeper through the molten fires deep inside the planet and then…they find their way into the solid metal core where they anchor themselves around the heavy iron ball at the very centre of the world……inside the very, very, centre of the Earth your roots reach the sacred and mystical milky white Ocean of Compassion… and there in the white waters of pure compassion…your roots can drink from the nectar of unconditional love and the sweetness of the never ending joy……now you are grounded and protected by the Holy Spirit and you are anchored into pure bliss……now you can sleep in tranquillity and in peace…knowing that Mother Earth has you safely in her arms and that you are surrounded by the protection of the magic tree……

Lucy came in a little while later to find both the children and Sophie fast asleep!

Joshua returned home the next afternoon tired and bruised.

Adela had not slept a wink the night before. Lancelot had stayed with them both at the hospital and brought them home as soon as Joshua was discharged. Adela put Joshua into his cosy bed and let him watch some TV in his room as a treat.

Joining Lancelot in the kitchen where he was making some coffee, she couldn't hold back her tears any longer. She had been strong up until then, and the relief that Joshua was going to be alright suddenly hit her - the flood gates opened. Lancelot took her into his arms and held her close. She leaned into him and let him support her. When she was all cried out, she looked up at Lancelot's kind, handsome face and noticed for the first time that his eyes, which first she had thought were silver grey, were a bright shining blue. She looked longingly at his soft lips and wished he would kiss her.

Lancelot could feel her energy racing through him like a sparkling fire. The love flowing from his heart seemed to swell like a tidal wave and he could no longer hold it in. He had to kiss her or he'd burst. His first kiss was so tender that Adela almost fainted. She gathered herself and returned his kiss with another which was followed by another and then another…until they became so lost in each other that they were whipped up inside a tornado of passion which neither of them had expected or could control. Adela hurriedly unbuttoned his shirt (now knowing the delights she would find beneath) only to pull back, remembering that Joshua was upstairs.

"We can't," she said reluctantly, and then kissed him again - which was a mistake because it just ignited their desire for each other even more. She felt him harden beneath her hand. Lancelot bit his lip trying to control himself but she pushed herself tightly against him. In spite of every fibre of his being crying out to lift her up, wrap her long legs around him, and throw her onto the couch he stopped himself. He pushed her gently away from him and slowly buttoned up her shirt and then his own. Then, gently kissing her one last time, he promised not to kiss her again.

Adela felt overwhelmingly disappointed - it was a promise she was aching for him to break!

Chapter 15
~ * ~

Easter Sunday is always a day of charity in Little Eden. Everyone puts their unwanted household items outside their houses, and neighbours can take what they want for a small donation towards the various charities in the town, including the Refuge and the Hospice. At the end of the day any leftover items are taken to the Charity Shop or recycled. This year all the money was going towards paying off Collins and Lucas - much to the dismay of all the residents.

Tambo was looking for a banjo; Alice was after a pre-used, mobile phone; Elijah was hoping there might be a skateboard going spare; and Joshua wanted to find a bike. It was a sociable afternoon with most of the town out in the streets, and everyone found pretty much what they had hoped for. Lucy came back to the café with an antique teapot decorated with rosebuds. Minnie had found a vintage sewing basket, and Mrs B was as pleased as punch with a stash of cake tins and a set of spatulas.

Over in the Pump Rooms, Iris was holding the annual Easter jumble sale. Shilty was not best pleased to have been asked to run the designer clothes stall, but her new role as the first lady required she participate in the town's events, so she didn't like to refuse. To rummage through endless, slightly ripe smelling, black bin liners in search of the best pieces was a task she did not relish. Once she had set up her table she was shocked to notice that a long queue had formed outside the door.

"Are there always this many people waiting to come in?" she asked Iris.

"Oh, to be sure!" Iris replied. "You'd be surprised at how competitive people can get when there are bargains to be had. People come from as far away as Brighton for our jumble, so they do."

Iris was in her element - she loved charity events.

Shilty, on the other hand, felt as if she had walked into the twilight zone.

Four hours later there was virtually nothing left on the trestle tables. Every coat, every pair of shoes, every dress, suit and pullover had gone, except for two fur hats and a pair of braces.

"Well done, my dear," Iris said to a dazed Shilty when the doors were finally closed and the mayhem had come to an end. "You look a bit tired, so you do. Perhaps you should have another sandwich? There's plenty left in the kitchen."

Shilty sat down and could hardly speak - she was shattered.

Iris smiled. "Let me get you another cup of tea," she offered, but Shilty shook her head. "Thank you but I think I'll just go home. I feel as if I need a shower and something stronger than tea." Shilty felt a little violated and distinctly grubby.

Robert popped his head around the door (he'd been going around the town all day supporting everyone and cheering them along). "Everything went okay did it, Iris?" he asked her.

"Oh, very well indeed. The best year yet, so it was. I think your lovely new fiancé drew in the crowds," she smiled.

Robert saw the look on Shilty's face and could see she was not a happy bunny.

"Do you need a pair of braces?" Iris asked Robert as he waited for Shilty to get her coat. "Or perhaps a fur hat or two?"

Robert laughed. "Not really," he replied. Then, in a more serious tone he added. "I want to thank you Iris. Since Lilly left us you have been such a rock - taking on all her work as well as you own. You're Heaven sent."

Shilty returned from the cloakroom hobbling along in her high heels. "If I'd known I'd be standing up for god knows how many hours I'd have worn kittens instead," she grumbled. "We'd better have made some serious money after all that effort. I've never seen anything like it. It was like feeding time at the zoo!"

"We'll have made a few hundred pounds, so we will," Iris told her.

"A few hundred?" Shilty exclaimed. "My god! Next year I'll personally give you a few thousand and we can throw all this junk in the bin and save ourselves the effort!"

Robert ushered Shilty out of the room as quickly as he could, knowing Iris wasn't too impressed with her attitude.

He walked her back to Bartlett Crescent.

"I can't believe your mother used to do this type of thing on a regular basis!" Shilty moaned.

"She did do some charity work," Robert admitted. "Although, she wouldn't have stayed all day. She'd have opened it and left after about ten minutes."

"I didn't need to stay all day?" Shilty lamented. "Why didn't you tell me!"

Robert laughed. "I thought you'd have left straight away anyway," he replied. He put his arm around her as they walked up the path through the crescent gardens.

Shilty sighed, "It's a beautiful old town, Robbie, but my god it's hard work. Collins said it was a noose around your neck and I'm starting to see why."

"Don't tell me you think I should sell!" Robert exclaimed.

Shilty kissed him saying, "All I know is, I can think of a much better use of my time and talents than helping at some smelly jumble sale."

To continue the day of generosity the café-bookshop always held a book sale in the evening, with ten percent of all sales going to the charities. Authors came to sign their books, some local and some world famous, and by seven o'clock the whole place was usually heaving with regulars and newcomers alike, all come to see their favourite writers, buy books and enjoy the tea and cake.

"I could do with some of those spirit women to help me," Lucy laughed, as hundreds of customers crowded into the place.

"Yes! Poltergeist help us," Tonbee laughed and put her hands into prayer position whilst looking up at the ceiling, as if friendly ghosts might descend from above and start pouring the coffee.

Mrs B laughed as she came out of the kitchen carrying some clean cups. "Can they wash up too?" she asked as she picked up a tray full of dirty crockery to take back. "We just can't keep up. I've never seen it so busy!"

"I think word is out that we are trying to save Little Eden and this year the whole of London has come to help us raise money," Lucy replied as she stuck her head in the fridge to find more milk. "Oh my god," she exclaimed. "Was that the last of the milk?"

Everyone looked around for some more, but they had just used the last drop.

"I'll go to the 7/11," Tonbee offered, but the clamour of customers was so overwhelming that she couldn't even get out from behind the counter.

"Do you need some help?" a customer asked.

"We need about another ten pairs of hands," Lucy replied. "Sorry to keep you waiting but we've never had this many people in here before,"

"I can go and get you some milk, if you'd like," the stranger offered.

Lucy was a bit surprised. She didn't like to say yes as he was a customer, but she really needed some assistance. He had a friendly face and a lovely smile. He seemed familiar but she didn't recognise him as a regular. Taking a chance, she took some cash out of the till and handed it to him. "Would you?" she asked. "The shop's just over on Castle Street, just at the end of the alleyway next to the Deli."

"How many pints?" he asked with a smile.

"Ten - if you can carry them," Lucy told him.

"Back in a jiffy!" he said, and managed to squeeze his way through the throng and out the door into Daisy Place.

"Who was that?" Tonbee asked as she took a plate of fresh cookies from Mrs B.

"No idea!" Lucy replied.

"Maybe he ghost!" Tonbee giggled.

"I've never known a ghost offer to go to the shops before," Mrs B laughed. "But, there's a first time for everything!"

"Well, if he doesn't come back with any milk, I guess we'll know he wasn't real," Lucy laughed.

They all tried to keep the customers happy whilst they awaited the return of the mysterious man. When he squeezed his way back through the cafe carrying a whole crate of glass bottles they were relieved to see him.

Lucy thanked him.

"It's the least I could do," he replied. "You look as if you're all run ragged." He looked a bit embarrassed for a moment and added, "I don't suppose Sophie Lawrence is around anywhere is she?"

Tonbee handed him a coffee and smiling began to say, "She upstai'…"

…Lucy interrupted her, "She's not here, she's…" Lucy suddenly couldn't think of a white lie so Tonbee finished her sentence for her…

…"She help at church" she told him. "I give her message?"

"That's okay," the man replied, "I'll go and see if I can find her."

"No!" Lucy exclaimed. "I mean, you can't. It's a private service - at the church."

Lucy felt as if he knew she was lying and she blushed.

"Could you tell her that Tobias Gilbert, from the museum, stopped by?" the man asked her with a smile.

Lucy gasped with delight. "Yes, yes of course," she replied. "I'll tell her. Does she have your number? You could give me it if you like, then she can get back to you."

"That's okay, I'll be in touch," he replied in a rather enigmatic way.

Lucy dried her hands on her apron and giggled. "So, that was Tobias Gilbert. I think Sophie rather likes him."

"He very handsome," Tonbee said.

"He's very kind and thoughtful which is more important," Mrs B declared.

"Why you not tell him Sophie upstairs?" Tonbee asked.

Lucy frowned. "Sophie doesn't like people knowing she's ill and she'd not want him to see her in her pjs. He doesn't know about the CFS."

Mrs B nodded approvingly. "That's something she'll tell him about in her own good time."

"He like her too I think," Tonbee said.

Lucy smiled. "Yes, I think he must!"

By eleven o'clock everyone had left, and Lucy turned off the lights in the bookshop and sighed. She'd been feeling dizzy on and off for weeks now and sometimes felt as if she wasn't in the real world anymore. She couldn't describe it easily, but it was as if she didn't belong in the human world at the moment and as if she was observing everything from a distance. With only the low glow of the amber street lights to give the store any form, the darkened balconies, nooks and crannies, seemed to disappear into the darkness. She could feel the sensation of disconnection from reality coming over her again, and she slipped into the haunting atmosphere and from one dimension into another.

From the shadows appeared the spirits of the café women, and many more besides, filling the aisles and alcoves with their ghostly apparitions. They were acting as if they were aware of each other now. Some were reading, some were talking in small groups and others were putting books on the shelves.

Quietly the disembodied chant of Elfenthal[10] whispered through the stacks, sending chills through her veins.

Materialising before her was Queen Bertha.

She didn't know what to do. She was so wholly surrounded by other worldly spirits she felt as if she had become one of them. She called for St Margaret and found her courage rise from deep inside. She remembered her psychic health and safety, which Sophie had taught her, and before Queen Bertha could speak, Lucy said the following three times in her head; *Are you a true light being working for and from the true source of all that is*

10 Cuncti Simus Concanentes, Elfenthal, 14th Century, Anon

good? She waited for a clear Yes in her mind each time, and when she was satisfied that at least the apparition of the Queen really was a holy one, she felt herself relax.

Queen Bertha was dressed in fine silk robes which cascaded to the floor like a waterfall. Her long, free flowing, silver hair was decorated with fine braiding, which shimmered with iridescent light, and she wore a delicate gold crown upon her head.

"Take this," Queen Bertha told her, offering a small silver coloured ring, set with an amethyst cabochon, to Lucy.

Lucy was about to reach out and take the ring when she felt a pressure on her hand. She looked down and realised that the etheric ring was already on her own finger. "What is it for?" she asked.

"You will know what to do when the time comes," Queen Bertha replied.

Before Lucy could ask anything more, Queen Bertha had vanished along with all the female spirits and the music had faded away.

Okay, she thought. *That was weird. I'd better let Sophie know about the ring.* Lucy rubbed her finger - she could feel the physical sensation of wearing a ring even though it wasn't really there. *It's the same one that we found in the wardrobe. I wonder what I'm supposed to do with it?*

Coming fully back into the real world, Lucy was aware of the comforting smell of books, old and new, and she let it envelop her as if it was helping her to ground her consciousness again. As she walked towards the café she noticed some poetry anthologies on the counter. One book had fallen from its display stand, she picked it up to put it back but the cover caught her attention. It was decorated with a beautiful purple swirl and was embossed with gold stars which were scattered all over it. She randomly opened one of the pages and, dear readers, on that page was this poem…

THE QUEEN

She removed her crown
melted it down
made a ring
for every finger in the kingdom

Knocked her castle to the ground
raised a city with the stones
a home for every tired body
tossed by the great storm

She walked the streets in plain clothes
ate plain food, smiled
at every face she passed
young or old, known or unknown

Dismantled her ancient oaken throne –
snapped it to pieces –
kindled a colossal fire
at the centre of the city

The blaze reached the sky
blew warmth into every open window
drew the people, one by one
to gather around the light[11]

Well, that's a sign if ever there was one! Lucy thought. *I'm not making all this up! Something is going on with queens and dragon portals and women who used to live in Little Eden - that's for sure. I wish spirit wasn't so cryptic though. I mean, why don't they just say…this is happening on such and such a day in such and such a way and can you please do this, that or the other! Instead, its half whispered messages and weird synchronicities. It's like everything is a mystery - until it's not.*

---

11 The Queen, Andrea Perry, 2019

Chapter 16
~ * ~

The next day was Easter Monday and Alice awoke with a flutter of excitement in her tummy. She climbed the bunk bed ladder and shouted into Tambo's face, "Wakey! Wakey! It's Easter egg day!"

Tambo moaned and was about to turn over when he realised what she had just said. He jumped up with such a start that he banged his head on the ceiling (he was getting too tall for the top bunk but was not ready to give it up just yet).

They raced into the living room but there was no one there. They grinned at each other and began to hunt under the cushions, behind the curtains, in cupboards, even inside the oven and the dish washer - but there were no eggs to be found.

Alice pouted. "You don't think they forgot this year, do you?"

Tambo was worried for a moment. "There's been a lot going on," he agreed. His heart sank. *Surely mum wouldn't forget to get chocolate eggs, would she?*

They carried on searching high and low. Tambo even climbed on the table to see if there was anything on top of the dresser, but - nothing.

Then Tambo had a brain wave. "Wait!" he exclaimed.

Alice stopped in her tracks.

"They always hide them in here…what if…this year…they're somewhere else? To make it harder?"

"Good thinking Batman!" Alice replied and they sped off into the bathroom, then the study, then their own bedroom, but still - nothing.

"I know!" Alice said, "I'll ask Jin - she'll know where they are."

Alice closed her eyes and looked for her new spirit friend with her psychic sight. The astral consciousness of Jin Keung was sitting on the window seat at the top of the stairs. She was reading a book of poetry that had a purple cover scattered with gold stars. She winked and opened the top of the wooden seat.

"They're in the window seat!" Alice proclaimed, and rushed to investigate. There inside were two enormous chocolate eggs. They both had initials iced on them - one had a T on it and one had an A. "Found them!" Alice shouted.

"They're huge!" Tambo exclaimed happily. "This'll last me 'til my birthday!"

Alice giggled. Hers was just the same size but she said, "This'll last me 'til lunchtime!"

"Come on," Tambo laughed. "Let's see if mum and Aunt Sophie can find theirs?"

They had both bought an egg from Devlin's Chocolaterie the day before. He did a special price for children so that they could use their pocket money. They had hidden them in the bookshop and as it was such a massive space it was like looking for a needle in a haystack! It took Lucy fifteen minutes to find hers: she finally discovered it under a bean bag in the children's book area. "Good job I found it before anyone sat down!" she giggled. "Now, I think Mrs B has hidden something for you," she told them. "Where could it be, do you think?"

Alice and Tambo looked at each other. "The kitchen!" Tambo shouted, and they went in search of more chocolate. When they opened one of the fridges, they couldn't quite believe what they found. There, on the third shelf, was a plate of chocolate food with a note which said:

Happy Easter, my loves, Mrs B xx

"There's chocolate fried eggs!" Tambo cried as he took out the plate.

"And chocolate baked beans!" Alice added.

"A full English breakfast all made of chocolate," Lucy smiled. "Can it get any better than this?"

You may think that the day couldn't get any better, dear readers, as chocolate for breakfast is never a bad thing (unless of course you are sugar or dairy intolerant) but you'd be wrong - for this was just the start of Easter Monday in Little Eden and, as you are now well aware, the residents of this special town never do things by halves...

The sound of church bells filled the air and the late cherry blossom was falling thick and fast like pink snow onto the cobbles. All the residents with children (and many of those without) gathered in the Peace Park just before eleven o'clock. From toddlers to teenagers, they assembled at the Cricket Pavilion, carrying anything from a bucket for the beach to big empty popcorn tubs, each and every one ready for an epic Easter egg hunt. They crowded around waiting for the town clock to strike eleven. Once they were off, they were off - running about and scattering all over the place. Some of the two and three year olds were not yet sure what they were doing but got over excited none-the-less as their parents guided them to the 'easier to find' eggs. The older children climbed trees and some became lost in the maze. Tambo and Elijah were joined by Joshua as they hunted for colourfully wrapped eggs of various sizes, and Alice took Blue around the Wonderland Garden. He had never seen anything like it before but he soon got the hang of it. At the end of half an hour there wasn't an empty receptacle left and nearly every hidden egg had been discovered. Faces were already showing signs of early chocolate munching and the kids grew more and more hyper as the sugar rush kicked in.

The weather stayed fine and the picnic blankets came out, as did wet wipes and hankies. The children played to their hearts content on the swings and the climbing frames, in the little fairy houses and amongst the statues of their favourite fictional characters. Egg painting in the Cricket Pavilion was followed by rolling them down the grassy slopes of the Telly Tubby garden.

India and Robert sat on the wooden porch of the Pavilion watching the fun. "It cost even more than usual this year," she told Robert.

Robert sighed. "It costs more each year it seems. We used to be content with finding one or two eggs - these days they want at least ten each!"

"I thought, with us needing every penny, you might have at least reduced the budget a bit?" she suggested.

"The Bartlett-Hart's have thrown an Easter egg hunt in Little Eden for hundreds of years, and if this is the last time, then it's going to be the best ever," Robert told her. "I want every resident to remember their last year in Little Eden as the best one they'd ever..." he couldn't finish his sentence. He felt overwhelmingly sad at the idea of never seeing such a happy sight in his life ever again.

India smiled sadly. "I understand," she replied.

Robert looked at the children, innocently playing, shouting and running about without a care in the world, and he remembered his own childhood. The excitement he and Collins had felt on Easter Monday was more thrilling than Christmas, and it had always been his absolute favourite celebration of the year. He didn't want the innocent joy of childhood to ever end.

~ * ~

Since his accident, Joshua had started to see the spirit women around Little Eden, and when he realised that Alice was not only seeing them but talking with them too, they were both relieved to be able to admit it to each other. Amongst the trees near the pumpkin house, Alice introduced Joshua to Jin, and some of the other ethereal ladies came to say hello. The park seemed hushed as they began to communicate in another dimension.

"So, you're the chosen one?" Theresa Sunshine said to Joshua.

"A fair haired little angel, that's what you are," Jin said as she bent down to greet him.

"He's a warrior king," Genevieve declared and winked at him. "You watch, there's more to him than meets the eye."

"He's so cute!" Delice Drake smiled as she clucked over him like a mother hen.

Angelica Montagne spoke to him seriously, but her eyes twinkled. "So, you are the one who wants to join the saints, are you not?" she asked him.

Joshua nodded. "More than anything," he replied.

"You will have to sacrifice something very precious," she told him.

"Anything," Joshua replied in earnest (although he was hoping she wasn't going to ask him to give her his chocolate eggs!)

"Why can only a few people see you?" Joshua asked them.

Jacqueline Gide smiled at them both. "Only the ones who believe in us can see us," she told them. "And we see only the ones whom we believe in."

"But momma believes and she can't see you," Joshua replied.

"Don't pay any attention to her," Netti White interrupted. "Those as can see, can see, and them as can't, can't and that's an end to it. It's all stuff and nonsense about believin'. I sees who I sees. I don't know the whys and the wherefores - it is what it is."

"Lucy saw you the other day," Alice said. "Can you see everyone in Little Eden," she asked the women.

"We can see all the guardians," Paradise Brightwater replied.

"The guardians?" Joshua asked, excited by the idea that there was something worth guarding, and that he might be one of the chosen ones. But before Joshua could ask her or any of the others about it, they disappeared into thin air and the park became noisy with laughter and games once again.

Chapter 17
~ * ~

The night of St George's Day was one which the residents of Little Eden would not forget in a hurry, and this time not for the right reasons...

In the park, bunting and flags had been fluttering in the wind, candy striped tents had been dotted around the lake, and the sweet scent of burgers and hot dogs had filled the air. There had been jousting demonstrations and craftspeople, dressed in 6th Century costumes, showed the children how to spin wool, weave baskets, cook over an open fire and even how to make wooden swords and shields. The kids had made themselves white tabards with red crosses on them and tinfoil helmets. Joshua had loved the giant papier-mâché dragon which was gracefully manoeuvred by ten talented puppeteers who reinacted the folk tale of St George and the Dragon. Instead of killing the dragon, St George tamed it, and the vicious, fire breathing monster became a friendly, loving beast which led the children in a procession to the World Peace Garden fountain, which sparkled and danced with a display of rainbow lights, to the rousing music of Pomp and Circumstance.[12]

Joshua, who had refused to take off his tabard, had gone to bed with his sword and shield beside him. When Adela looked in on him a couple of hours later, she had found his bed empty. At first she wasn't too worried. Since his polo accident Joshua had started sleep walking (as he had been prone to doing on and off when he was younger), but so far had gone no further than the kitchen. However, this night, as she ventured downstairs, her heart stopped for one awful moment - the back door was wide open!

Scared to death, Adela quickly pulled on her cardigan, and still wearing her fluffy slippers, she dashed out into the cold night air, hoping to god that her boy was still in the garden and had not gone towards the road or the canal. She called for him as she ran down the path and out of the gate which lead into the woods. In the moonlight the bluebells shone like sapphires amongst the trees and lit her way along the path towards the Vicarage. Still calling for Joshua, she came out onto Old Pasture Lane, but then, she didn't know which way to go! In the darkness she couldn't see very far left or right and she began to panic.

She couldn't cut herself in two - which way?

---

12 Pomp & Circumstance, Military Marches, Sir Edward Elgar, 1901 - 1907

Feeling helpless, she instinctively reached for her phone, but she had left it back at the house. A light was shining in the Vicarage window and she rushed through the gardens towards it. She hammered on the side door. It was Iris who came, wrapped in her dressing gown, to see what all the fuss was about. Seeing the look on Adela's face she sprang into rescue mode.

Within minutes Johnathon had been alerted, and within a few more minutes, Lancelot arrived.

"Adela's gone to the canal," Iris told Lancelot. "Johnathon is checking Dovecote Street and Cubby is combing the woods. I'll get dressed and help you look," she offered.

"Thank you, Iris," Lancelot told her. "I'll go and find Adela. Someone should go to her house in case he comes home."

"I'll go," Iris agreed and rushed to put on her outdoor things.

Lancelot found Adela in front of the Dutch Houses talking anxiously to Noddy, who had been sitting on his canal boat having his last cigarette of the day.

"He hasn't passed this way," Noddy assured her. "I'd have seen him if he had. I've been here half an hour already and I can see the whole footpath from here."

Between them Noddy and Lancelot persuaded Adela to return home whilst they continued the search along the waterside.

As Adela entered the kitchen she met Iris, and they didn't even get chance to greet each other before they heard a phone ringing. Adela's heart leapt at the thought it might be Josh. With Iris in tow she rushed upstairs to her find her mobile.

But it wasn't Joshua on the other end - it was Elijah.

"Elijah?" Adela answered in surprise.

She looked at Iris in puzzlement.

"Yes. Yes. No! Wait there. Yes, we're coming now," she said, and before she had even turned off the phone, she started to rush out of the house again. Iris called to her, to ask her where she was going, but Adela didn't reply and just kept on running through the trees, past the Vicarage, and into the Rue des Fees. She stopped, out of breath, when she realised that an iron fence barred her way into the Abbey complex. She looked frantically around to see if there was a gate.

Lancelot suddenly stepped out of the shadows - scaring her half to death!

"Where are you going?" he asked her. "You said you'd stay at home in case he came back."

"He's in the church," Adela gasped, still trying to catch her breath, desperate to carry on.

"The nearest gate is in the gardens," Lancelot told her. "It'll be quicker to climb over," he suggested.

Lancelot easily stepped over the open barred fence then lifted her into his arms and carried her over the rails and the nettles. He didn't put her down until they were in the middle of the Chappelle graveyard, when he realised that maybe he had been carrying her too long without good reason.

The tombstones and sepulchres shone like pale alabaster in the moonlight. The sudden call of a barn owl startled them for a moment and brought them back into focus. Lancelot knew the way and gave her his hand. They ran together across Lady Well Walk and into the churchyard.

The heavy oak door of St Mary's was ajar. It groaned on its old hinges as Lancelot pushed it open. The moon's pale blush illuminated the stained glass windows, and Adela could just make out two small figures standing in front of the altar.

They were Elijah and Joshua.

She rushed down the aisle towards them.

"What happened?" she cried reaching out to hug her boy but as she did so she realised he was still asleep. Joshua's body was rigid. He stood bolt upright, like a zombie, with a strange, glazed look in his eyes.

Adela felt a shiver down her spine.

She turned to Elijah for an explanation. "I came to check the church when mum told me he'd gone missing," Elijah told her anxiously.

Lancelot put his hand on Elijah's shoulder to comfort him and was pleased to see Iris had just arrived. He rang Johnathon to tell him to call off the search and to let him know that all was well.

But Lancelot was wrong - all was far from well.

Chapter 18

~ * ~

Adela couldn't seem to get Joshua to wake up. He was in a deep trance, rooted to the spot, transfixed by the golden carving of the crucifixion on the altar screen, which was glinting in the moonlight.

Lancelot begged Adela to let him call an ambulance, but she refused. "Not yet," she told him. "He's just asleep. He's done this before when his dad left us. It wore off after a few weeks. I think it's just because of the stress of the fall. If we leave him long enough he'll wake of his own accord."

"Perhaps if we could get him to sit or lie down?" Iris suggested, thinking how unnatural and ghoulish Joshua looked as he stood there paralysed and mesmerised in the gloomy cold church.

"Good idea," Lancelot agreed.

Elijah cleared the candlesticks from the altar and Iris took up one of the kneeler cushions for a pillow. Lancelot lifted an almost lifeless Joshua onto the heavy, red embroidered cloth. He looked around for something to cover him with and the nearest thing to hand was a St George's flag. Reaching up he pulled it down and laid it over Josh to keep him warm.

They all sat down in the front pew and waited in silence. Amongst the whispering shadows the church seemed insubstantial - ethereal somehow - as if they were in someone else's dream.

The dream, however, was about to become a nightmare.

The sudden rattle of a heavy metal door handle made them all jump!

With bated breath they all wondered who it was that was entering at this time of night. With no lights on in the church, a passer-by would not have known that they were there. Rationally they knew nothing could harm them, but the spector of fear crept between the pews, enveloping them all in an ungodly aura of uneasiness. At the other end of the church the old oak door creaked and groaned…

…It was just Johnathon come to check on them. "Is he okay?" he asked as he walked up the aisle. He suddenly stopped short. He was shocked to see little Joshua laid out like a corpse upon the altar. "What the f**k is going on?" he asked under his breath.

Lancelot reassured his friend. "Joshua won't wake up. We're just keeping him warm 'til he wakes of his own accord, that's all."

Johnathon shuddered. There was something irreligious about the curious scene and he felt uneasy. "We should take him home and call the doctor," he told Adela. "It's not right leaving him here like this." He had an overwhelming urge to pick Josh up in his arms and carry him away from this unearthly scene.

"I'll stay with him here until he wakes up," Adela told them all. She had no idea why she felt such a strong desire to remain in the church. She turned to the others saying, "You all go back to bed, I'll stay." Although her heart sank at the thought of being left alone amongst the dead.

Elijah shook his head. "I don't think he is asleep in the normal way this time," he said. Iris could tell by the look on his face and the tone of his voice that Elijah had been told something by his spirit guides.

"Do you know something, my pet?" she asked him. "Has someone spoken to you from the other side?"

Elijah nodded. "St Hilda is telling me that someone had better go and get Sophie," he added quietly.

They all looked around, expecting to see an apparition of St Hilda glowing through the gloom, but it was only Elijah who was aware of her angelic presence. He was also aware that streaming into the church were hundreds of ghosts - all women, of all ages, and from all eras, and they were filling the chapel with their spectral forms. Unafraid, Elijah welcomed them all, but he didn't want to frighten the others by telling them that they were now surrounded by other worldly phantoms.

"I'll go call her," Johnathon offered (he was glad of an excuse to get out of the spooky atmosphere).

"Wait!" Elijah called to him as he turned to leave. "Tell her to bring the treasure she found in the wardrobe."

Johnathon showed his surprise. He motioned to Lancelot to go out of the church with him. As soon as they were out in the graveyard he turned to Lancelot, "What the hell?" he asked.

Lancelot seemed to be taking the nightmarish events in his stride, which disconcerted Johnathon even more. "What treasure? And who the bloody hell is St Hilda when she's at home? Everyone's gone mad in there! We need a doctor alright, but not for Joshua - for you lot!"

Lancelot shrugged and pulled out his phone.

Johnathon shuddered as a large crow flew out of nowhere and landed only a few inches away from them both. Stepping back in alarm, he kicked at it to scare it away, but it seemed unafraid of him and even pecked at his feet. Johnathon wasn't easily scared, he was an ex-Royal Marine, but right now he felt overwhelmed by a feeling of insidious evil which he had never experienced, even in combat, and he had a strong desire to run away.

Lancelot held up his hand to let Johnathon know to be quiet. They waited, for what seemed like an age, for Sophie to pick up her phone. Finally she answered...

..."Sophie," Lancelot said..."Is that you?...Yes, it's me...Sorry if you'd already gone to bed but there's an issue at the church with Elijah and Joshua...Adela is wondering if you'll come...Yes, straight away...And this might sound a bit strange, but can you bring the treasure you found in the wardrobe?...Really, at the museum still?...I'll ask. Hold on..."

He turned to Johnathon saying, "Go and ask Elijah if he is sure he needs the treasure. It's still at the British Museum being valued."

Johnathon shook his head in amazement. He didn't want to go back into the dreadful funereal church. His legs felt as if they were trying to prevent him from going through the door. He looked at the crow again and his heart turned cold, but like any good soldier, he did as he was asked. He returned saying, "Yep, Elijah says the treasure is the key - whatever that means. Bloody bonkers the lot of you," he added and shivered with fear again as several more huge crows landed in the graveyard and began walking sedately around the white stones as if they owned the place.

Lancelot put the phone to his ear again..."Sorry, old girl, but it seems we can't do without the treasure. I don't know what to suggest...I know no one will be there at this time. Can you call that chap, Gilbert was it?... Tobias, yes. He might be able to let you in?...Alright...Yes...Call me when you know." He shut off his phone and sighed. "Look, I know this all seems rather odd to you," he told Johnathon, "But it's complicated. Things have gone rather astral here lately and after what happened with Alice and Marcus I'm not willing to take any chances. These kids are different from you and me. They seem to know things that we don't. Sophie knows things too. She'll know what to do about Josh and if she doesn't wake him up - then we'll ring an ambulance."

Johnathon shook his head in bewilderment, but he had always trusted Lancelot's judgement even if he didn't understand it, and Lancelot was usually right.

"Go and help Sophie," Lancelot told him. "She'll need a lift to the museum and back - if that Tobias chap can help us."

Bemused, but glad to be out of there, Johnathon set off to Daisy Place. "Bloody crazy," he muttered as he set off up Dovecote Street. "Bloody crazy the lot of 'em."

Chapter 19
~ * ~

Sophie stumbled out of bed and went to find Lucy who was cleaning her teeth ready for bed.

She explained what Lancelot had just asked her to do.

Lucy looked amazed for a moment and then shrugged in resignation. There had been so many freaky goings on lately, she realised that she was pretending to be surprised rather than actually being so.

Sophie looked as tired as hell. She was going through a period of hyper-insomnia which meant that her adrenal glands were so fatigued that she couldn't sleep and was locked in a vicious circle - a common symptom of CFS. Her hair was lank and unwashed - she hadn't been able to take a shower in days. She felt nauseous all the time and was too tired to eat. Her body ached all over as if she had the flu and she hardly had the energy to hold her head on top of her body.

Sophie really didn't want to go to the museum right now.

"Will you go instead?" she asked Lucy.

Lucy shook her head. "I think this sounds like something you have to do. If Elijah asked for you then I reckon it'll be something *only* you can do."

Sophie wanted to just sit down and cry - she was so past it.

Lucy rallied her sister. She sprayed her with dry shampoo, handed her some baby wipes and washed her face with a flannel as she might have done Tambo when he was three years old. Whilst Sophie dressed Lucy made her some hot chocolate and took a large piece of chocolate fudge cake out of the tin.

"Right! First of all you need sugar and caffeine," Lucy said, handing Sophie a can of coke and the piece of cake. She put some rosemary oil on Sophie's temples and wrists and then sprayed her with Ruby Rainbow Rescuer. "Dig deep and you'll last about an hour, then you'll crash and feel even worse, I know. I'm so sorry, but we just need to keep you going long enough to do whatever needs doing."

Sophie nodded as she tried to eat.

"Has Tobias replied yet?" Lucy asked her as she drank her own cup of hot chocolate and helped herself to a 'small' slice of cake.

Sophie checked her phone again and there was a txt. "He'll meet me at the side door in fifteen minutes," Sophie replied.

Lucy smiled. *He must like her*, she thought, *To come out late at night to help her - and without a rational explanation too. I hope he asks her out this time. Shame she doesn't look more awake. I wonder if I should put some make-up on her?*

But before Lucy could suggest doing so, Johnathon arrived.

Johnathon explained the strange goings on he had witnessed in the church as they went to look down Castle Street for a taxi. There were none on the rank, and he thought he was going to have to fetch the van from the security office, when suddenly they heard the clatter of horse's hooves and the rattle of wooden wheels. Out of the shadows, the tourist carriage came into view. Its driver had just dropped his last fare at the hotel for the night and was heading back to the stables.

"Wait! Doryu!" Johnathon called. "Give us a lift to the British Museum, will you?"

Doryu pulled up the horses and stopped to let them get in. Although he didn't normally drive outside the walls he agreed to take them.

"I'd ask you what the hell is going on," Johnathon said to Sophie as the carriage moved off up Queen's Gate. "But I really don't want to know."

Sophie laughed. "Even if I did understand why Joshua needs the treasure at this time of night or why he's asleep on the altar, you'd be unlikely to believe me, so probably best not to try to explain."

Within a few minutes Sophie spotted Tobias waiting for them on Gower Street. "Drop me here. You'll wait for me won't you?" she asked Johnathon.

Johnathon nodded and helped her down.

Tobias seemed happy to see Sophie and was intrigued as to what was going on.

Sophie felt excited to see him again but she also felt frumpy and ugly. Her heart was fluttering and sinking at the same time as he led her to the side door.

"We are not supposed to come here after hours," Tobias told her. He tapped a code into the door keypad and it beeped. As it opened a light came on. "But the Security Chief owed me a favour," he explained as he led her inside. "Try to look confident," he added. "There's CCTV everywhere and you need to look as if you are meant to be here. They can't hear us but they can see us. No! Don't look at the cameras. Just walk with me and act as if you know where you're going, and they'll think you are my colleague and this all is legit'. Okay?"

Sophie tried to act normal but she found it really hard. Firstly: she felt like she was breaking the law and secondly: she couldn't stop wondering if he felt the frisson that she could feel between them or whether she was just imagining it. *He did come to the café and ask about me the other night - that could be a sign he likes me? She thought. But he's never txt or emailed me since we first met so maybe he's not interested in me in that way? Don't they say that a man usually asks you out within twenty four hours of meeting you if they really like you? I bet it's all just a bit of old karma between us and we've been married in a past life or something like that. I'll be picking up on past energy between us and as usual I'm imagining it might lead to more in this life. Stop thinking about it! We're here for Joshua. Focus woman, focus!*

Tobi asked her what the treasure emergency was and she tried to come up with an explanation which didn't involve spirits, saints and sleep walking. She needn't have bothered however, because as it turned out, Tobias Gilbert also had spiritual depths to him, and he had already guessed that this was no ordinary situation.

They went through several doors and corridors until they came out into the Egyptian exhibition and she recognised where they were. The dim and scarce security lights made for deep shadows and the gallery felt eerie and unsettling. As they passed the giant carved head of Ramesses II, Sophie suddenly stopped. She could feel an invisible force field ahead of her. Usually, she felt this type of tangible resistance in the doorways of haunted rooms, and it was a warning not to go in; but right now, she had to continue walking whether she liked it or not. *I don't have time for this*, she said in her head to the unknown spirit.

She felt her hands tremble and prickles of heat ran up her arms and around the back of her neck. She did not get a good feeling from whoever this spirit was. To her surprise, Tobi suddenly said, "It's a bit spooky in here in the dark isn't it? I sometimes think old Ramesses wakes up and walks about the halls at night."

"You've seen him?" Sophie asked. "His spirit, I mean?"

"If I tell you a secret will you keep it?" he asked her.

Sophie nodded.

"I can feel him right now," Tobi admitted.

"How does it feel when you sense him?" Sophie enquired.

"Like hot needles on your skin and a shiver down your spine," Tobi replied.

She looked at him sideways. "So you believe in spirits and ghosts?"

Tobias nodded. "I know some people think it's all hocus pocus, and as a scientist I am not supposed to believe anything I can't prove empirically, but you don't work with ancient artefacts every day and not start to feel the difference between the ones which are still alive with energy and the ones which are empty and dead. Some of these statues are replicas so you'd think they would be void of all consciousness, but even copies can still hold the energy signature of the person they represent or the person who owned them. I can't explain it but I can sense it."

Sophie couldn't believe her ears. Here was a man who believed in the existence of consciousness beyond the human body but was still sane and rational at the same time, and who didn't wear flip flops in winter. Is he for real? she wondered. *Has the universe finally sent me my perfect partner?*

"It's in the safe room," Tobi explained.

"What is?" Sophie asked, having lost track of what she was there for. She was too busy thinking about marrying Tobi and imagining they might take a cruise down the Nile on honeymoon.

"The treasure," he smiled. "That's what we came here for isn't it?"

Tobias opened a glass door which led into a large room in which there were safety deposit boxes along one wall. He opened one of the boxes and turned on a scanner. On the box was a barcode, which when it was read, flipped the lock.

Sophie could see the jewels were inside - individually wrapped.

"You really should sign them out," Tobi told her. "Can you bring them back tomorrow to sign them out officially?"

"I hope so," Sophie replied. Although she wasn't sure what they were going to be used for between now and then.

"What do you really need them for tonight?" he asked her again as he put them in a bag for her.

Since his declaration in the Egyptian gallery Sophie felt she might be able to tell him the truth. She thought for a moment of how to put it. "You know you said that consciousness can be trapped in any object?"

"Yes," he replied as he locked everything back up.

"Well, these jewels are not just jewels."

"I know," he said. "They're holy relics. I could feel the energy when I examined them. I've handled enough of these types of objects to know when they are the genuine article. I've identified the St Cuthbert cross as one of the Lindesfarne crosses. I believe it may have belonged to St Hilda of Whitby."

Sophie was overjoyed to be able to speak openly with him. "What do holy relics feel like to you?" she asked.

Tobi thought for a moment. "They feel to me as if they have a heartbeat of their own and the energy around them hums in my hand. Their aura is full of electromagnetic energy and I feel an overwhelming sense of peace when I handle them. Sometimes I don't want to put them down because I feel as if the energy inside them is so compassionate - so precious - it's awe inspiring. I've never told anyone any of this before," he admitted. "But sometimes it feels like I want to kiss them."

Sophie wished he would kiss her and, just for a moment, it seemed as if he was about to.

But then he didn't.

"Did they all carry a peaceful energy?" she asked him.

"They are all full of beautiful energy. I can understand why Buddhists say spiritual energy is like a precious jewel. To me it feels as if I would die to protect it, and it wouldn't feel like a sacrifice, but a great honour," he replied, and smiled. "In energy terms they are priceless, but.in monetary terms you've a small fortune in that bag as well, so don't lose it," he joked. "Come on, I'll take you back."

They returned via the Egyptian gallery and Sophie felt uneasy again. She tried to walk a little quicker, eager to get out of there, and she clung to the bag of treasure as if someone might try to steal it.

Tobias could feel her anxiety and hurried too. He wanted to take her hand but thought he'd better not as he hardly knew her, although something deep inside him told him he was there to protect her. He kept looking from side to side as if expecting someone to jump out and attack them.

They had nearly made it out the other end when Sophie felt a hand touch her on her shoulder. She wanted to scream but she froze. Her breathing quickened as if she was no longer in control of it. Nausea washed over her.

It wasn't a human hand.

Tobi felt goose bumps rise over his arms and pin and needles prickled the soles of his feet. "Can you feel that too?" he whispered.

Sophie nodded. She couldn't find her voice to speak. She held tighter onto the jewels and could almost feel them burning her hands through the cloth bag.

"What is it?" Tobias asked her in hushed tones. He stood as close to her as he could. He was captivated by the warmth of her body and he lost his breath as her fingers brushed against his.

Sophie was trying to focus on what was happening but Tobi's presence was distracting her too.

Suddenly Tobi felt her quiver with fear. He instinctively he put his arms around her from behind and held her against him. She leant into him, glad of the support. The statue of the Pharaoh filled her with an overwhelming terror.

Ramesses II did not look happy!

Chapter 20
~ * ~

The terrible head of Ramesses II was alive with fire. A blinding golden light radiated through the marble with such intensity that it made Sophie's physical eyes water.

His ravenous etheric hand reached out and grasped her heart so savagely that her chest actually hurt.

The human pain caused by a supernatural phenomenon petrified her to the core. Usually, the astral and the physical dimensions appeared separate, but right now she was realising how evil could squeeze the life force from a person leaving them just an empty shell. Once drained of all hope and all belief in the Light, only fear would remain, and there would be no defence against the dark side taking over one's heart and mind.

Tobi felt a splitting pain shoot up the side of his head as if someone had just driven a spike through his temple and straight into the back of his eye. "What's happening?" he whispered, feeling instinctively that he should not talk loudly in case he was overheard (though he had no idea who he thought might be listening).

Sophie tried to speak but found herself struggling for breath. She was terror-stricken.

If she had never felt pure evil before she now knew that this was it. As the all-pervading darkness started to take her over, it felt as if her body was disintegrating into ashes and that death itself was devouring her.

She called to Aunt Lilly but there was no answer.

Sophie didn't know what to do. *Has the Light abandoned me just when I need it the most?* she wondered. *Is fear stronger than love after all?*

The psychic energy of the Pharaoh felt more forceful than anything she had ever experienced before. He wielded centuries of patriarchal power. A belief in male supremacy had been implanted into the dragon lines and was now held within the DNA of all mankind. It had grown like a thorny tree through the spinal cord of every human being. Countless spells, repeated, generation after generation, through mantras, prayers, hymns, psalms and all forms of black magic had built a web of lies and deceit which were hard to counter. He had the upper hand.

The human world is run by fear, that's obvious. Sophie thought. *If you add up all the fear would there be more than all the love?* She thought of the world leaders who were liberal minded and in the service of the people - she could have counted them on one hand. The balance of power was skewed in favour of the darkness.

Sophie called to Alienor but again no answer came.

The dark side was playing tricks on her mind. She couldn't control her thoughts. A stream of self-loathing began to infiltrate her psyche. *I'm not worthy*, she thought. *I'm nothing. I'm not a world leader. I can't fight this power. I'm just a woman. How dare I challenge a king? How dare I challenge the power of Adam and of Amun Ra? I should just kill myself and go home to my stargate. Humans don't want my help. It's hard work to be a good person and care about others and the planet. No one likes hard work. Why update any keys to make a new matrix of consciousness? The Star Children will probably end up corrupting it anyway in the end just like everyone has always done. Why not just let humans blow up the Earth just like Siriens blew up theirs? Why should I bother to save anyone or anything when they don't even want to be saved?*

In her despair, she called out to Dr G and he answered her call.

The idea of 'like for like' floated into her mind and she remembered what Dr G had once told her. *Fighting against witchcraft is always an eye for an eye and a tooth for a tooth. It is not about taking revenge, as many might interpret it, but means that poison is also its own antidote - as in homeopathy or in vaccines.* She realised she needed to tap into the same energy the Pharaoh was using and she needed to use it against him. He was harnessing the spells of the Grail, of Amun Ra and of Atlantis so she must do the same.

Sophie was reluctant to engage with pure evil. It was a dangerous business and she knew it. She was already having second thoughts about fighting back. Giving in would be the easier option.

Luckily, dear readers, Sophie rarely took the easy option. It was one of the reasons she had been chosen as a portal guardian!

Tobi suddenly gasped in astonishment! Sophie didn't look like Sophie anymore. In his arms he now held a regal Egyptian goddess.

Sophie had begun to channel the goddess energy of Isis. It was no more pure or holy than that of Amun Ra, but she was now the female to his male.

The Pharaoh spoke to her telepathically; "I can give you untold power and the protection of the priests and priestesses of Atlantis. You are a powerful sorcerous, you have lived with us many times, you have learnt the ways of the craft. You could be one of the most powerful beings on Earth. Use the Grail with us and you can manifest great riches and attract to you everything you want."

It was tempting. *Maybe I could save Little Eden if I had the same power as he seems to wield*, Sophie thought.

Sophie was shocked at herself. *What am I thinking? This isn't me! Argh! He's got inside my head. Get out! Get out!* Sophie shouted back at him with her mind. *"I don't want your fake power. Your power is the darkness. It's manmade. I will only use the Light even if it kills me to do so. I would rather die than use black magic."*

Sophie's determination to channel only holy energy transformed the whole chamber into a portal for the Holy Grail. A phantasmagorical golden liquid flowed through the gallery and up the walls. The shining elixir streamed between the statues and the glass cases like a river of everlasting light. The glistening waves made Tobi feel unsteady and dizzy, and the pain in his head was still relentlessly jabbing at him.

They both watched in horror as the ectoplasm of Ramesses burst forth in terrible vengeance from his marble effigy. The angry apparition of the Pharaoh towered before them, twenty feet tall, brandishing a wooden Ished staff. A monstrous red and black double helix serpent coiled around its shaft, spitting venom with every flick of its tongue, and a metal sun disk, mounted between two horns on its zenith, sent out a protective golden shield around the king. His regal face was hard and evil and, as with his statue, he had no eyes.

"You dare to use the power of the Grail against me?" Ramesses bellowed into her mind. "You are no-one. How dare you challenge my power? Do you think we let the Pleiades take this planet from us? We, the Atlanteans, have wielded the power of the dragon lines for millennia and we will keep control of the human world for eternity. You will regret your defiance."

His presence was paralysing. The stench of death and decay seemed to hang on his tortured breath.

*"F**k,"* Sophie thought to herself. *"I'm out of my depth here."*

She was torn between wanting to run and wanting to stay and stand up to him. He terrified her and yet something deep inside her wanted to conquer her own fear.

"You know you said you thought that Ramesses wakes up and walks around this room at night?" Sophie whispered to Tobi.

"Yes," he replied.

"Well, you're right and he's wide awake right now. Can you see him?" Sophie asked.

"I can feel him," Tobi replied. "I don't want to sound over dramatic, but if I ever wondered what the mouth of Hell felt and smelt like - I think this might be it!"

"You're not wrong there," she replied. "I think we're standing at the gates to the underworld. Ramesses holds the key I need to take to Josh but he doesn't want to give it up."

"What do we do?" Tobi asked her.

"Let the angels work through us and use the Holy Grail," Sophie explained. "But we must let go of the outcome - be prepared to die if needs be - that's what letting go really means. If we get too entangled in our own fear we'll lose."

Reluctantly she looked the hideous Pharaoh in the face again. Black adders were now writhing from his mouth as his face shape shifted into a hideous skull hanging with rotten flesh. He seemed to be gathering his energy from the realms of the dead and was growing stronger by the minute.

"He's just a tinsy bit pissed off," Sophie told Tobi in a hushed voice, trying to make light of it. "I think it's got something to do with the jewels. I think he wants them or at least he doesn't want me to have them."

"What do you need me to do?" Tobi asked her.

"I've no idea what to do," Sophie admitted. "I've not had a scary mother f**ker of a Pharaoh try to suck the life out of me before."

As she said that she felt her heart being wrenched from her chest again, and only by chanting the words, 'I am the Light,' 'I am the Light,' 'I am the Light,' over and over in her head did she prevent her etheric heart from being completely snatched from her. The keys in the words created a glowing, green, heart protector shield which just managed to hold the Pharaoh at bay.

"Okay," Sophie thought to herself. *I've got to get a grip! Angels and saints where the hell are you? I need help and I need it NOW! This evil bastard isn't going to get the better of us. Come on! Whatever happens I'm staying with the Light.*

Sophie's determination sent a blast of white light through her body and channels of information began streaming through her. She took a deep breath and let herself be guided by the Light. "It's definitely something to do with the jewellery," she said to Tobi again. "We need to take a matrix code from the Pharaoh so that we can upgrade it for the Star Children. It's to do with changing the DNA of the human body and of the planet. I need something to hold the code inside. The Ankh! I need the Ankh."

Sophie frantically searched inside the bag but each piece was wrapped in paper and she couldn't tell which was which. Tobi helped her unwrap each piece. They went as fast as they could, but they just kept uncovering cross after cross. "Hurry!" Sophie urged him. "This energy is draining me and if I'm not careful he'll take me with him into the darkness and I won't be able to come back out. I'll end up like Linnet - trapped in my own fears forever."

"Who?" Tobi asked her, thinking she meant a mythological queen.

"Just someone I know who hasn't recovered from over exposure to evil yet," Sophie replied and kept unwrapping.

As is always the case - the Ankh was the last one they unwrapped.

Sophie looked at it. It was unremarkable. The golden surround had dulled with age and the black onyx inlay was plain. The finely carved reliefs of a serpent and the eye of Horus were so worn they were hard to make out. A winged scarab beetle decorated the handle, and down its shaft, two lotus blossoms flanked a female Pharaoh who was holding up another Ankh to the face of a half-naked man in front of her. She wasn't sure what to do with it at first but then she felt that if she could place the Ankh against the statue of Ramesses, just as the queen was doing in the depiction, it might have some effect.

That didn't sound so hard, but between her and his marble face was the miasma of every angry man in the universe. Sophie recoiled at the thought of having to put her hand through such insidious hatred. *I can't do it*, she thought. *My hand. It's paralysed. I can't move it.*

"What's going on?" Tobi asked her again. He could feel her trembling, and the room around them felt like ice yet he was in a cold sweat.

"I have to touch the statue with the Ankh to capture the key to the consciousness of Nun inside it," Sophie explained. "Then I can pass it to the Pleiades Council to be upgraded. The old matrix has to be folded up and we have to build a new matrix from its foundations. I think there are many keys we will have to gather and this is just one of them. Souls can decide whether to stay in the old Atlantis matrix and no longer reincarnate or come into the new Pleiades matrix, but either way it's time to end it all."

Sophie tried to be brave but the menacing Pharaoh loomed over her like a gigantic genie - his robes flowing with serpents and his lifeless body oscillating with the faces of countless enraged ancestors. She could feel the centuries of male oppression pressing down upon her. Self-doubt began to plague her again and she was haunted by the impression that she would never be strong enough to win a battle against this great and powerful Pharaoh who carried centuries of corruption inside him.

"I don't think I'm strong enough to take on so much darkness," Sophie admitted to Tobi.

"You have to be," Tobi replied. "Looks like it's up to you. I've got your back. I won't let you fall."

Sophie was suddenly fearful that maybe Tobi was in on it and that this was a trap. He was a man after all and carried the same spells of patriarchy as any other.

I need more divine female power, she thought. Not just any women, but women who carry the Light - women who can rise above the spells and are prepared to let go of everything they have ever known. She remembered all the spirit women who had been gathering in Little Eden over the last few weeks and, at last, something made sense! *If a woman accepts that she is not worthy of equality then the spells holds fast, but if she can see through the illusion, she can break it. I have to use the pure power of Nun.*

"Ladies," Sophie called out loud, "I need your help!"

At Sophie's cry, the resplendent spirits of Egyptian priestesses, draped in fine white cotton robes embroidered with threads and patterns of all colours, materialised out of the display cases, statues, funeral vases and even the mummies. Sophie recognised some of them as followers of Isis, Hathor, Bast and Maat by their headdresses and their jewellery. But as the divine feminine energy flowed through their hearts their appearances altered. Their old amulets and charms fell away. Their robes disintegrated as they walked and they shape shifted into naked, shimmering blue beings of light, free from all trappings of religion.

Now, with them by her side, she felt invincible.

Ramesses raised his staff again in wild fury as he felt their submissiveness transform into equality. Inflamed with outrage, his face seethed with indignation, and he looked more terrifying by the second. The women had abandoned his cult and he could no longer control them.

"Come on girls," Sophie said out loud. "We've got this! Let's take him down."

Harnessing all the strength of the sovereign women, Sophie now reached through his ectoplasm; it felt thick like cold custard, but she pushed on through to the searing hot fire of the sun inside. Her hand began to burn, and just as she felt she couldn't stand the heat any longer it transformed into the biting sensation of ice.

Finally, her hand was only half a centimetre from the bust of the Pharaoh. Willing her hand to press the Ankh to the stone she found the golden force field of the corrupted Grail was completely impenetrable!

Chapter 21

~ * ~

Tobi could see that Sophie was struggling to make contact with the statue. On impulse he put his hand on hers and pushed. The Ankh moved through the final layer of golden energy and ancient metal met ancient stone. A terrific blast of white light shot out from the point of contact and the Pharaoh's degraded skull transformed into clear crystal. Sophie could see strings of hieroglyphs running through the crystal like computer code.

The hearts of the women swirled together in a whirlwind which grew in size and ferocity until the force of their love blew the etheric Pharaoh and his staff to smithereens.

Both Tobi and Sophie were nearly blown backwards by the force. Tobi had to use all his strength to keep himself and Sophie upright.

Then the space was suddenly peaceful again.

The golden liquid of the Grail, still flowing all around them, coalesced into a glorious giant lotus flower in the shape of a chalice. A stream of gilded holy water bubbled up from an infinite well spring at the centre of the sacred flower and a delicious amber nectar flowed out from the petals in a constant stream of divine feminine consciousness, enveloping the two of them in total bliss - the like of which neither of them had ever experienced before.

"If I knew what being in the arms of the divine Mother felt like," Sophie whispered. "I imagine this would be it."

Sophie wished she could be suspended forever in this ocean of compassion and felt heartbroken with disappointment as the soothing sensation of the Holy Grail slipped away.

Tobi felt himself come back into reality too, and to his eyes, Sophie looked like Sophie again. His head still ached and he felt physically exhausted. He felt as if his mind had been shaken and stirred leaving him with a sense of confusion and of being lost in a new world. Holding Sophie in his arms felt as if she was his anchor in the storm. Then abruptly she pulled away from him - she had remembered why she had come here in the first place!

"We must go quickly," she told him. "This isn't over - Joshua needs us. We must get back to Little Eden as soon as possible. The energy in the

Ankh must be the key they need at the church. Whilst we are holding it we are in danger of being corrupted by it. The sooner we can get it to the Star Children and the Pleiades Council the better."

Tobi led her by the hand through the darkened corridors and back out to the bright lights of Montague Street where Johnathon was still waiting in the horse and carriage. As she climbed in Sophie apologised for taking so long. Johnathon looked confused saying, "I thought you'd be longer. You've only been about fifteen minutes."

It was Sophie's turn to look confused. "It seemed like hours to us," she told him.

Tobi said goodbye and watched as the carriage headed back to Little Eden as fast as the horse could trot.

As they drew up outside St Mary's church Lucy rushed out of the lych gate to greet them.

She was shaking.

"What is it?" Sophie asked, surprised to see her sister there and looking so distressed.

"Come quickly," Lucy told her. "After you left for the museum, I came over to see what I could do, but there is nothing anyone can do. I wanted to ring an ambulance, but Elijah and Iris keep saying it's you they need to wake Joshua up."

Lucy led Sophie into the church. She had lit some of the larger candles to give the place a semblance of warmth, but in spite of the mellow glow the atmosphere was soaked in dread. Sophie gasped in horror as she saw little Joshua laid out on the stone altar as if for a human sacrifice.

Elijah, Iris, Adela and Lancelot all sat in silent vigil around him. Sophie's heart went cold.

Was little Joshua dead already?

Adela, seeing Sophie, grasped hold of her hand. "What should we do?" she asked desperately.

Sophie shook her head and placed the bag of treasure down beside Joshua. Quickly she scanned the church with her psychic sight. She could see the hundreds of spirit women and looking at Elijah she knew he could see them too. Comforted for a moment by the presence of St Hilda, Aunt Lilly and Alienor she tried to speak with Joshua telepathically, but his lifeless corpse did not respond.

Joshua's spirit was no longer in his body, yet he was still faintly breathing.

Sophie looked down at the bag of treasure. *Well, here goes nothing*, she thought. She took courage in the fact that if Joshua was so near death already there would be little she could do to make it worse.

Sophie let herself be guided by Alienor and stopped thinking logically about what she should do. She let go of the outcome and gave herself completely into the hands of the angels. She knew that she and Joshua were just being used as human vessels by spirit and that it was the Pleiades Council, whom she had met at the Giza pyramid, that was leading the way. She opened the cloth bag and took out the half-unwrapped packages. Placing the Ankh on Joshua's chest she crossed his palms over it.

Adela, Iris and Lucy picked up one of the crosses each on Sophie's request.

"Which one should I take?" Lucy asked her sister.

"Choose without thinking," Sophie told her. "Just pick the one that you feel most drawn to. Do it instinctively. Let your higher self and the good spirits guide your hand."

When Lucy unwrapped hers, she took in a sharp intake of breath.

"What is it?" Sophie asked her.

Lucy held out the parcel to show her. It was not a cross but the amethyst and tin ring - the very one that Queen Bertha had given her astrally in the bookshop. Lucy realised that she had selected the right piece and that being here now, in the chill of the dark church, was no co-incidence.

This night had been planned a long time ago.

Iris opened her parcel to find she had chosen the ornate St Cuthbert Cross. It felt strangely familiar to her as if she recognised it from a past life. St Hilda felt closer to her than ever.

"What do we do now?" Lucy asked Sophie.

"It's all to do with male and female energy and how unbalanced it has become," Sophie explained. "All I know is that this Ankh holds the original key of Nun which has been corrupted by manmade spells from Atlantean priests and priestess, kings and queens and religions of all kinds," Sophie explained. "I think Joshua has to give it to the Pleiades Council who can remove the spells and use the pure key to create a clear stream of consciousness for the Star Children to use."

"Joshua!" Iris suddenly said. "Of course! In the Bible Joshua was known as the son of Nun. He helped Moses with the exodus from the rule of Ramesses II. Perhaps 'Joshua' has been a guardian of this key all this time?"

"Or perhaps only someone who once corrupted the key can hand it over?" Sophie mused. "If Joshua is willing to let go of the Atlantean spells which gave him power and embrace the Pleiades he can change the code."

In the gloom they all waited with bated breath expecting something momentous to occur. The candles flickered in the unseen draughts but all remained as quiet as the grave.

"We need music," Sophie said suddenly.

"Why music?" Adela asked.

"Sound," Sophie told them. "Some energy keys are activated by sound waves."

"Yes, that makes sense, so it does," Iris said. "In the Bible story of Jericho, Joshua had to surround the town with trumpeters, and when they blew their trumpets the walls fell."

"Yes!" Sophie added, "It's symbolic of using sound to activate and deactivate spells. The dragon portal of Jericho would have been full of spells from a plethora of gods and pagan beliefs. Joshua wanted to change the key so the people would agree to unite under one unified god. Although, I'm not sure his spells were any less corrupt than anyone else's."

They all looked at Elijah to provide some music.

"I don't have a trumpet with me," Elijah said.

"Any music will do as long as the intention is right," Sophie replied. She nodded over towards the organ.

"What should I play?" Elijah asked as he went to sit down.

"Whatever comes out of your fingers," Sophie replied. "Let the angels guide you."

Elijah took a deep breath and imagined that he had given his hands over to Mother Mary. He began to play the macabre notes of Toccata and Fugue in D Minor[13], which sent chills through them all.

Johnathon felt as if he had stepped into some kind of low budget horror movie and was none too impressed by the spiritual shenanigans. "I don't understand," he said. "All this is just fairy stories. You don't actually believe that Joshua from the Bible, who probably never even really existed anyway, conquered a town with some trumpets and now our Joshua is somehow the same person do you?"

"It is all symbolic of the greater human truths," Sophie said. "We have to re-code the DNA of the planet and of mankind so that the Star Children no longer carry the illusions and lies of the ancestors. How do you set up

---

13 Tocacata Fuge D Minor, Johann Sebastian Bach, c1704

any belief system? You do it through words, images, songs. You tell or write down stories. If you tell them often enough they become spells and people start to believe them! From all those wishes and spells a stream of consciousness is created and generation after generation make it stronger - or they change it if they can."

Sophie looked at the large leather bound bible on the lectern and frowned. "That book has a lot to answer for," she said. "Just like any story it's one big jumble of spells which make us believe things which are not true. It has made us afraid of the idea of God and of each other. God is just Love. The love has been hidden over the years by false prophets and manmade deities. I guess it's time to go back to the beginning and write a new story."

"You mean Joshua has to take the old codes and merge them with some new ones to build a new set of beliefs for the Star Children?" Adela asked.

Sophie nodded. "I don't know how all this works exactly but that sounds about right!"

Adela had always known her boy was special, but this was not what she had expected at all.

Elijah stopped playing the doleful tune for a moment. The haunting notes lingered in the air. "I don't think it's working," he said. "Josh is still asleep."

Sophie looked around the shadow filled church for inspiration. She could see the spirit women sitting in the pews eagerly awaiting her next move; she had felt that the music was doing something as she had seen astral musical notes dancing from the organ to the altar and they still hovered over Josh. She looked at the Ankh in his small cold hands but there was no light coming from it and she knew it wasn't activating.

Then the next piece of information downloaded into her mind.

"Lucy!" she said. "That ring. It's a key."

"Is it?" Lucy replied, looking down at the simple piece of jewellery. "Queen Bertha said that I would know what to do with it when the time came, but I'm just not sure what to do with it," she admitted. She ran her finger over the amethyst cabochon wondering what to do next - not realizing that that was all she needed to do.

Lucy had inadvertently activated the key and all hell let loose.

Chapter 22
~ * ~

The flagstone floor began to vibrate and everyone, even Johnathon, could feel the soles of their feet buzzing. A cold breeze quivered in darting wisps around them, and Johnathon, thinking the door had opened, went to close it only to find it was firmly shut. He looked around the eerie church, but no windows were open either. He could have sworn that Elijah was still playing the organ as the melancholy notes echoed faintly through the rafters, but to his bewilderment, Elijah was now standing by the altar - nowhere near the instrument.

Lancelot felt the familiar sensation of the Holy Spirit passing through him, which he had often experienced in Quaker meetings; it grew stronger and stronger until his hands were literally shaking. He took hold of Adela's hand: partly to protect her, partly because he felt a little unsure of what was happening himself and partly to stop the quaking.

Adela had drawn a small Maltese cross from the treasure bag and was clutching it in her freezing hand. Decorated with pearls and turquoise it reminded her of the ocean and she could feel ripples of gelid water flowing over her palm. She felt the urge to say the St Hilda prayer and started whispering it to herself.

Sophie gasped as she simultaneously felt and saw an etheric pure white dove fly out of her own heart. The sacred bird glided into the Ankh, illuminating the black onyx at its centre. The crystal's dark-light pierced Joshua's chest with an otherworldly glare which dispersed into the altar, turning the whole church as black as pitch. The friends gasped in horror as the candles blew out leaving them in eerie darkness.

The spectral inky light of the onyx began to spiral into a whirlpool in front of the altar. The earth shook as the gigantic jaws of an etheric blue dragon burst from the opening portal, shattering the stone floor and threatening to swallow the whole church.

Lucy began to pray in earnest to St Margaret for courage. She could not see the dragon but she could feel evil all around her. The ring on her finger became so cold it felt as if she had put her hand in a bucket of ice. She badly wanted to take it off but knew she should not - she felt a deep resolution to stand against the darkness in spite of her fear. As gusts of frosty air began to flow through her blood, she realised Queen Bertha was manifesting through her body in order to anchor the Light as close to the third dimension as was humanely possible; her clothes changed from her jeans and padded winter coat into the opulent rich velvet robes of a queen and a simple but glorious golden crown appeared upon her head.

Sophie and Elijah witnessed this miraculous transformation and took hope from the presence of Queen Bertha.

Iris took hold of Elijah's hand and told him to pray. As the prayers began to take effect, Sophie could see that along with Lucy's ring, the crosses Iris and Adela were holding created a startling bright blue-white pyramid of light above the dragon's head, which was now writhing and squirming out of the yawning abyss. Like fine laser beams the blue-white rays flipped over and created another triangle, this time pointing into the ground. Sophie felt the need to put her hand over the Ankh but was reluctant to step into the swirling pit of hell and into the dragon's jaws. Taking a deep breath, she braced herself and stretched out her hand. As soon as her palm touched the magical onyx the ethereal trines combined into the shimmering hologram of a six pointed star.

To her amazement and relief, Sophie saw Joshua's spirit appear inside the sacred star.

At first, his body was that of his seven year old self, but within seconds he had transformed into a mighty warrior, clad from head to toe in shining silver armour and brandishing a colossal, glistening, golden sword. Before she could get used to Joshua in this regal form he shape-shifted again into a white Storm Trooper, and the ancient sword transformed into a glowing green lightsaber.

Joshua's spirit wasted no time. He plunged his reverberating lightsaber into his human body, which lay as still as death on the altar slab. The resounding saber penetrated his chest, passed through the altar and plunged its full force into the mouth of the dragon.

Sophie's heart leapt with hope that Joshua had activated the key of Nun and could now pass it to the Pleiades Council, but to her dismay, instead of elation, she felt a familiar and ghastly grip within her chest - she knew Ramesses was back.

The Pharaoh's sickening ectoplasm oozed out the Ankh, his hand grasping at Sophie, trying to drag her etheric body back into the jewel with him. Lucy involuntarily stepped in front of her sister, and with the consciousness of Queen Bertha, she formed a shield between them both and the ferocious King.

As the pain in Sophie's heart abated she gathered herself. *Bloody hell*, she thought. *Why don't they ever just give up? The darkness always has to fight it out to the bitter end.* She mustered all her strength - at least this time she knew what to do.

"Ladies!" she called out to all the ghostly women in the church who had been watching and waiting all this time. "Do what you have to do to take the old misogynist bastards down," she told them.

Their response was miraculous. Simultaneously standing up, they took hold of each other's hands, and their combined power sparked a chain reaction. Flashing through them like a bolt of lightning, a blinding blue-white light shot through the six pointed star and a vision of Mother Mary manifested alongside Joshua. Her serene and beautiful face lit up the church with the magical golden glow of the Grail, and for a moment Sophie hoped all would be well.

The women channelled the compassionate consciousness of the Holy Mother with such determination and force that Ramesses could not pull his entire body from out of the Ankh. His maliceful, eyeless face writhed with anger as he hovered, trapped halfway between the two dimensions.

Mother Mary filled Sophie's etheric body with so much Love that she shimmered with a deep cobalt blue light and grew in size to match the terrible, sneering face of Ramesses II. He tried to scare her into defeat with his rage and terror, but he did not succeed. Sophie was no longer just Sophie. She was now a vessel for the full force of the divine feminine, and the combination of all the hearts of all the women of Little Eden anchored so much compassion that even the deepest evil in the world didn't stand a chance against such Light.

Sophie now felt no fear. She was so wholly overwhelmed with bliss that she felt invincible. She gently opened her hands upwards to the sky and let a million enchanted rose petals fly out of her upturned palms. The delicate petals whirled and swirled about the vile Pharaoh and began to form a dynamic tornado around him. They spun so intensely that he could no longer see. He was completely disorientated by Love. He tried to muster his millennia of magics, but it was to no avail.

The pure compassion of the divine feminine was too strong for him.

Sophie watched in awe as the spirit of Joshua ran his galactic lightsaber through the archaic King, but what happened next, Sophie did not expect…

… Joshua pulled Ramesses II into the centre of the blue-white star which was still hovering over the dragon's open jaws. They became one being, merging together as if they were one soul - glowing as golden as the sun.

Mother Mary evaporated into the rose petals, followed by all the spirit women who vanished into the liquid ball of amber light. The shining star collapsed in on itself and the dragon's teeth snapped shut around it. The portal closed.

In her mind's eye, Sophie saw the iridescent, scaly tail of the dragon flip and dive miles away into river Thames; and at that moment, over by the river, a group of tourists looking down from Tower Bridge saw a tiny flash of golden light flicker beneath the surface of the dark waters and thought it to be only the reflection of a street light!

Elijah was involuntarily smiling now, as one does when bliss has taken over. He could feel the Light had triumphed and he had seen what Sophie had seen. He felt as if he had been initiated in some way and felt privileged to be working so closely with the holy spirits. "It's done," he told them.

Sophie nodded in agreement.

The church was quiet now.

Lancelot and Adela bent over Joshua, expecting him to wake at any moment, but he was still sleeping.

Sophie felt a spirit presence flutter over her arm and she focused in to see who it was. To her surprise it was Joshua. He was his seven year old self again, dressed in his St George's tabard and holding the wooden sword and shield he had made that day in park. Sophie looked over at his body on the altar and was puzzled.

"Shouldn't you go back into your body?" she asked him telepathically.

Joshua shook his head making his blond curls dance around his cherub like face. Sophie had always thought Josh was cute, but at this moment he looked beautiful; so innocent, so adorable, she could have mistaken him for an angel.

"I think you'd better go back - your mum will be sad if you don't," she told him, holding out her hand to take him to his now almost lifeless body.

Josh shook his head again and took the hand of St Hilda instead.

"I'm going with the saints," he told her, smiling.

"I don't understand," Sophie frowned.

But Sophie was lying to herself. In her heart - the heart of the divine feminine - she did understand.

Joshua was dead.

Chapter 23
~ * ~

Sophie's human heart was breaking as she watched Adela try to wake Joshua. In the half-light of the church he seemed as lifeless as a marble effigy upon his own tomb. As his mother tenderly stroked his cheek, she realised he was cold to the touch.

"My boy!" she cried out in anguish. "No! Joshua! No!"

Adela lifted him up and held him close against herself as if her own body heat might revive him.

Lancelot felt his pulse, not daring to believe that Josh had slipped away whilst they were holding vigil over him. He shook his head in dismay.

Iris, Lucy and Johnathon watched in horror as Adela screamed out in bone crushing pain.

Sophie fell to her knees and began to pray silently to Mother Mary. *Take me! Bring him back*, she pleaded. *Take me! I've nothing to live for and nothing to lose. What are you doing to Adela? Why are you making her suffer? Why take Joshua? Why not just use his body and leave him here with us? You're as cruel and as heartless as those damned Pharaohs. How can you call yourselves angels when you can do this to an innocent little boy and his mother? Take me instead, please! I beg you, take me and give Joshua back to his mother.*

St Hilda, Aunt Lilly and Alienor tried to comfort her. "He is with his Mother, the Holy Mother," St Hilda tried to tell her, but Sophie would not accept their loving thoughts and instead she closed her heart to their wisdom and held firm to her human grief. *I hate you*, she told them. *You're evil.*

As Adela began to sob, everyone else found it impossible to hold back their tears too, and only Johnathon had the presence of mind to call for an ambulance.

The next hour was a blur for everyone as the paramedics came calmly into the sorrowful church and sombrely took Joshua, Adela and Lancelot away.

Iris and Elijah walked slowly in the pale moonlight back to the Vicarage. Sophie and Lucy carried on towards Daisy Place, in silence.

Words seemed irrelevant, empty and pointless.

~ * ~

Sophie tried to sleep but she couldn't. She kept checking her phone but it didn't ring. It had been several hours since Joshua's body had been taken to the hospital and they had heard no news.

In the living room, Lucy hugged her mug of tea and laid her head on Jack's shoulder. "It's three o'clock," she said. "We should have heard something by now."

Jack kissed the top of her head and flicked through the TV channels trying to find something amusing to absorb them; every programme seemed to be about death, horror or war. He turned it off and pulled the duvet over them both. "Try to sleep," he told her, but he knew neither of them would.

A few minutes later, Alice came wandering into the living room. "What's the matter, sweetie?" Lucy asked her and tucked her in between them on the sofa bed.

"I had a bad dream," she said. "Joshua was a knight and I was a great queen. There was a horrible battle and when I looked for Joshua - he was dead."

Lucy looked at Jack in alarm and put her finger to her lips. She took Alice back to bed and they said the St Hilda prayer together, which had the desired effect of calming Alice down enough for her to drop off back to sleep.

Just as Lucy returned to the living room, three phones rang at once.

Sophie reached out to grab hers and sent it flying to the floor - she fell out of bed trying to rescue it. "Hello…Yes…Okay, see you in a few minutes."

Lucy's phone was over in the kitchen area, and as she went to get it, she tangled herself up in the duvet and had to throw herself towards the breakfast bar to grab it. "Hi. Yes...Come here… No, of course it's not. You have to come here. I wouldn't have it any other way…Ten minutes…Yes."

Jack rooted around in his jeans pocket and pulled his out. "Yes, old boy. Okay. See you at Lance's in ten."

Sophie came through from the bedroom. "Minnie just called. She's coming over with Adela."

"Yes, I know," Lucy replied. "Adela just called."

"I have to go to Lancelot's. Robert's already there," Jack told them as he pulled on his coat. "You girls will okay on your own?"

They nodded.

"Did Adela say anything?" Sophie asked. She was scared to death that she had killed Joshua somehow. She wasn't sure that you could actually kill someone from the astral realms - other than by sending them mad or pushing them to commit suicide. To actually stop someone's heart beating - she hoped that was not possible.

The next ten minutes seemed like hours.

Finally, a shaken and tired Adela arrived with a supportive Minnie. Before she could speak, she burst into tears, and Lucy made her lie down on the sofa with a cup of sweet tea.

"It was an aneurism," Minnie told them, "Caused by the fall at the polo match. There had been a blood clot and they hadn't seen it at the time. He died instantly once it…He wouldn't have…" Minnie began to cry… "He wouldn't have…" she tried to breathe through the tears…"He wouldn't have felt a thing. There was nothing anyone could have done."

"If we'd rung for an ambulance sooner would he have...?" Sophie began to ask.

Minnie shook her head. "They said he would have died at the hospital even if he'd got there hours earlier. By the time they'd have realised what it was, it would have been too late." Minnie had to gather herself again and whispered, "Adela said she was glad he died in the church and not at the hospital because at least there he was already with the angels and the saints."

Adela was persuaded to take a bath with some Pink and Emerald Rainbow Rescuer, and Sophie poured as many Apache Tears and Rose Quartz crystals as she could find into the water along with one of Alice's pink fizz bath bombs. Adela could hardly even feel the warmth of the water. She was numb.

Her heart was broken.

Over at Lancelot's house the decanter of whisky was empty. Robert, Jack and Lancelot sat in silence as they watched the dawn break over the eastern wall.

Lancelot felt as if someone had plugged him into an electrical socket; adrenalin and cortisol ran through him with such force that he thought he might explode. He knew he was to blame.

He looked at his phone in the hope that Adela had txt him but she had not. He was desperate to see her, to be with her, to hold her. His body ached with her pain, and the energy between them, which had felt like a sea of tranquillity warmed by flames of passion, now seemed to be a tempest filled with shards of glass.

He threw his own glass across the room, shattering it against the wall.

Lancelot needed to do something physical. Robert suggested he come over to Bartlett Crescent to use the pool. Whilst Robert prepared them both some breakfast, Lancelot went onto the roof and undressed in the cold morning air. The sharpness against his skin was less than he deserved to feel. He dived in and held his breath under the water for as long as he could bear - punishing himself with the sensation of near suffocation. He did laps until he was so tired he could hardly move his arms anymore. Exhausted, he floated on his back, looking up at the pink morning sky and prayed for Joshua's soul.

~ * ~

Back at Daisy Place, Sophie lay on her bed. *I hate you*, she kept repeating to the angels and all her spirit guides. *How could you take him?* But as she felt the familiar presence of Aunt Lilly surround her she began to feel her heart melting and floods of tears came. *They should have taken me instead*, she told her Aunt. *Why Joshua? Why so young?*

In reality, Sophie didn't need to ask these questions as she knew the answers, but she felt guilty that real truth wasn't humane enough. She couldn't help but feel that if she accepted the spiritual meaning of life it would make her sound like a monster to everyone else. How could she be happy for Joshua when everyone else was devastated? Adela had lost her only child to the spirit world. And yet Sophie knew that life on Earth is a terrible journey of suffering through karma and fear, and the sweet release of death is a welcome relief for many. And most of all, she knew that Heaven is our real home. She began to smile involuntarily as she thought of Joshua in Heaven, surrounded by the bright white light of the Holy Spirit, living in such love, such peace.

As she listened to the dawn chorus outside her window, she opened her heart again to compassion and she couldn't feel sad for him, try as she might; all she could feel was joy.

Chapter 24
~ * ~

As the devasting news of Joshua's sudden death spread throughout Little Eden a hush of sadness descended over the town and the school was closed for a period of mourning.

Adela began arranging her departure from Little Eden. Her parents and sister were arriving on the next available flight and all she wanted to do was to go home. The charms of England seemed dulled now and the beautiful town she had fallen in love with felt morbid and gloomy to her bereaved soul. Feeling like an alien in a foreign land for the first time, she found no solace within the sanctuary of the walls and longed for the wide open horizons of the Pacific Ocean.

As dusk enveloped Accoucher Lane, the last rays of sunlight lit up the canal like a ribbon of fire; exhausted with grief and shock, Adela met Lancelot on the Seven Sister's Bridge.

She blamed him for Joshua's death.

"If you hadn't encouraged him to learn to ride, he'd still be here," she told him bitterly.

"I know," Lancelot replied pensively. "It's all my fault. I'm so sorry. I don't know what to say or how to ever make amends." He wanted to magically bring Joshua back to life and right now he would have sold his soul to the devil to do so.

"When are you going back to California?" He asked her.

"In a few days' time," she replied in a faint voice. Her eyes were red from crying and her hands visibly shook. Lancelot wished he could hold her in his arms and comfort her. He reached out his hand to take hers but pulled back. He knew she didn't want his kindness. She seemed a million miles away from him now.

"If there's anything I can do?" he began to say.

"Nothing," she told him despairingly. "Just do nothing. Don't try to call me," she added. Lancelot was about to protest, but before he could speak she told him again, "Don't speak to me. Just don't."

Reluctantly, Lancelot walked pensively away into the shadows down the towpath. He glanced back for a moment and saw Adela still standing on the bridge, her hair glistening gold in the last rays of sunlight, looking as beautiful as an angel and as fragile as glass.

He knew he had lost her forever.

Adela took a deep breath. She had been forgetting to breathe since Joshua passed away. She wanted to stay outside in the cold air - its sharpness made her feel alive at least. She looked down into the silent black water of the canal and in her grief she called out into the chill of the night, "Joshua. Come back."

A shiver ran through her as she realised that the spirit of her little boy was manifesting through the water as a glowing orb of light. She did not doubt it was him. She held out her hand as if to touch his invisible fingers and felt a flicker of warmth against her palm. Her poor fractured heart suddenly felt suspended in total peace. "My boy," she whispered. "My little boy."

The comforting sensation of Joshua's presence lasted a few minutes and the respite it brought was much needed. As his spirit faded away, she didn't want to go home to her house, filled only with memories now, so she let her feet take her to Daisy Place, where she found Minnie closing up Buttons and Bows.

Minnie heard the shop bell tinkle and turned to see a depressed Adela standing in the doorway. She seemed unsure whether to come in or not. Minnie closed the till and went to hug her friend. Not really knowing what to say, she offered her a chair and continued with her tidying, waiting for Adela to speak first.

Adela ran her fingers through some ribbons and smoothed down some fat quarters which Minnie had been cutting out of vintage fabrics, but she didn't say anything.

After a few minutes Minnie felt she should break the silence, but small talk seemed ridiculous considering the circumstances so she went straight to the point. "Robert asked me to ask you about the funeral. He says he'll pay for you and Joshua to go home or he'll arrange whatever ceremony you would like here. What would you like?"

"I don't know," Adela replied, as if she wasn't actually thinking about it. "The flight's booked for next week."

"Do you want to go home?" Minnie asked her.

"I don't know," Adela admitted. "I loved it here in Little Eden. I thought I'd found my real home but my parents want Joshua to be buried in California." She looked up at Minnie in desperation. "I want someone else to tell me what to do."

"We would all love it if you and Joshua stayed here in Little Eden with us," Minnie told her kindly. "But you have to do what's best for you."

"Everyone here is so lovely," Adela replied, arranging some cotton reels into neat rows. "I don't want to leave the school when I've only just started. I thought it was destiny that brought me here. It felt so right. Now part of me wishes I'd never come."

"Sophie would say it is our karma which leads us to people and places and that there's not much we can do about what happens or where we end up or who we end up with," Minnie replied.

"Fate," Adela smiled sadly. "Is the fault in our stars or in our own hands?"

Minnie sighed. "Peony would say you have total control over everything that happens. But I can't think that can be right. It seems to me that it's a bit of both. What happened to Joshua - whether it was pre-ordained or just a pure accident - I'm not sure we can ever really know. But what happened was no one's fault. Not yours, not Lancelot's…"

Adela looked up at her - she knew what she meant. "I know it's not really his fault," she admitted. "But, oh god, Minnie, I'm so angry! Why Joshua? Why me? Why us? Why now? Why here?"

Minnie frowned as she locked the door and turned off the main light, leaving only the window illuminated with fairy lights. "I think the only answer to all those questions really is just fate."

The next day, Sophie and Lucy took Tambo, Alice and Elijah into London, to try to keep them occupied and cheer them up. Wandering under the trees by the river Thames, with the Tower of London just behind them, they tucked into fresh donuts bought from a street vendor nearby. Robert had given Sophie his wheelchair and this was her first trip out in it. It felt strange and she was aware of people looking at her. It hadn't been very easy to use on the Tube, but it had meant she could have a day out of Little Eden for the first time in a long time.

They found a bench to sit on to watch the boats go by.

"Can I sit with you guys?" Lucy asked them.

"Of course, but don't sit there," Alice told her as she pointed to the space between her and Elijah.

Lucy paused, "Why not?"

"Joshua's sitting there," Alice replied, as if it was a perfectly normal thing to say. She shuffled over to give Lucy some room on the end.

"Okay!" Lucy replied, a little surprised.

"So, are you guys all okay?" Sophie asked them - trying to sound casual. "I mean about Joshua only being with you in spirit now,"

They all nodded.

"Alice, are you sure? You were worried everyone was going to die after Aunt Lilly left us. Do you feel the same now?" Sophie asked her.

Alice shook her head. "I don't mind about death now," she replied in all seriousness.

"Well, that's good," Sophie said. "What's changed?"

"Now I know for sure that death isn't scary and you go on living in Heaven afterwards. Josh can't play with us like he used to but he says it's so cool to be with the saints. Plus, I met all those women who had lived in Little Eden and they were awesome. They just don't have a body like I do. When I die I'll be like them."

"Are all the spirit women still around Little Eden?" Sophie asked her.

Alice shook her head. "No, they all went with Joshua when he died."

"Do you know where they went?" Sophie asked her.

Elijah pointed to the river. "They went back in time and into the water," he told her. "They went to change the keys."

"Can you see and speak to Joshua?" Sophie enquired.

Tambo shook his head. "I can't speak to him but I know he's here."

"I can sometimes," Elijah replied.

"Do you miss him?" Sophie asked them.

"I miss that he can't play the drums in the band anymore," Tambo admitted.

"He told us not to worry about it," Alice said. "He says he is happy and wants us all to be happy too."

"You all seem rather glum today though," Lucy observed.

"Josh told us he doesn't want his ashes to go back to America," Elijah told her. "He needs to stay here with us in Little Eden. He's a saint now and he needs to be here to help guard the dragon portal."

"Can you ask Adela to stay so she'll let Joshua stay with us?" Tambo asked his mum.

"I don't think we can stop Adela taking him home if that is what she would like to do," Lucy replied. She felt the wind getting up and shivered as some yellow catkins blew down around them. She suddenly felt a cold sharp sting on her right hand and looked down. She was still wearing the amethyst ring. She twisted it slightly and got a small electric shock. "Ouch!" she said and took it off.

"What is it?" Sophie asked.

"This ring - it just come alive again like it did in the church," Lucy told her.

Suddenly Sophie saw a huge watery dragon's head rush up out of the river and hover in front of them. At first she wasn't sure if they were in danger, but when the dragon smiled at her she felt a rush of love through her body and giggled. "I think the sisters would like their ring back!" she told her.

"Are you sure?" Lucy asked her, a little sad to let it go.

"When we are given power we must use it wisely, as we are guided to do, and then give it back to where it came from," Sophie explained.

Lucy grimaced. "When I was channelling Queen Bertha I felt invincible," Lucy admitted. "It was rather intoxicating I have to admit. I felt like a queen for hours afterwards."

"Power is borrowed from the planet and from other people," Sophie explained. "If you start to imagine that it is yours to keep it will take you into the dark side of yourself."

"Like the ring in Lord of the Rings[14], " Elijah added. "You have to give it back."

Lucy had no desire to end up like Gollum. Without hesitation she threw it into the waiting water.

The friendly dragon gladly swallowed the ring. It burped and winked then dipped back into the Thames and disappeared into the flowing stream again.

"Are those old male oppression keys upgraded now?" Lucy asked.

Sophie shrugged. "I don't know," she replied.

"What difference will it make anyway?" Lucy wondered.

"I think the Star Children will be less concerned with male and female. Gender neutral is more appropriate now, but all the oldies need to start to think like that too if the world is to be a more inclusive and equal place to live. It's the oldies who want it to stay the same as it ever was."

"Too right," Tambo agreed. "A boy, a girl - what's it matter - we're all the same."

---

14 Lord of the Rings, J.R.R. Tolkien, 1937- 49, Allen & Unwin

"Just because I'm a girl doesn't mean I'm less worthy than a boy," Alice agreed. "I can do anything a boy can do if I want to." She remembered at her old school how sometimes the girls would tell her she was too much of a tom-boy. At the Star Child Academy it didn't seem to matter anymore.

"I sometimes feel like I'm not sure if I'm a boy or a girl," Elijah admitted. "It's hard to say what it is to be one or other don't you think?"

"We still have boy's bits though," Tambo laughed.

"I think it would be good to be both," Alice pondered.

"I don't think I'd like to have a girl's bits as well," Tambo grimaced.

Alice giggled at the idea.

Lucy laughed. "It sounds to me as if 'anything goes' from now on, and whatever 'bits' you have or don't have shouldn't define how you are treated."

Alice suddenly caught sight of a balloon seller in the distance and all philosophical thoughts went out of her mind. She begged to be allowed to buy one. Lucy let them go and watched them dodge and weave amongst the tourists along the riverside.

Sophie sighed. "We might not live to see the day that women and men in every culture are free and equal, but that's the hope I suppose. A new globally inclusive matrix is where the Star Children want to live, and if we can help them build it, so much the better!"

"We just have to convince everyone else too," Lucy smiled.

"That's why we have to change the DNA codes," Sophie replied. "Until we do that, the old ways will remain programmed in people's minds and hearts. Humans get very upset when their beliefs are challenged or threatened because their survival instinct kicks in and the programmes they believe in trigger fear. Being a human sucks. I'll never understand this whole 'incarnation' obsession. The world is pretty I'll grant you - the sky, the oceans, the forests, the architecture - it can be attractive I suppose as long as the weather is good, but a few nice views aren't worth the hassle of being human if you ask me."

"I don't mind being human," Lucy mused. "I'm not sure I'd want to keep coming back here forever though. It'd be nice to go live with the angels like Joshua one day, just not yet."

Alice, Tambo and Elijah returned, laughing and giggling, with a bright balloon bouncing behind each of them. Sophie smiled at their innocence and their ability to find the fun in the small things. She was glad they were with her to teach her to lighten up when her mind sank into depressive thoughts.

The air turned chilly in the late afternoon and they all headed home through the ancient narrow streets. As they passed by the fine, tall, green spire of All Hallows, one of the oldest churches in London, Sophie shuddered. Its grimy walls were soaked in a thick aura of human thought forms. Thousands of years' worth of prayers had woven a web of deception within the stones, which was now so potent it was tangible. The sacred site was steeped in millennia of spells; generation after generation adding to the idea that God is wrathful and that humans are sinful. The all-pervading belief that the only way to Heaven is with the permission of a clergyman had firmly taken root. Fear had replaced Love a long time ago.

Sophie didn't like to say what she was thinking out loud in case it scared the children, but she couldn't help but ponder on the strength of etheric keys and codes within the human psyche. Once they were woven into the mind and then into the DNA via initiations, ceremonies, attunements and false blessings, they seemed almost impossible to remove. *I don't think this transition from one matrix to another is going to be smooth*, she thought. *Half the world feels safe in their nationalistic identities, their religious rules, their tribal beliefs and their family ways. Just like we want to hold onto Little Eden, everyone wants to protect their life as they know it. Ramesses and his cronies might want to keep their power over the planet and the human race, but whether they like it or not their time is up! I just wish they would bow out gracefully, but knowing human nature I very much doubt they will.*

138

Chapter 25
~ * ~

Joshua's funeral did take place in Little Eden after all. It was held in the charming crematorium near Devil's Gate. Intimate and beautiful, the tiny chapel holds only twenty people, and it can be used by anyone of any faith or of no faith at all. The delicate stained glass window depicts a small wooden boat, sailing on ribbons of a watery blue ocean towards the enchanting amber glow of the setting sun. Above this serene scene the arc of a sparkling rainbow glints in the incoming light and the words beneath read:

The world's thy ship and not thy home[15]

The sorrowful band of mourners sheltered from the drizzling rain under the sombre branches of the ancient yew tree, waiting for the black, horse drawn hearse to arrive. As the small coffin was carried slowly into the chapel on the shoulders of Robert, Jack, Johnathon and Adela's father, Tambo quietly sang Tears in Heaven[16], accompanying himself on his guitar.

Adela's father stood before the mourning congregation. He was visibly grieving and his usually strong voice broke from time to time as he spoke about his grandson - recalling such happy memories as when, less than a year old, Josh had taken his first steps on Santa Monica beach; and when, on his first birthday, he had said 'grandy' for the first time (which meant granddad) - a name that had stuck ever since. He was heartbroken that he would never see his little grandson graduate from college or start his first job. He had hoped the next speech he would give would be at Joshua's wedding. He had never dreamt it would be at his funeral.

---

15 St Therese of Liseaux
16 Tears in Heaven, Eric Clapton, 1991, Warner Bros

Too upset to speak, Adela had asked her sister to recite a poem, and this, dear readers, is that very poem:

Do not cry for me momma,
For I am in Heaven now.
Far beyond the rainbows and the soft clouds in the sky.
I was born of angels and to them I now return.
My time on Earth was fleeting but I am home, momma, I am home.

Do not be sad for me, momma.
For I am in Heaven now.
Playing amongst the daisies and the sparkling waves upon the shore.
I was born of fairies and to them I now return.
My time on Earth was but a moment but I am home, momma, I am home.

Do not grieve for me momma.
For I am in Heaven now.
Flying through the universe and sailing upon the Milky Way.
I was born of the Stars and to them I now return.
My time on Earth was just a glimmer but I am home, momma, I am home.

At the end of a touching ceremony the weeping mourners walked silently from the chapel, comforted by the soft tones of Sissy and Ginger singing, Let It Be[17].

In the empty chapel of rest, Adela lingered a while by Joshua's coffin. Minnie came to stand beside her. The scent of roses was soothing and the silver stars scattered upon the coffin seemed to twinkle as if they were waving to her from above. As Minnie took her hand she seemed to be jolted back into reality, and it dawned on her fully that Josh was never coming back. She desperately wanted to rip open the coffin and using any magic she could, bring him back to life. She prayed hopelessly for this all to have been a bad dream and that she would wake up to find her boy asleep in his bed again or hear him rushing down the stairs, two at a time, eager for his breakfast. If only she could turn back time and start all over again. She begged the angels to return him to her.

---

17 Let It Be, Beatles, 1969, Apple

Adela felt sick to her stomach and her legs would hardly hold her anymore. Minnie helped her outside into the sunshine. The rain had stopped, opening up the sky to a cloudless horizon and the air was deliciously scented with freshly cut grass and the gentle nodding heads of golden daffodils. Adela needed to sit down, and she perched for a few moments on the steps of the Little Eden Cenotaph, just beside the gate.

Absently running her fingers over the names of the soldiers engraved upon the obelisk, Minnie realised something, "Sometimes sacrifice is needed for a better world," she mused. "There are hundreds of heroes and heroines who die every day in many unsung ways. I think Josh would have been proud to be one of them," she said. "My boy is a hero, isn't he?" Adela nodded. "We can't put his name on a monument like this, but in a spiritual, other worldly way, he is a hero," Minnie said. "He should have his own inscription somewhere in Little Eden."

A fleeting gust of wind whistled through the leaves of the yew tree and a small white feather floated down from the sky landing just by their feet. "Joshua?" Adela whispered, "Joshua is that you?"

Her little boy's voice floated through her mind. "Momma," she heard him say. "It's me, momma. I'm here."

A tear rolled down Adela's cheek. "Momma," she heard Joshua say again. "Don't be sad, momma. I'm safe. I'm with the saints. I'm home."

Adela could feel her heart physically disintegrating inside her as she spoke to her darling boy in her mind, "I shouldn't have let you learn to play polo. I'm so sorry my love. Lancelot persuaded me," she told him remorsefully.

"I told you Jedi[18] had to learn to ride horses, didn't I, momma?" Joshua's voice replied cheerfully. "I wanted to learn, didn't I?"

Adela could not deny that he had begged her to let him ride, and she smiled to herself, remembering his insistence that Jedi would become, for the Star Children, what the Knights of King Arthur were for the ancestors, and that he had to be one of them.

"Don't blame Lancelot, momma. He's a White Knight. He's one of us. He'll always be on our side," Joshua told her.

"But why did you have to go?" Adela asked him in despair. "Why couldn't you stay here, with me?"

"I'm still here, momma. I'll always be in Little Eden. Bury me in the

18 Jedi, Star Wars, George Lucas, 1977, Lucasfilm/Disney

church. I'll be the first saint of the new age."

Adela half laughed at the ridiculousness of it all. "You got what you wanted then Josh. You're where you wanted to be?"

"I am, momma. I'm so happy. Be happy for me. Thank the saints for letting me join them for this awesome ride. And it is an awesome ride, momma. I am a chosen one. I'm so lucky, momma, I get to help everyone forever. I get to be an angel."

Just for a fleeting moment Adela thought she caught a glimpse of Joshua amongst the grave stones and darted up to move towards his spectre, but before she could take a step the shimmering vision evaporated.

She sat back down in sorrow. Looking up at Minnie, who was still reading the names of the heroic dead unaware of Joshua's ethereal presence, she said, "I think Josh and I need to stay in Little Eden after all and you're right - we need to make a memorial for him. I feel it needs to be in the church so that everyone who needs help can find him, and he'll do what he can for them from the other side."

Minnie put her arm through her friend's as they walked to the gate. "I'm glad you're both staying," Minnie told her. "We all are - especially Lancelot. You will forgive him one day won't you?"

Adela felt a dagger through her heart at the mention of Lancelot. She knew she had a long way to go before she could forgive him, herself, or the universe. "Maybe, one day," she replied. "Maybe."

~ * ~

A few days later, in the kitchen of No.1 Daisy Place, Mrs B was baking a cake. It was for Buddha's birthday. She had designed it so that it looked like a stupa with a bobble on the top and she had decorated it with bright colours, glittering sprinkles and edible gold leaf.

"We need some cheering up," Mrs B told Lucy as she made lotus flower petals out of pink fondant.

Lucy was feeling extremely fed up. Not just because of the terrible tragedy of Joshua's death but also because she knew the day was approaching when she had to tell Jimmy that she knew of his affair. She had started to run out of excuses as to why she couldn't sleep with him. She wasn't exactly missing him but she was afraid that she might never meet anyone ever again and die an old maid.

"Life is full of trials," Mrs B said, rolling out some more icing. "We must balance sorrow with joy and loss with generosity otherwise we will all drown in despair."

Lucy sighed as she applied some more gold leaf to the cake. "I wish life could just be the happy bits. It seems we're having more than our fair share of bad times in Little Eden since Lilly left us. Maybe she was our lucky charm?"

"You always pull through, my love," Mrs B reminded her.

Lucy sighed again. "I'm tired, Mrs B, tired of always having to pretend everything's okay when it's not."

Mrs B sighed. "You can scream and shout and cry and wail all you like, my love. I believe it does us good. But then we must remember to smile and laugh and love and have some fun too."

"Peony says we should be positive no matter what happens," Lucy replied, standing back from the cake to check where it needed more touching up.

"Well, my love," Mrs B replied. "If you think Peony is wise - then follow her advice."

"I don't think it's healthy to always be positive," Lucy decided. "I think you are wise. We have to yell and cry sometimes too."

Mrs B came and gave her a sugary hug. "What helps me when I'm despondent is to think about someone else. There are others in Little Eden who need cheering up just as much as you do."

"You really are the wise owl of Little Eden, Mrs B," Lucy told her.

"Perhaps I'm channelling some of Buddha's wisdom whilst I'm making this cake!" Mrs B laughed.

"You sound like Sophie when you say things like that," Lucy giggled.

"Talking of Sophie," Mrs B said. "I hear she may have a new beau?"

Lucy smiled. "Tobias Gilbert. Yes. I think he likes her. I'm so excited for her Mrs B but she won't get excited for herself. She says he'll drop her as soon as he finds out about her illness."

"Well, my love, if he does then he isn't worth having anyway," Mrs B replied and put the final touches to the cake. Wiping her hands on her apron she admired her handy work.

"It's a masterpiece of joyfulness and yummy sweetness!" Lucy smiled.

"It'll do, won't it?" Mrs B nodded. She washed the sugar off her hands and put on her coat. "Now, all I have to do is get it to the Buddhist Centre in one piece!"

The World Peace Centre gladly opened its doors to everyone who wanted to come for Buddha's birthday party. The park was full of visitors from all over the world, and there was a joy filled atmosphere combined with a serene calmness which is always particular to sacred Buddhist sites.

Devlin had made white sugar mice to give out to the visitors, and Dr G led a group meditation in the outdoor theatre to which over five hundred spiritual seekers came; consequently, there were not quite enough white mice to go around. Hope and compassion filled the air along with laughter and some gleeful giggling sparked off by Dr G who had a lively sense of humour which he could not contain once he was channelling the consciousness of Buddha. To finish the happy day, candles were lit and placed in white paper lanterns, which were floated out upon the dark waters of lake to welcome the Light into everyone's hearts and minds.

Chapter 26
~ * ~

Sophie had been too tired to join in the celebrations so Dr G invited her to join him that evening for some private meditation. When she arrived however, the tranquil peace she usually felt in the inner sanctum was replaced with a powerful invisible force she had never experienced there before, and she felt a rush of energy which nearly knocked her off her feet. She could swear that the room, usually bright white, was filled with a pale blue hue and the air seemed to hum around her.

The moon could be seen high in the sky through the long Georgian windows and Sophie had the uneasy sensation that the moon was watching her; she felt a shiver run down her spine. Dr G put his finger to his lips as a sign for her to remain silent and motioned to her to sit down on a big floor cushion.

Blue was sitting, like a mini Buddha, robed in a dark maroon and bright orange robe, in the middle of the lotus flower rug. He seemed to be in a trance, unaware of Sophie's arrival, and he remained perfectly motionless as Sophie sat down.

Sophie felt as if she had just entered the eye of a storm.

The whole chamber was awash with watery light, the colour of lapis lazuli, which shimmered and sparkled with such intensity that Sophie felt overwhelmed by it. Blue was surrounded by droplets of water which began to coalesce to form the Thames dragon. Its huge shimmering head bubbled up as if it was appearing out of a big hot tub in the floor. The sensation it brought with it was compassionate and loving. Sophie felt a sincere and powerful wave of kindness flow through her.

Suddenly a frisson of fear, followed by an oppressive darkness, shook the room.

Sophie recognised the presence immediately. It was accompanied by the familiar reek of dank tombs and the stench of death. The evil, rancid, fearsome face of Ramesses II materialised through the portal in the floor, his crystal skull aflame with indigo fire.

Sophie feared for Blue's safety as she felt a freezing hand trying to wrap its icy fingers around her heart once again. She grasped hold of Dr G's hand and could feel the sensation of a warm pink energy emanating from his palm into hers. Coral coloured streams of light were pouring from Dr G's heart, and she saw the embroidered lotus flower in the carpet come alive and wrap its precious petals around Blue, holding him safely within its golden bud.

Sophie realised that Blue was sending a key into the dragon portal, and unlike her - he felt no fear.

The Pharaoh and the dragon grew bigger still and faced each other in anger as if the Atlanteans and the Pleiades were about to go into battle again - just as they had in the church. To her horror, Blue didn't look so calm anymore, and his usual straight spine seemed to crumble as he folded in on himself.

At that moment the wrath of the Pharaoh was more powerful than the Light.

What had happened to Joshua flashed before her eyes. She wanted to reach out and whisk Blue out of the mouth of the dragon portal to safety.

Dr G's hand tightened in hers and she realised by the look on his face that he had not expected Blue to fail.

The Pharaoh's hellish smile chilled her to the bone. She could hardly breathe. *Don't take Blue*, she begged the universe. *Don't take him too.*

Sophie prayed for help.

There was a collection of highly coloured and different sized Buddhas displayed around the room, some fierce, some serene, some male, some female. Her eye landed on Blue Tara and she knew that was the one who could help her.

Blue for Blue, she thought.

Sophie took up the Tara figurine, which was only a few inches high; as soon as she touched it a portal opened with a blast of scintillating blue light. The force which shot out of the statuette belied its physical size. A million silver spinning disks flew out of the icon, and just before they reached the Pharaoh, they merged into one giant blade which sliced his head clean off.

His evil face fell to the floor and shattered into thousands of shards of glass which were immediately sucked down into the portal in the floor.

Blue suddenly sat bolt upright again - he was back in the game.

The Thames dragon, friendly, smiling and compassionate, with eyes that shone like diamonds, bent its head gently down towards the young Tulku. Blue reached up and stroked its neck, as he did so he smiled with such joy that his whole body seemed to glisten with pearlescent light, and he sat like a twinkling jewel within the gleaming lotus flower.

Sophie felt all the fear and dread flee from the room and the familiar sense of pure peace washed over her.

Then, just when she thought it was over, from the dragon's mouth stepped an apparition of young Joshua, shimmering like a hologram before them. Tears of joy trickled down her cheeks as her heart swelled with love. Joshua asked Sophie to give him the statuette of Blue Tara and she handed it to him. Taking the etheric energy it contained with him he smiled at her, stepped back into the dragon's mouth and vanished. The dragon winked and then it too disappeared into the floor.

Over the pool of glistening water a large golden wax seal appeared, with a curling dragon and a delicate lotus flower stamped upon it, and it closed the portal down.

Blue remained seated in meditation for a while longer, drinking in the bliss.

Sophie looked at Dr G for an explanation, but Dr G seemed a little dazed and neither of them spoke for several minutes.

Finally, Sophie broke the serenity, "What just happened, Dr G?" she asked him.

Dr G shook his head. He sighed. "The female consciousness of Tara comes from the same god consciousness as your Mother Mary - the divine feminine," he told her. "They are becoming one again."

"I thought Buddhists didn't believe in God," Sophie said.

Dr G smiled. "What you call God we call consciousness. What you call Heaven we call the Pure Lands. We have different souls and different homes, but when we incarnate into human form we all are one, united by being human. There are many aspects of the diamond heart of the goddess, but all life comes and goes through the Mother."

"I thought they might take Blue to the other side as they did Joshua," Sophie admitted.

Dr G reassured her. "They did not take Joshua. Joshua chose to go with them. He did great service to mankind by being the anchor for the light beings to work through."

"He was a sacrifice?" Sophie asked.

Dr G smiled sadly. "Joshua does not see death as a sacrifice. He is released from samsara - he is free. To live as a human - that is the sacrifice."

Sophie thought it all sounded topsy turvy.

Dr G smiled. "Life is precious, but only because it is a way to further enlightenment. If death, or the manner of death, increases our merits, it becomes part of our enlightenment."

Sophie nodded. "Joshua wanted to be a saint more than he wanted to be human. He knew that life after death was more rewarding than life on Earth could ever be. He wanted to be enlightened and I guess now he is enlightening others too."

"That is why I came here to the West and why Blue is here in Little Eden," Dr G explained, "To help reunite our Tara and your Mother Mary. I learn from you and you learn from me, and together we create a new belief system that everyone can understand and be part of. We must not separate ourselves from each other with religions and tribal cultures. We are all human beings. We must learn to live with compassion for each other and ourselves - this is the way to ensure world peace."

"The Star Children already understand that, I think," Sophie said. "But children quickly learn to hate each other from their parents and peers."

Dr G nodded his head in agreement. "The Star Children need new mantras, new teachings, new prayers. Listen…"

Dr G began to recite a prayer which took some of the energy from Buddhist mantras and some of the energy of the Holy Spirit and made them flow as one…

Heart Jewel

In you, great Goddess of Compassion & of Perfect Wisdom,
I go for refuge until I realise myself in You.
My earthly life is transient and is purified by the waves of your eternal
wisdom, knowledge & bliss.
Walking the path of Truth before me, revealing all that is false & fake,
cutting through all karmic ties.
Releasing me from all suffering you shine the light of the Holy Spirit
amidst the darkness
so that I may dwell forever in your diamond heart and in your holy
embrace.[19]

When he had finished, Sophie felt that the etheric diamond in her heart had grown too big for her chest and that her brain was expanding so much it made her head hurt. She also felt waves of pure bliss washing through her mind, body and spirit and understood for the first time what unity really felt like.

---

19 Heart Jewel Prayer, KT King Prayers, Book Two, 2016

Chapter 27

~ * ~

Since Joshua had passed away Iris Sprott had sensed an unfamiliar energy flowing through the church. She began to feel dizzy whenever she approached the altar. To her it felt as if there was something invisible whirling around and around over the top of her head whenever she got close to the centre of the dragon portal. At night, her dreams had become startlingly vivid, to the point where she was waking up not sure what day or even what year it was. One particular vision dream had lingered in her thoughts for days afterwards - the sky behind the vicarage had been filled with crystals instead of clouds, and the air was shimmering with rainbow light, yet it was not raining. As with vision dreams, when she was in it she believed it to be reality and the supernatural atmosphere seemed perfectly normal. A towering and glowing image of Jesus appeared to her, his arms outstretched as if to welcome her into his heart, but when she had tried to embrace him, he had melted away like wax in her arms. In his place a six foot tall man of about thirty years old, dressed in white robes with long dark hair and bare feet took hold of her hand and transported them both to the rolling sands of an infinite desert. There, in front of a tiny crag of a cave, which seemed to protrude out of the ground all by itself, an ordinary Jesus sat down with her, in front of a blazing fire pit, and put his arm around her. The brotherly love she felt enveloping her was so beautiful and blissful that her body fell into a profound state of relaxation and peace. She felt completely safe in his presence, his consciousness being the epitome of male protection: strength, kindness and compassion. This was the real Jesus and he was just a saint like any other. And just like all other true saints, he had anchored divine love and his guidance in a dragon portal - his being situated in the golden sands of Arabia.

Iris didn't realise that the oscillating sensation above her head was her crown chakra opening and downloading new levels of consciousness. The lucid dreams were visions of other dimensions and time frames. She had started to become aware of her multi-dimensional self but didn't yet know what she was doing. Thanks to being released from the old Atlantean patriarchy spells, her belief system had started to involuntarily shift.

The day after Buddha's Birthday she was rearranging some blossoms in the chancel when her eyes began to water. She assumed it was an allergic reaction to the pollen (not that she had had hay fever in her life before). As her sore eyes began to blur, she felt the rotation above her head once again and had to hold onto the lectern to steady herself. She heard the external vestry door bang shut; the sound seemed to trigger a flash of clarity and she remembered another vision she had had on the night of Joshua's death.

Usually Iris kept her emotions well under control through regular prayer, especially her favourite - the St Hilda prayer. Now for some reason, she could not hold the rising anger down any longer.

That is it! she thought to herself. *Enough! I can't do this anymore. I'm lying to myself, to the congregation, to everyone in Little Eden and most of all to God. If I hide the truth any longer I'll be as culpable as he is, so I will. I'm going to tell someone!*

Slamming down the unfinished flower arrangement, she didn't even wait to take off her apron but marched staunchly out of the church and over to Adam Street.

In his office, Robert was elbow deep in paperwork, not least because he was going through a petition to banish his mother, which many of the residents had signed.

Iris knocked briskly on his door.

"Come in," Robert called out, relieved that someone might give him an excuse to take a break. "Iris, how lovely to see you," he said. "Can I get you a cup of tea?"

"No, no thank you," she replied anxiously.

Robert was a bit taken aback - she looked harassed and not at all her usual self.

"What can I do for you?" he asked as he invited her to sit down.

"This is hard for me to say, to be sure," Iris began. "But in all fairness to myself and Elijah I have to say it, so I do, and say it I will."

Robert waited in trepidation.

"I want you to sack my husband. The Reverend," Iris announced.

"Do what now?" Robert asked, aghast.

"I have come to the decision, so I have, and not lightly I might add. I've decided that he is not fit to be the vicar here in Little Eden and well, anywhere for that matter!"

Robert was speechless.

"I know you might think it harsh of me to say so. But I think you know why we came here in the first place..." she paused and looked at Robert for reassurance.

Robert leant back in his chair and sighed. "Well, yes I do," he agreed.

"Well then," Iris continued. "In light of what happened with poor Joshua, and what is happening with Little Eden, and all this ascension everyone is talking about, I feel you would be better with someone else to lead the church. Someone more forward thinking - someone more honest."

Robert had to admit to himself that Erik Sprott had a slightly repugnant aura about him, but he had let him be the vicar as a favour to his Aunt Elizabeth.

"Go to the vestry at five minutes past two today," Iris told Robert. "If you need a reason to dismiss him you'll find it then, so you will. There's an internal window above the door from the curate's office - he always forgets it's there, so he does. You'll have a good view."

Before Robert could ask her anymore questions (which he was dying to do), Iris hopped up out of her chair, said a hurried goodbye and left Robert to wonder what he might find Erik up to at five minutes past two.

The clock struck two as Robert sneaked into the small curate's office and waited. The church was deserted. He listened to hear if anyone was moving about but heard no one. Five minutes later, just as Iris said he would, Erik appeared. He came into the vestry, followed by the curate, Cassie Lossett.

Robert watched them sit down at the desk. They seemed to be going through some accounts. *Is he guilty of embezzlement?* Robert wondered. But that theory didn't really add up as there was hardly any money to embezzle! After a few minutes of conversation, which Robert could not quite make out, Cassie came over to Erik's side of the desk and leaned over him to point out something in a large ledger. Robert was a little taken aback at her low cut blouse and he saw a great deal more of her than he wanted to.

It was Erik, however, who got the real eye full, and before Robert had had chance to blink, Cassie was seductively unbuttoning her blouse. Erik didn't hesitate; he lifted up her skirt, sat her on the desk, spread her legs and unzipped his flies, revealing his...

151

Oh god! Robert thought and put his hand over his eyes. *I can never un-see that!* He winced at the scandalous scene but couldn't help taking another look just to make sure. He closed his eyes again wishing he had just trusted his first glance! *What do I do?* he wondered. *Do I barge in there whilst they are...or wait till they've finished?* He didn't really have to decide as Erik was finished a great deal sooner than Robert could ever have imagined, and he sat back in his chair, red in the face and panting.

Robert couldn't believe it!

If he was honest with himself however, he wouldn't have been surprised at all.

Robert waited a few more minutes hoping Cassie would leave, but instead, she put the kettle on and took out the biscuit tin as she rearranged her clothing. She was obviously staying a while.

Well, Robert thought. *I can't wait any longer! Once more into the breach as they say!*

He took a deep breath and swiftly opened the door to the vestry.

A surprised Erik greeted him affably. It was clear that he had no idea that Robert had been watching them all this time.

"Erik. Cassie. I have some bad news," Robert said without ceremony. "I think you might want to hear it privately Reverend."

Cassie offered Robert a cup of tea and a hobnob, but knowing where her hands had just been, he cringed at the thought of taking either from her. "No thank you," he told her. "Perhaps the Reverend and I could..."

"Oh yes, of course!" Cassie said, realising he wanted her to leave. "I'll go and restock the towels in the toilets, excuse me."

Robert waited impatiently for her to go - he just wanted to get it over with. As soon as she had shut the door behind her he plunged in with, "Look Erik, there's no easy way to say this so I'm just going to say it: I know what you and Cassie are up to and it's not on. Not in your position." He had a flash back to their passionate scene and his stomach churned.

Erik blushed and looked flustered. "I'm sorry?" he answered. "Up to..?"

"Oh, come off it!" Robert replied brusquely. "As vicar you are supposed to set an example, and shagging your curate, in the church, I might add, is not the right example now is it?"

Erik blushed like a naughty school boy.

"It was a mistake!" Erik pleaded. "She seduced me. I couldn't help

152

myself. You see, Iris and I, we…"

"I don't want to know!" Robert replied (and he really did not want to know!). "You need to sort out your private lives between yourselves, but as far as your public duties and Little Eden are concerned, it's over. It's not just about your infidelity. I know you are against women entering the clergy and I overlooked it. I know you are against same sex marriage and I overlooked that too. And I know you don't really like homosexuality either. I did not appreciate the fuss you made about the Mayday celebrations including the drag queens this year, but freedom of speech and all that, I let you have your opinion. I don't agree with bigotry, racism or misogyny, you know that. I run Little Eden now. What I say goes."

Erik looked shocked. "I don't believe in…"

Robert stopped him there, "You don't believe in progression, enlightenment, change, compassion, inclusivity or basic human rights."

It was Robert's turn to be a bit shocked - at himself. He had had to take a firm stance with residents from time to time over the years but he had never been quite this assertive before and it felt strange – amazing, but strange.

Erik didn't respond.

"You're not practising what you preach," Robert added.

"You don't understand what being a Christian really means," Erik tried to tell him. "There are rules. We must follow the doctrine."

"Well, maybe I am not a good Christian then!" Robert replied, "But if being a Christian means being a bloody awful human being, then I'm sorry Erik, I want nothing more to do with it."

Robert regretted that last statement a little as he thought maybe he had been too harsh, but he didn't want to show any sign of backing down, so he continued…"Lancelot will send you the necessary paperwork and your position is terminated forthwith. You will leave the vicarage within a week and find alternative accommodation outside Little Eden."

Robert felt a stab in his heart as he really did think he was being a bit rough, and he hoped that Erik had somewhere to live - he didn't want to make the man homeless - but he was determined to stick to his guns, not least for Iris's sake.

"The dragon portal needs a protector and you are not the man for the job," Robert told him. "You just don't have the balls…" Robert stopped himself as he realised what he was saying… "You don't have the courage to fight the darkness - the dark side has already got you right where it wants you."

Erik didn't protest anymore and just sulked.

As Robert turned to go Erik suddenly asked, "What's a dragon portal?"

Robert rolled his eyes and shut the door behind him.

As Robert walked back into the church he could feel that something had changed. The imposing gold crucifix above the altar caught his attention and he was overtaken by a sudden urge to pull it down. He couldn't quite reach it as it was hoisted high into the rafters so he looked around for something to stand on but could find nothing that would take his weight. Finally, he climbed onto the altar, and stretching as far up as he could reach, he unhooked the dust filled chains which suspended the cross on both sides. It was much lighter than he had imagined as it was made of wood - the metallic effect was merely trompe d'oeil.

Nothing is ever what it appears to be, he thought to himself.

Holding the cross firmly against his chest, he climbed back down and walked up the aisle with it. As he passed the lectern he noticed the grand, ancient bible open at Colossians 1:15. Shoving the cross under his arm he took up the heavy book. He wasn't sure where he was going with them but he just knew he wanted them out of the church.

~ * ~

Later that afternoon, Robert sat alone in a green leather wing arm chair, amongst the rows of neatly bound legal books in the Law Offices, wondering what to do next.

The crucifix and the bible were lying, dejected, on the floor.

India came in looking for Lancelot. "You okay?" she asked Robert.

Robert looked up and shook his head.

"Want to tell me about it?" she asked him as she looked at the religious items on the floor and wondered what on earth was going on.

Robert shook his head again. "Not really. I'd like to forget the whole thing if I'm honest, but I can't, as usual."

India put her files in Lancelot's in tray and sat down in the other wing chair. "Anything I can help with?" she enquired.

Robert sighed. "I have to sack Erik Sprott."

India looked shocked. "What? Why?"

Robert rolled his eyes. "Because he's an adulterer."

India didn't look shocked anymore.

Robert thought it was a bit strange that she didn't exclaim.

"Why aren't you surprised?" he asked her.

India shrugged. "I don't know. Maybe because he's that type. You know, holier than thou and sanctimonious as hell but underneath it all he's hiding a dirty little secret. The slimy git. Oh, god he's not a pedo…" she began to say…

…Robert interrupted her, "No! Thank god it's not that bad! He's been having an affair with Cassie Lossett."

India pulled a face. "Cassie Lossett?" she said. "Ooo, that's not decent. Does Iris know?"

"She's the one who told me about it," Robert replied, and grimaced as he had another flash back to the grubby little scene. "Aunt Elizabeth only let him come here as a favour to his dying mother and she hoped he'd change his ways under our influence, but it seems temptation was just too strong," Robert explained. "I just found these letters in his file."

He handed them to India…

Dear Lizzy

Thank you so much for arranging for Erik to take the position of Vicar in Little Eden. I believe the Bishop has been less than generous about his current situation but I know in my heart that it was not his fault. He is a temptation to women wherever he goes and his kindness can be misinterpreted so often. I have his assurance that it will never happen again and that he is determined to turn over a new leaf in Little Eden.

If I don't write again before I go, know that I love you and if I meet McIntosh in Heaven I shall say hello. If I see Frith I shall try to get a message to you somehow, if that is at all possible.

All my love
Besty-Ann

This was Aunt Elizabeth's reply:

Dear Betsy

My dearest friend, please do not distress yourself, I will make sure that Erik and Iris are cared for here in Little Eden and under my watchful eye he will not repeat his usual behaviour. I am sure the general goodness of Little Eden will have a positive effect on him. Everything will be just fine and I hope I will see you again before you leave us but if God comes for you before I do I shall look for your signs from Heaven and I know that we shall all be reunited there some day.

I love you my dear friend and thank you for all the years of support and love you have shown me. I shall take care of Erik and keep him safe.

Love always
Lizzy

"I need some coffee!" India said when she had read them, and went over to the percolator to get them both a cup. "The idea that Erik is some kind of lady magnet is a bit of a leap," she added. "I wouldn't throw myself at him if you paid me a million pounds." She shivered at the very thought of it.

Robert sighed. "Men in positions of power are always attractive, even when they themselves are not particularly attractive."

India had to concede that it did seem to be the case in general but she had never fallen for the charm of high office herself.

With that, Lancelot arrived, looking dishevelled and as if he hadn't slept in days (which was pretty much the case). India handed him some coffee too. He listened to them about Erik but couldn't really concentrate.

"You're not really listening, are you?" India reprimanded him.

Lancelot rubbed his head. "Sorry, I just can't seem to concentrate at the moment."

"Maybe you should take a few days off?" Robert suggested. "We can manage without you for a week or two."

Lancelot frowned. "I'm fine."

"You're not fine," India told him. "You're love sick and still blaming yourself for Joshua's death - which was not your fault! Being in love sucks when you've been rejected - believe me I know - it sucks the life out of you. It's like your insides have been ripped out and replaced with a black hole which devours you hour by hour until you can't feel anything anymore."

Lancelot just looked at her. That was exactly how it felt but he was too tired to talk about it.

The phone rang and he was saved by the bell.

Robert stood up to go. "That was Stella," he said. "Mother is having a meltdown, I'll have to go and sort it out."

"Maybe you could tell your mother to leave as well?" India suggested.

Robert didn't even respond. He was feeling a lot like Lancelot - past caring, past getting upset, past giving a f*ck what happened next.

Chapter 28
~ * ~

Robert walked over to Hart Crescent with a heavy heart. The lilacs were in full bloom and their voluminous wands of white and purple flowers filled the air with delicious scents but he paid little attention to the beauty around him - he was deep in contemplation about what to do. His mother was still refusing to leave Little Eden, yet at the same time she was threatening to go to the Caribbean to be with her 'only son'. Although Robert had thrown her out of Bartlett Crescent he had not had the guts to go the whole hog. The petition handed in from the residents, demanding her removal from the town, had more than enough signatures to make it binding and Robert knew he had to listen to them. He was hoping however that fate would intervene and she would just leave of her own accord.

When he arrived at the crescent, Stella's front door was wide open. Suitcases and matching bags were spilling out from the hallway into the porch. He could hear Stella, somewhere inside, trying to calm an irate Jennifer.

Don Freeway, one of the Little Eden taxi drivers, sitting in his black cab, his window rolled down, was pretending to read a newspaper, but it was obvious that he was listening to the debacle going on only yards away and that he was finding it mildly amusing. He had signed the petition and he knew he would become a bit of a hero for being the one who would literally drive her out of the town gates!

Robert stepped over the luggage and called to Stella. He could still hear his mother ranting and followed her shrill voice to the kitchen, where Stella was listening patiently whilst Jennifer shouted the house down.

"I won't apologise!" Jennifer yelled. She stamped her foot and was so red in the face that she looked as if she might have a stroke. "It's Robert's fault…" she tailed off as she caught sight of him in the doorway. He hoped she would end her tantrum at that point but instead, she turned from yelling at Stella, to shriek at him…"You're so selfish! You're the most selfish child in the whole world."

"Mother! Calm down," Robert said in a stern voice.

"I am calm!" she roared back.

"You're not calm, you're shouting," he replied.

"I'm not shouting," she shouted.

Robert glanced at Stella with a look of despair on his face.

"Why don't we all just sit down and talk about this sensibly?" Stella suggested, "And have a cup of tea?"

"I don't want tea!" Jennifer squawked.

"What is it you do want mother?" Robert asked her. "Do you want to stay or go? By the looks of things (referring to the large amount of luggage) you've decided to go to live with Collins and Varsity after all."

"I'm not going to your brother's," Jennifer screeched. "He's as bad as you! He doesn't want me anymore. No one loves me. No one cares if I live or die."

"If you're not going to St. Lucia, where are you going?" Robert enquired.

"To Italy to marry a Duke, that's where, and I'll be richer than Collins," Jennifer smirked. Then she turned to Stella and shrieked, "And richer than you too!"

Stella sighed and poured some tea into a pot - she was used to Jennifer's outbursts and had learnt over the many, many years of dealing with her not to take her too seriously. She would be as glad to see the back of her as everyone else would however. Since Melbourne had run off with his third wife, Christabelle, Jennifer's outbursts had become uncontrollable and that was a long time ago now. Some therapy may have helped Jennifer but she had no wish to change her behaviour as she saw nothing wrong in it at all.

In Italy they won't notice her uneven temper quite so much, Stella thought. *They are much more volatile in general. They will probably say she's just passionate. I could do with a little less 'passion' in my golden years, thank you very much.*

Robert on the other hand felt responsible for his mother's behaviour. The old familiar feeling of guilt and shame began to creep through his veins. He had upset his mother again. He had to make it right...or did he?

Since his coma he had felt less inclined to support her roles as victim, harpie and bully but had not quite got to the place where he could really cut her loose. Suddenly he felt a kind of epiphany wash over him. He heard himself raise his voice and say, "Leave then! Just leave! I don't want you here and no one in Little Eden does either. Do you know how many names I've got on a petition to have you banished? Over five hundred! If you're going to behave like this, shouting and screaming, for the rest of your life, then just go and good riddance."

Jennifer looked shocked. She wasn't used to anyone challenging her authority. In a panic she became even more irrational and incomprehensible than usual, "You don't know what I've sacrificed for you boys, what I have gone without so that you could have everything. All I wanted for us was to be free of this place and have enough money to get by. Everything I do I do for you - not me. I never get anything I want. I went without a life so you could have everything."

Robert took a deep breath and wondered what Alienor must think of his mother, and as he thought of her grace and love he felt a deep sense of zen like calm inside him. "You are a bully!" he told Jennifer. "You are going to leave Little Eden and never come back, do you hear me? We have zero tolerance on abuse, bullying and violence and you have violated every rule. Just because you are at the top of the tree doesn't give you the right to act anyway you want to. The rules apply to everyone."

Jennifer looked at him - she was stunned into silence at last.

"Do you understand me?" Robert said, raising his voice again. "I've had enough! You are leaving and never coming back."

Jennifer was frightened of him for the first time in her life but she was still so churned up that she couldn't calm down. "Get out of my way," she exclaimed, and pushed past him into the hall. She picked up her handbag and clambered, rather clumsily, over her suitcases and trunks.

"Get my bags," she screamed to the taxi driver, who didn't exactly rush to open the door for her. "Hurry up, you idiot," she snapped. "Take me to the airport, now!"

Don found himself overwhelmed by Jennifer's obvious anger and the large number of bags. Robert came out to help him load them all into the boot. The song, Listen[20], was playing on the car radio and the lyrics caught Robert's attention for a few moments. He wasn't sure if he should say goodbye to his mother or not but then decided it would be churlish not to. He opened the passenger door and said dispassionately, "Goodbye mother, I hope you'll be happy in Italy with all your money."

Jennifer did not reply.

Robert slammed the car door shut.

As the taxi drove off, Robert could feel the crippling emotions of regret and sadness which usually followed an outburst by his mother, but to his surprise, they did not last more than a few seconds. He thought he could

20 Listen, Various, 2007, Musicworld-Columbia

see the apparition of Alienor standing by the front door and a huge sense of relief and freedom came over him. Puzzled, he walked back into the house. His new inner resolve was somewhat disconcerting - but very welcome.

Stella handed him a cup of tea and offered him a chocolate nutty square. He took both absent mindedly - he was still preoccupied with why he didn't feel absolutely dreadful.

"Something's happened," he said to Stella. "I don't feel...I don't feel... well I just don't feel...anything really."

"Well, I am glad to hear that," Stella replied.

"Are you? Why?" Robert asked.

"Because she's been in your head and your heart your whole life, and she's controlled and bullied you, and worst of all, she's played on your kindness and your goodness. It's about time you found your own voice and followed your own path. You've been trying for months to conquer your fear of her," Stella told him. "Now you've broken free - don't ever go back into her nest of machinations and emotional blackmail."

"But she is still my mother," Robert said. As he said the word 'mother' he sensed it now meant something different to him and he realised that the Holy Mother was his real mother. Jennifer had given birth to him in this lifetime but that only meant that she was playing a role - a temporary, earthly mother was not supposed to be a replacement for the everlasting compassion of the divine feminine.

"Who's this Duke she was talking about and why is she going to Italy instead of St Lucia?" Robert asked Stella.

"The Duca di Pitti has proposed marriage," she explained.

Robert was aghast. "The Duca di Pitti? He must be nearly a hundred years old by now. I thought he was dead!"

"Apparently there is life in the old dog yet," Stella giggled. "He wants a trophy wife, another one, and your mother seemed the perfect fit. Shilty's father has arranged it."

Robert wasn't sure what to think. "He's richer than Rockerfella that's true," he admitted. "But marrying my mother? Her marrying him! That just seems..."

...Suddenly Robert felt something shift in his chest as if his heart had just jumped sideways and moved to the left. *That was weird!* he thought to himself. *God, I hope I'm not having a heart attack.* He put his hand to his rib cage. *I've been under a lot of stress. Maybe I've got something wrong with my heart? Why do I feel so differently about throwing her out? This chocolate square is really nice, I wonder if I can have another piece? Come to think of it I've been feeling different since the coma and that past life clearing Silvi did with me, and to be honest, since Josh died I've realised nothing really matters. Poor little Josh - maybe him taking those old spells with him into the dragon portal to be upgraded has helped me see things in a new light? The idea of mother marrying the Duke is kind of creepy but it's always about money with her - everything comes down to money in the end. She's never gone without anything, I don't know why she even says that all the time? Maybe I'd better see a doctor about my heart? I hope Stella offers me another piece of this chocolate thing so I don't have to ask.*

"Another slice?" Stella asked him as she offered up the plate of squares.

"Do you think Joshua's death has changed how we see the world?" Robert asked her as he took one.

Stella smiled. "I wouldn't like to say, but I believe Dr G thinks little Joshua did a great service to mankind by taking some old spells over to the other side. He says the spells clouded our judgement when it comes to money, power and equality of the sexes. I don't understand it completely but I always find a death, especially a young death, brings things into perspective for most people - for a while at least."

Roberts's phone started ringing.

"Sorry," he said, "It's Shilty - she wants to see me - says it can't wait."

"Perhaps since Joshua took the spells away you might wake up to quite a few things - not just your mother," Stella suggested.

Robert wasn't sure what she meant but he was about to find out.

Chapter 29

~ * ~

Robert arrived back at Bartlett Crescent to find Shilty Cunningham in the snug, casually dressed in jeans and a white t-shirt, helping herself to a whisky and soda.

"Bit early for that isn't it?" he asked her as she offered him one.

Shilty shrugged. "I think you're going to need it, Robbie," she told him as she handed him his drink. "Sit down - I've something to tell you."

"If it's about my mother and the old Duke, I already know," Robert told her. "She's just left for Italy."

Shilty sighed. She felt sad - which was not an emotion she felt very often. She wanted the melancholy sensation to pass as soon as possible so that she could get on with being happy again. "It's not about your mother," she replied. "Although you can thank me for the Duke later." She paused and downed her drink. She perched herself on his knee and kissed him.

"It's a bit early for that as well!" Robert laughed.

"Be serious," Shilty scolded him. She stood back up and poured herself another drink.

Serious? Robert thought. Serious was not something Shilty usually was. His heart started racing again. He put his hand to his chest in alarm.

"I'll get straight to the point," Shilty announced. "I can't marry you after all."

"What?" Robert exclaimed.

"I woke up the other morning and I just had a change of heart," Shilty explained.

"When?" Robert asked her. His heart was racing even faster now.

"The day of that little boy's funeral actually," Shilty replied.

"Joshua," Robert reminded her.

"Whatever his name was, that one, yes," she said. "Not that it matters when," she added.

Shilty was puzzled by the strange look on his face.

"Are you alright?" she asked him.

Robert nodded, but he was secretly convinced he was going to have a heart attack.

"Sorry to shock you, Robbie darling, but you see - I don't think I'm cut out for being lady of the manor after all."

"I don't understand," Robert replied, now feeling a little short of breath as well. "You did all the chasing this time. You said you wanted to be like…" he stopped short in horror, realising what he was about to say…

…"Like your mother?" Shilty said finishing his sentence for him. "That's the problem! I don't like your mother - no one does frankly - but it's not just that. It's all those smelly jumble sales and endless parades, and quite frankly very weird funerals as well - I thought I could stand them if I had to, but I can't."

Robert didn't reply. He wasn't really listening now - he was far more concerned with how his body felt. *I really think I might have a heart attack, he thought. These palpitations are worse than ever! How fast can your heart beat before it explodes? What is she going on about?*

"I'm not cut out for the W.I.," Shilty continued. "I'm more, well, I'm more about the big events, the balls, the celebrity weddings - that kind of thing."

Robert still didn't reply. Just as he thought his heart might flip inside out due to its crazy rhythm, his body stopped churning and calmed down. He felt, as he had done at Stella's, an immense wave of relief.

"I love you and you love me!" Shilty carried on saying, and came to sit on his knee again. "Only, sometimes, a girl has to do what a girl has to do. I realised I don't need a husband at all really. I thought I did but I don't need to get married. I don't want children (Robert looked at her in amazement as she had led him to believe she wanted at least six kids) and I don't need money or security from a man." She pondered for another few moments and added, "I'm going to be like Elizabeth I and become a virgin."

"Definitely a bit late for that!" Robert blurted out and downed his drink.

"Not that kind of virgin silly," Shilty replied. "A Virgin Queen - like Eleanor of Aquitaine or Queen Matilda. I have my own power, my own income, my own status - why would I give that away to a man?"

She waited for Robert to say his piece but he stayed silent.

"So, that's that," Shilty said finally - getting tired of waiting for a response.

"What is?" Robert asked, a little unclear.

"Good god man! Haven't you been listening to a word I've said? I've had an epiphany and I'm going to be my own woman and do just as I please for the rest of my life."

"I think we are all having an epiphany or two this week," Robert said ponderously as he lifted her off him.

Shilty had been hoping for a few tears from him at least and was more than a little disappointed.

"The day of Joshua's funeral you say?" Robert suddenly asked her.

"What?" Shilty asked exasperated.

"When you had this epiphany," Robert prompted her. "You said it was the day of Joshua's funeral - when you realised you wanted to be a virgin queen."

"Yes, it was," Shilty nodded.

"Mmm, that's interesting," Robert mused as he poured himself another drink.

"Why is it?" Shilty asked, a bit disconcerted by his bewilderingly calm attitude.

"You're right, of course, as you always are, Shilty darling," Robert announced. "We're not meant to be together - not in this life anyway. You want more than I could ever give you and Little Eden needs more than you are willing to give it, so..." he paused as he didn't know what else to say..."Well, goodbye Shilty, my love, it's been a blast." He lifted his glass to her and then downed its contents.

Shilty was astonished! She had had a big dramatic ending planned for her departure and this certainly wasn't it.

"Aren't you even a little bit sad?" she asked him.

Robert looked at her and smiled. His heart suddenly swelled with love for her then began to beat faster again, which worried him. "I do love you Shilty, you know I do, but I was only marrying you for the money and that wasn't right was it? I shouldn't have used you like that."

"No, that's an awful thing to do to me!" Shilty exclaimed. Her shock was feigned as she knew only too well that her money had been the reason he had taken her back.

"Still," Robert added as he poured himself yet another drink. "You did sleep with my brother so I guess you could say we're even."

Shilty was startled. "You knew?" she asked him flabbergasted.

"It's surprising how much you can hear when you are in a coma," Robert chuckled. His relief and his fourth whisky were starting to make him slightly giddy.

Shilty suddenly realised she'd been played and couldn't help but laugh out loud. She was almost sorry she wasn't going to marry him after all.

"Well, I may have done a few things I'm not so proud of, but I got your mother off your back, so I reckon that cancels out the little business with Collins doesn't it?" she asked cheekily.

Suddenly Robert felt as if the whole room had morphed into another time zone and all the furniture, the walls and the floor were four dimensional. It appeared to him as if he was in a computer game and he realised that if you were shot down, what did it matter? You just rebooted and started again. All life on Earth felt astonishingly clear for a few moments. Then the sensation faded and the powerful moment of lucidity was gone.

"Oh Shilty, you are such good fun to play with," he admitted, and putting his drink down he grabbed her by the waist and pulled her into him. Kissing her one last time he felt aroused yet totally numb at the same time.

Shilty actually felt a tear roll down her cheek.

Robert gently wiped it away. "I'd rather have you as a friend than an enemy but you're right, you are a tour de force and no one should try to fit you into their little box. If you try to live someone else's life you'll suffocate and die."

"So, we're still friends?" she asked him.

Robert smiled. "Always and forever," he replied and kissed her gently on the forehead.

Shilty went out into the hall.

Dyson had just brought her cases down.

"This is the second time today I've been faced with a pile of luggage and a goodbye," Robert told her.

"Must be something in the air," Shilty laughed. "'Til next time?" she said, and with a little wave of her hand she followed Dyson out to the car.

Robert stood and watched her go, from the porch. When the car was out of sight he leaned back against the door. *I really think I might have a heart attack*, he thought. *I need to Google palpitations.*

Chapter 30
~ * ~

The third departure that week from Little Eden was that of the Reverend Erik Sprott who skulked off, taking nothing with him except some clothes and the entire contents of the family's bank account.

Cassie Lossett claimed she had been seduced by Erik. Robert gave her a choice of either going for therapy or finding employment elsewhere. She chose the elsewhere.

A few days later, Iris stood alone by the Vicarage door waiting for the removal men to arrive. An oppressive sky enclosed the town in a haze of grey which left a feeling of depression and isolation in every corner of the town. As fine rain soaked the flowers, the air was filled with the rich scent of rosemary, but Iris was too unhappy to notice. Even the early pink roses, now blooming around the porch way, which usually made her smile, had no positive effect on her today.

She was angry with herself for having lived a lie for so long; and because she was not outwardly an angry person, she turned the blame inwards and it manifested as sadness and self-loathing.

Fifteen minutes earlier, Robert had received a call from Stella informing him of Iris' imminent departure and he had raced into India's office. India was just having her morning health shake, but on hearing the news, she left her bright green drink and pulled on her coat.

They both raced over to the Vicarage.

"What are you doing?" Robert called over to Iris as he was almost forced into the hedge by the removal van which was having trouble backing up the narrow lane.

"We just heard!" India said a little breathlessly. "You don't have to leave because of Erik."

As they reached the porch it was clear Iris had been crying, "I presumed you'd want Elijah and me to leave too, so I did," she admitted.

Robert went to put his arm around her but two of the removal men got in his way and he nearly hugged a burly chap with a bald head and a variety of rather racy tattoos.

"Iris. Of course I don't want you and Elijah to leave!" Robert called over the head of another couple of blokes who were carrying a sideboard out of the front door - trapping Iris behind it. "It isn't your fault," he added.

"It is my fault," Iris replied from behind the furniture.

India suggested they go into the summer house - out of the rain and out of the way.

They all went across a soggy lawn to the little wooden shelter.

"How can it be your fault?" India asked her.

"If I'd been enough for Erik he'd have been faithful, so he would," Iris sighed.

"That's just rubbish and you know it!" India exclaimed. "You're the most wonderful woman in Little Eden. You're the kindest, the most generous and the most hardworking, and if Erik doesn't find that to be enough then that is his problem not yours!"

Iris blushed. "I'm a liar," she told them. "I'm as bad as him."

India paused for a moment and looked earnestly at Iris. "You are not going to get back with him are you?" she asked her.

Iris looked a bit sheepish.

"Oh my god, Iris, don't you dare!" India scolded her. "This is your chance to make a clean break and have a new start. You asked Robert to get rid of him. You 'outed' him and now you're going to stay with him? Are you mad?"

"Hold on, India," Robert said, "That's a bit harsh. Iris has to do what she thinks is…"

…India didn't let him finish his sentence but took Iris by the hand. She yelled over to the removal men to stop what they were doing. "The move's off!" she shouted. "Put it all back!"

India led a bewildered Iris across the graveyard towards the Abbey and marched her inside.

A rather bemused Robert followed them.

In the Abbey, Stella and several others from the W.I. were preparing for Ascension Day. They were surrounded by fresh cut flowers and lush green garlands which they were arranging over the archways and hanging onto the pews.

The Gospel Choir, who were rehearsing one of their numbers in the side aisle, fell silent at the sight of Iris and India.

The ladies were surprised to see Iris being led like a lamb by India but they were very glad that she had not yet left Little Eden. They had been planning an intervention, thinking Iris wasn't leaving for another few days, but she had tricked them and had planned to disappear without them realising and until it was too late for them to talk her out of it.

"Tell her she's got to stay here in Little Eden and not to go with that bastard of a husband of hers!" India told Stella and the others.

Robert interjected. "Iris, India might be a little lacking in tact sometimes…"

…India looked at him in disdain and interrupted him…"Don't try to sugar coat it," she remarked. "If I see a spade I call it a spade! If a man's a lying cheating bastard then that's what he is!"

Robert attempted to carry on talking to Iris…"I was going to ask you to be our new vicar," he told her. "I was just waiting for the paperwork to be done. I was hoping you would stay," he explained.

Iris nearly fainted with the shock.

Stella took her arm and sat her down. She shooed India and Robert away as she and the other ladies rallied around Iris in support.

"Why didn't you tell any of us you were planning on leaving today?" Stella asked her friend. "I only got wind of it when Noddy told me you'd asked him to keep a set of keys for you. I got suspicious and rang Robert immediately."

Iris began to cry. "I didn't want to be any trouble to anyone," she explained. "Erik threatened to take Elijah off me if I didn't go back to him."

"He can't do that," Stella reassured her.

"I don't have anywhere else to go," Iris sobbed. "Erik said that without a house of my own, Elijah won't be able to stay with me. He said the courts would be on his side, so they would."

"Now, my love," Mrs B said. "Robert just told you, you don't need to go anywhere. You can stay here as vicar and live in the Vicarage. You'll have a good wage and all your friends around you. There'll be no way Erik can take Elijah away from you. He's the one with the bad character not you."

Iris sobbed with gratitude for their kindness.

"Iris, don't go," Sissy urged her, and the whole choir nodded in agreement. "You're the reason we get to sing every week in the church. You're the reason people still attend this church at all. You're our Guardian Angel. You're everyone's Guardian Angel."

"I have to leave," Iris replied sadly.

"But why?" Ginger asked her.

169

"Because I feel like such a fool, so I do, such a fool." She wiped her eyes. "You must all think I'm a silly old woman who can't even keep her own husband."

Stella shook her head. "Now you listen to me, darling. Not one person in this town thinks you're a fool, but they will think that if you go and live with Erik again."

Iris looked at them all. "I'm not good enough for Little Eden," she explained.

Stella grimaced. "What are you talking about Iris? There isn't a person in Little Eden more worthy to live here than you."

The rest of the ladies agreed enthusiastically. "Don't go, Iris," they all encouraged her. "What would we do without you?"

Iris felt so comforted in that moment. She couldn't remember a time when she had felt so surrounded by human love.

"But I lied to you all, so I did. I lied to myself," Iris admitted. "That's a sin."

"You don't believe in sin," Stella reminded her.

"You are always telling everyone that it's never too late to put things right and to make amends," Mrs B said. "If you truly believe that for others then you have to believe it for yourself as well."

Iris gradually felt as if the veil of despair and self-hate was lifting. She knew that Mrs B was right. She could forgive anyone anything but she couldn't forgive herself. She laughed a little through her tears. "I suppose you're saying I have to practice what I preach?"

"Exactly!" Stella nodded. "No one's perfect. We're all human. Even you!"

Iris laughed again and wiped her nose.

"What would Mother Mary say to you right now, my love?" Mrs B asked her.

Iris smiled sadly. "She'd tell me I was loved no matter what I'd done and to get over my self-pity so that I can help others, which is why I'm here on Earth. She'd say that trials are an opportunity to practice forgiveness and compassion."

"Exactly!" Stella said again. "You're an earth angel Iris and earth angels never get an easy ride, but you know what they have that no one else does?"

"What?" Iris asked, and sniffed into her now rather soggy tissue.

170

"They have the ability to weather every storm that life throws at them and they always come out the other end stronger and even more compassionate than when they started. This is your opportunity to shine, Iris. As vicar you'll be able to help everyone and like you said - that's why you are here in the first place."

Iris did like the idea of being vicar but it also scared her half to death. "I can't help thinking I'm not up to the job," she admitted.

"Nonsense," Stella told her friend. "You've been running this place behind the scenes for years! The only difference now is that you'll get the recognition and the respect you deserve."

"Plus we'll not all be falling asleep during sermons anymore," Mrs B smiled. She handed Iris some flowers to put into one of the urns and Iris automatically stood up and started arranging them. "I should have left him years ago," she admitted as she placed some delicate white Solomon's Seal into a half made arrangement. She looked over at the statue of Mother Mary which was standing by the altar, waiting to be raised up on Ascension Day, and sighed. "She came to me you know," Iris said.

They all waited for her to explain.

"Mother Mary came to me in a vision after Joshua's death, so she did. I couldn't sleep, waiting to hear from the hospital, so I came back to the church and I prayed all night long for his soul." She sighed and picked through some fern leaves to find the best ones. "She brought all the nuns who had ever been here at the Abbey with her." She pointed to the pews. "They filled the church, so they did. I knew they were here. It felt so comforting, so protective. Queen Bertha came too and she asked me, 'What have you been blind to Iris?' I didn't know what she meant at first, but then she showed me all the women Erik had been unfaithful with. I saw every one of them from each parish we'd been in, so I did. All lined up along the aisle they were…" her voice tailed off as tears welled in her eyes. "I didn't think I had been blind, you see," Iris continued. "I'd forgiven him, as a dutiful wife and Christian should, but I suddenly realised that Erik's heart wasn't filled with the Holy Spirit but with darkness. When I saw it so clearly I felt sick, so I did." She held her stomach as she felt it flip at the memory. "The next morning I couldn't bear to look at him or even be near him. He repulsed me." She lowered her voice and made the sign of the cross before adding in a whisper, "I saw the Devil in his heart and I felt ill that I had lived with him so for long, shared a bed and a home with him - with the Devil himself."

"Come now," Stella told her. "Erik is not a good man in many ways but surely he is not the Devil?"

"Oh, but he was!" Iris exclaimed. "Don't you see? What is the Devil but the absence of goodness and truth? Mother Mary and the nuns - they made me see that he didn't respect me - he didn't care for me, he didn't honour me as his wife or as a human being. No one should be treated in such a way and I was too blind to see what was happening to me. I was blinded by duty and by what I thought was love."

"They do say love is blind and blind faith is never a good thing in my book," Mrs B agreed. "Don't upset yourself, my love. We all have an epiphany at some point in our lives and when we do we always wish we it had happened years before."

"Exactly! Stella said, "We resist change even though we are suffering. Heaven knows why we do it but we do. We are all blind - until the day we are not!"

"That's why I left the Catholic Church you know," Iris admitted. "I found out about all the corruption and I could see the core of compassion had been buried so deeply underneath the evil deeds that I just couldn't stand it. Then I met Erik and he said The Church of England didn't put up with corruption, but it does. When Elijah came to us, he had such new ways of seeing things. He asked ever so many questions which I just couldn't answer other than by quoting scripture, and when I heard the words coming out of my mouth they sounded like nonsense. I think I've been clinging onto the idea of needing a religion because it felt safer to be told what to do than to work it out for myself."

"You never lost your faith though," Mrs B reassured her.

"That's the funny thing, so it is," Iris replied. "The more the rules began to crumble, the more faith I had. It was as if the more lies that were uncovered the stronger my compassion became - the stronger the true saints and Mother Mary became for me."

Mrs B smiled. "Perhaps, the more we go back to the beginning, the more compassion we find?"

"I think that's what Queen Bertha was telling me," Iris said. "Together we must go back to the beginning. There is a source of compassion in the heart of the goddess and there is no religion there."

"As the great Desmond Tutu would say, 'God is not a Christian[21]',"

21 God Is Not a Christian, Desmond Tutu, 2011, HarperOne

172

Stella smiled.

"That's why you'll make such a wonderful vicar," Sissy told Iris. "Faith doesn't have to be tied to a religion. Faith is about finding the compassion we have inside us. We don't need some old men telling us how to live. What we need is to stay connected to the Holy Spirit, which is constantly reminding us how to love each other, through prayer and meditation and song."

Sissy began to sing the first few bars of the song, Shackles[22], and the rest of the choir soon joined in. The song of freedom and faith resounded through the Abbey and at last Iris was convinced she had to stay.

---

22 Shackles, Mary, Mary, 1999, Columbia

Chapter 31
~ * ~

With all the recent goings on in the town, emotions were running high. Lucy and Sophie were constantly bursting into tears at the slightest thing. The initial feelings of shock and disbelief at Aunt Lilly's passing had faded and were replaced with anger and despair at the realisation that she really was never coming back.

It didn't help that Lucy was struggling to keep up the pretence with Jimmy. She was half relieved and half devastated that tonight was the night on which she would be free to tell him what she knew. One moment she wanted to forgive him and the next she wanted to bash him over the head with a skillet. She knew she had to end it with him, not least because of Iris having had the courage to give Erik the boot, and she couldn't stand the thought of not being as brave. She knew in her heart that Jimmy was 'a wrong 'un,' as her father would say, but her heart strings were also being tugged by the love-karma between them. She was convinced she had had a past life with Jimmy in which they had lived happily ever after and she was sure that they were soul mates.

Knowing Jimmy's predilection for fame, the high life, himself and the ladies, it is likely, dear readers, that Jimmy had far too many soul mates from past lives which he kept coming across in his present lifetime - the curse of having too many soul mates can be a heavy one to bear!

That evening, Lancelot, India, Robert, Sophie, Minnie and Mr T (with Cedric of course) all sat around the living room whilst an agitated Lucy made drinks. Jack lit the log burner whilst Jimmy Pratt set up the video camera ready to show them the documentary he had made called 'Finding Frith'.

Before the proceedings could begin, Sophie received a txt from Tobias Gilbert asking her if he could pop over to discuss the sale of the treasure. She couldn't help blushing as she asked the others if he could join them. She received a resounding 'Yes' as well as a few winks, nudges and 'oooos'. As they waited for him to arrive Lucy, Minnie and India helped Sophie change out of her comfies and into something a little more, shall we say, appropriate to having a potential boyfriend drop round!

"Why am I so nervous?" Sophie asked, as Minnie curled her hair with straighteners.

"Because you like him so much!" India teased her.

"I don't know him!" Sophie protested but found it hard not to smile.

"Well, if you don't like him, I'll have him!" Lucy laughed. "I'll need a strong shoulder to cry on later tonight."

Sophie held her sister's hand. "Sorry," she said. "I shouldn't be excited about Tobi coming round this evening when you have to..."

..."Don't be silly!" Lucy laughed and then started to cry again. "Just because I won't have a boyfriend doesn't mean I don't want anyone else to have one."

"I'm considering being 'self-partnered' for good," India said as she picked out something from the wardrobe for Sophie to wear.

"That's just a fancy way of saying you're single isn't it?" Minnie asked.

India shrugged. "Being labelled as single always sounds like you are unlovable or a lesbian." She realised what she had said. "Oh, god, Minnie I didn't mean..."

Minnie laughed. "I know you didn't mean anything by it," she reassured India. "But our sexual preferences or our relationship status shouldn't be something that is judged. I suppose people judge each other all the time based on all sorts of things," she added. "You can't please all of the people all of the time."

"We don't even know if Tobias likes me yet," Sophie told them as she pulled on some skinny jeans. "He doesn't know much about me. He might judge me on all sorts of things too when he finds out."

There was a knock at the conservatory doors and Sophie's heart fluttered. They all looked at each other.

"Quick!" Lucy said to Minnie. "Go make him a drink and I'll finish Sophie's make-up. India, can you find Sophie's best slipper socks? They're in that basket over there by the wardrobe."

Tobi had a hot cuppa in his hand when Sophie came into the room, trying not to look as if she had just changed her clothes and done her hair for him. She knew he'd find out one day about the chronic fatigue, but she just wanted a little flirty fun for one more night at least.

Everyone made sure that Sophie and Tobi sat next to each other, and they were not very subtle about it either, which embarrassed Sophie, but Tobi didn't mind a bit. Sophie couldn't help but notice he was wearing a very fine-cut striped shirt and well-fitting jeans. She particularly liked the after shave he was wearing which evoked the scents of neroli and bergamot - two of her favourite essential oils.

God, he even smells divine! Sophie thought to herself. *I could just rip that shirt off him right here, right now, but I won't. I hope I smell okay. I forgot about perfume. Oh my god, what if I don't smell nice? I'll have to ask Lucy to smell me but how do I get her attention without it looking weird? Great! Now I'll have to sit here and watch the film hoping I don't smell of old potatoes or something.*

A rather impatient Jimmy turned on the documentary and everyone hushed as they watched.

The show seemed to be more about Jimmy than about Uncle Frith, but to be fair, it did make it look likely that Frith was alive somewhere in the world and that he could be found if enough effort was made to track him down.

When the lights came back on, Lancelot thanked Jimmy for his efforts. Making sure he had a copy of the tape to show to Collins' and Lucas's lawyers, he nodded the all clear to Lucy.

She could finish with Jimmy anytime now. However, she kept putting the inevitable off by keeping the conversations going and the drinks flowing.

India and Jack finally cornered her in the kitchen. "When are you going to tell him?" they asked her.

"I don't know," Lucy replied. "Maybe not tonight after all, I might wait 'til tomorrow."

"Where's your courage?" India asked her.

"I don't know!" Lucy admitted. "When I see Jimmy it seems to disappear into thin air." She felt herself welling up again and reached for some kitchen roll.

Jack put his arm around her. "You want me to punch his lights out?"

"No," she sniffed. "I'll tell him myself in a civilised manner."

"And then can I punch his lights out?" Jack said again and winked.

Lucy took a deep breath and asked Jimmy to join her in her bedroom.

He thought he was going to get lucky but he was sorely mistaken.

Everyone pretended not to listen as they heard shouting.

A door banged.

Footsteps were heard running down the stairs.

Lucy sat on her bed crying.

Jimmy had left the building.

Chapter 32
~ * ~

Lucy felt so upset that she wanted to be alone. She went to bed early, leaving the others to carry on talking about the future of Little Eden.

The conversation in the living room turned to the treasure from the wardrobe. Jack had had confirmation from Brindisi Thistle that a prospective buyer was now a sure thing and that Brindisi, in his usual indomitable style, had negotiated the original offer of one million pounds up to one and a half million. Tobias and Jack assured Robert that it was unlikely to reach any higher and it was most definitely a generous offer so it was agreed that they would sell the bullion and coins.

Brindisi Thistle, who had lived in Little Eden all his life, had one of those ramshackle, Aladdin's cave, impossible to walk through, type antique shops, specialising in militaria, bullion and curios. He always wore an old sea captain's uniform (although it was rumoured that it was just a uniform he had found in a house clearance box many years ago and the older residents knew he had never been to sea in his life). With a big bushy white beard and a deep booming voice he gave an air of authority to everything he did and this commanding performance leant itself to persuading unwitting customers to pay far more for items than they were actually worth. He had therefore gained a reputation for being rather 'tight'. On this occasion though, his deeper kindness had floated to the top - he had waived his usual commission and donated it straight to the Save Little Eden Fund. Brindisi loved the town as much as any resident and wished he could do more to protect the only home he had ever known.

Tobi was quizzed about the rest of the treasure. He had come round, after all, on the pretext of passing on the good news about the St Cuthbert Cross, which was being fought over by various international museums. He was expecting it to fetch in excess of one hundred million dollars.

Everyone in the room was gobsmacked for a few moments then positively delighted!

As for the rest of the crosses - Tobi thought they would bring in around fifty million pounds altogether.

"That's great news," India admitted, "But still so far away from the four billion we need."

Sophie sighed, "Every day it seems to sound a larger amount than it did

177

the day before. The more we raise the worse it sounds - four billion pounds - it just seems so impossible."

"We will have Shilty's money as well, don't forget," Jack reminded them. "Once old Robbie here ties the knot that's at least one billion we won't have to find, isn't that right old boy?"

Sophie frowned. "So, you're marrying her for definite then?" she asked Robert.

"Er, didn't I tell anyone?" he asked and looked a bit abashed.

"Tell us what?" India replied.

"Ah, well, there's a slight change of plan where Shilty's concerned," he admitted.

"What now?" India exclaimed.

Robert felt bad about having lost the town Shilty's money but he couldn't lie - he was relieved that he wasn't going to be marrying her after all. His heart began to pound and his anxiety about having a heart attack returned. "Shilty has decided...we decided...mutually...that perhaps marriage wasn't the best idea when all was said and done."

India and Sophie breathed a visible sigh of relief.

"No Shilty! No money!" Lancelot grimaced, but he also felt a sense of reprieve. "Still, it wasn't fair to expect you to marry her just to save the town," he added.

"A hundred years ago it would have been expected of me," Robert admitted.

"Marriage for a lot of people is still business not pleasure," India said.

"As we well know," Robert tutted, thinking about his mother and then realised that he had been doing exactly the same thing as her, albeit to save Little Eden rather than for his own personal gain.

"We'll just have to find the money another way," Jack reassured everyone.

"Perhaps Jack could marry an heiress instead?" Minnie giggled.

Jack smiled. "I'd rather steal the money than marry for it," he laughed. "Although I suppose I'd take one for the team if I had to. Got anyone in mind?"

Everyone shook their heads - no one could think of anyone!

It was getting late and they all decided it was time to go home to give Sophie and Tobi some space for their budding romance to bloom.

"I really hope it works out for Sophie," Minnie whispered to India as they put on their coats.

"So do I," India nodded. "She deserves some happiness. She's had a terrible time of it."

"Shame he's not a billionaire!" Minnie winked.

Sophie and Tobi suddenly felt a little awkward and shy of each other when left alone. All Sophie could think of was to offer him another cup of tea - her mind was blank - partly due to fatigue and partly because she was so aware of his presence. It was as if an invisible, but very physical, magnetic force was radiating off him and she just wanted him to pull her into his arms - it was very distracting.

"So," Tobi began to say, but he too was distracted. He watched her make the drinks and couldn't stop thinking how pretty she was.

"So," Sophie replied as she handed him a mug of tea.

"So, I was going to ask you if you felt okay about selling the crosses" Tobi responded. "They seem priceless to me - it seems a shame to sell them to the highest bidder. Collectors don't often understand the spiritual energy in artefacts; they're more interested in the investment value of them."

Sophie shrugged. "The energy keys in the crosses have been used. Joshua took them over to the other side so now they are just trinkets really. Come and see for yourself."

She led him into her bedroom and opened a small writing bureau. From a secret compartment she took out the jewels and laid them out on the duvet. Tobi held each one in turn and tried to tell if they were humming, buzzing or making him feel a sense of peace; he could feel no sensations from any of them.

She's right, he thought, *They've all been deactivated. It's like the holy energy has been dissolved and they're just gold and precious stones now - only worth what someone is willing to pay for them.* He felt a little disappointed and yet amazed at how the energy had worked its magic.

"What were the energy keys held inside them?" he asked.

"They were the keys of the original divine feminine. These days we say Mother Mary or Tara or Parvati amongst others, but a long time ago they called it Nun," Sophie told him.

Tobi thought for a moment. "That makes sense I suppose," he said and sat on the edge of the bed. "In the western world one of the earliest gods was Nun, but that consciousness became corrupted over the centuries until the masculine energy of Amun Ra was the main focus of worship and the female moon aspect was demonised. The divine feminine was known by many names such as Isis, Hathor, Skemet and Maat. You looked like Isis at the museum - it was kind of freaky! You weren't you anymore, you were..."

...Sophie suddenly felt dizzy and the colour drained from her face..."Oh no!" she exclaimed. "You've opened a portal by saying that!"

These episodes were starting to be a regular occurrence for Sophie since returning to Little Eden. Dr G had reassured her that this was now part of her job on Earth - to be a portal guardian, key holder and ascension conduit. Sophie was not really very pleased about her new role - it was tiring, unpredictable and more than a little bit scary at times.

Tobi didn't quite know what to do so he pushed aside the crosses and helped her onto the bed. She lay down and he instinctively lay down next to her, taking hold of her hand as a vision began to form in their minds and their astral bodies went travelling together.

They were only out of body for about five minutes in Earth time but, dear readers, as some of you may know, it is amazing how long a vision quest can seem...

To her surprise, Sophie realised she was flying over Africa on a magic carpet. She was aware of gliding through a warm breeze and was awe struck by the majestic ribbon of the Milky Way far above her head. As the woven carpet flew above mountain ranges, deep gorges, white water rapids and then desert sands, she could make out Orion's belt overhead and the tops of the great pyramids below were illuminated in the white moonlight.

Aware that she was not alone she could feel Tobi's presence, not just on the bed, but also on the flying carpet.

Having an astral travelling companion felt very reassuring.

She gazed down at the scene below her; suddenly the carpet began diving sharply downwards - so rapid was the descent that it made her stomach flip. The carpet swooped towards the Great Pyramid of Khufu and for a moment she thought they were going to crash into it, but to her relief they came to rest upon the sands just in front of the gigantic paws of the Sphinx.

When she looked up at the magnificent statue, she realised that is was not as she had seen it on the television or in images. This Sphinx had the head of a lion and was in perfect condition. As she stepped off the carpet, she realised that there wasn't one lone Sphinx but two of them, flanking the corners of a great sandstone wall, which seemed a mile away.

Two colossal wooden doors, over twenty feet tall and decorated with carvings of plants and animals, opened in front of them, allowing Tobi and

Sophie to walk out of the desert and into a lush, green oasis. The shimmering garden which welcomed them was an opulent sanctuary of sparkling white stone terraces, pyramids and pergolas, with palm trees lining the long avenues. Marble rills flowed with crystal clear water which seemed to glow with a golden halo as it tinkled and splashed through the centre of each walkway. Intoxicated by the perfume of exquisite flowers and hypnotised by whispering trees, they processed through the dazzling, walled courtyard. The whole necropolis glittered and gleamed with heavenly light. Sophie realised the slightly eerie sensation she was experiencing was due to the complete lack of bird song and the absence of any human presence.

At the other end of the complex stood two more majestic Sphinxes - one to guard each corner of the oasis.

Why are there no remains of these other sphinxes today? Sophie pondered. *I wonder where all these buildings have gone as well? Were they here before the pyramids we see today? Were they ever really here? Am I at the real Giza back in time or maybe this is the etheric realms which humans can only see in meditation and the Giza complex was built as a representation of what exists in another dimension?*

Sophie wasn't sure which dimension she was in.

In the right hand corner of the luxuriant courtyard stood three pyramids which were carefully aligned with Orion's belt above. In perfect condition, silky smooth and gleaming, they dazzled in the moonlight with a blinding whiteness. When Sophie reached the base of the largest one, she was suddenly confronted by a wall of etheric fire which barred her way. She didn't think she would be able to penetrate the flames but her soul guided her forwards. She cringed at the thought of the heat against her skin but she and Tobi walked through the dancing flames unharmed.

To her amazement, instead of there being an opulent entrance into the pyramid, there was an insignificant half hidden door at the bottom of some narrow stone steps. She could hardly make it out as an optical illusion made the stairs seem invisible from all angles except one.

Aware that she should never go through doors or portals without asking if it was safe first, she paused and asked in her head three times, *In the name of the true source of all that is good, is it safe for me to go through this door?* After receiving a resounding 'Yes,' each time, she felt confident to step through the portal. On the other side she was greeted by a small, red elemental, who stood only three feet high, sporting a goatee and wearing the scarlet crown of Lower Egypt.

Sophie asked him three times if he was a true light being, and getting a strong affirmative, she knew she could trust him.

The little crimson spirit led her downwards into the pyramid tunnels. After a few metres she became aware that Tobi was no longer with her. He had had to wait outside. On asking the guide why he had not joined them, she was told that Tobi 'was not worthy'. She thought this a little strange but was distracted by having to bend down to get through a narrow passageway which was illuminated with an otherworldly light. On the walls were depictions of Egyptian gods and goddesses, palm trees and animals and hieroglyphs she did not understand. So tight was the walkway she could hardly make sense of the paintings, but the reoccurring images of Ma'at, carrying an Ankh and a staff with a feather in her hair, made Sophie feel as if this pyramid might lead to the gates of Heaven itself.

She realised that the further she walked the steeper the tunnel became. She was a little apprehensive but not afraid. It felt familiar in a strange way and it was at least brightly lit. The air began to heat up and she found it harder to breath. Beads of sweat began to form on her neck, and just as she was getting too uncomfortable to carry on, she stepped out into a dark room where the heat dissipated to be replaced with an almost freezing blast of air.

Chapter 33
~ * ~

The black basalt room was so dark that Sophie had to strain her eyes to make out its size. It was small and deserted except for a plain sandstone sarcophagus which lay near the wall on the far side. This pitch black, mysterious chamber was in stark contrast to the bright whiteness of the gardens and it gave her the creeps: this was not a welcoming place. As she tentatively stepped deeper inside, she shivered. Enclosed within the oppressive gloom she felt instinctively that this was no ordinary space despite its simple appearance. She realised it was the notorious Kings Chamber which had been used as an ascension chamber for millennia. She was rather unimpressed by it as it didn't look fit for royalty - it was without decoration of any kind and its austerity reminded her of a prison cell.

She felt uneasy not knowing why she was there or what to expect, and she really didn't want Ramesses or any other Pharaoh to suddenly jump out and start getting man-angry with her again. She felt compelled to stay however so she asked three times in her mind if it was safe to remain and to her surprise, she received an affirmative response.

Her heart sank as the little red guide explained that she was going to have to step into the cold stone coffin. In trepidation she lay down inside the roughly hewn tomb and was glad there was no lid. The open trough was not very big and she could feel the chill and coarseness of the stone pressing against her arms, the top of her head and the soles of her feet. She began to ask why she was there when without warning her mind went blank - she lost all sense of time and space.

Suddenly, the hollow darkness transformed into a blinding blue-white light. She was no longer in the Kings Chamber but standing on a glass platform which was open to the star filled heavens above. She felt dizzy as she looked downwards - she was standing hundreds of feet above the garden. This otherworldly etheric terrace projected from the side of the great pyramid just below the capstone. Vibrating faster than the speed of light, no human could see it. It seemed to Sophie to be like some kind of landing pad. As soon as that thought had come into her mind, to her astonishment, a humming and flashing spaceship - in the shape of a classic flying saucer – appeared, hovering overhead.

Sophie was taken aback and began to doubt her vision. In spite of her belief in the Star Children and the next generation of humans, she had never felt one hundred percent convinced that a new galactic consciousness was taking over mankind. Sometimes she wondered if she'd been watching too many sci-fi movies, but now, standing on this galactic docking station, she realised it was a sky portal and, just like a dragon portal in the Earth, it was a doorway through to other dimensions.

An aura of crystal clear energy surrounded her as a group of five shimmering star beings walked out of the scintillating ship to greet her. They were tall and slim, almost human looking; only their eyes were larger than usual. They wore glittering blue capes with high collars which seemed to be part of their physical bodies. They showed no emotion or expression but they exuded pure bliss which wrapped itself around Sophie like a comfort blanket.

Her heart swelled as the memory of 'home' flowed through her.

As she tried to communicate with the cosmic beings they began to fade. Frustrated, she tried harder to stay focused on them, but the more she tried the less she could hold the vision.

Abruptly she was surrounded by lapis blue, and as she opened her eyes, she realised she was back in her bedroom with Tobi lying motionless next to her. The intensity of the blue remained for a few precious moments as three dimensional reality and the etheric realms blended as one; then as her physical eyes adjusted to the present, the blue evaporated and the room returned to 2012 normality.

Sophie squeezed Tobi's hand.

"Did you feel or see anything?" she whispered.

Tobi took a deep breath and didn't speak for a few moments. He felt as if he was levitating and wasn't sure where he was. As he grounded back into his body he said, "I saw blue; blue everywhere; the oceans, the sky, the stars, they all became one and I was flying through the Milkyway so fast I thought I'd died and gone to Heaven."

Sophie giggled. "Then you saw what I saw?" she asked.

"I don't know," Tobi replied. "What did you see?"

Sophie told him of her vision.

Tobi was a bit disappointed. He had not seen or felt all that she had. "I was whizzing through the galaxy," he explained. "There were star portals - millions of them. Geometric shapes and crystals were floating all around me and I knew that every star was a gateway to some other dimension. I can't explain it but I knew that my consciousness was expanding further than it ever had before, and..." he paused to gather his thoughts..."I don't know what I learnt exactly, but I feel as if my brain is three times the size it was before. It's bigger than my skull can hold, it's so full of knowledge. I've a thumping headache."

"You've had a transcendental meditation," Sophie told him. "Your conscious awareness has expanded exponentially and you've opened your mind to higher vibrational information. Our human minds haven't built the synapses to process that knowledge yet. Dr G says we'll have to build new links in the brain so that we can make sense of galactic energy, and whilst we do that it'll make our heads and our bodies hurt. He calls the process Ascension and the pain ascension symptoms."

Tobi was still awestruck. He had never experienced anything like it before. He felt privileged to have witnessed the glories of the outer-most cosmos, whilst on a human level, he felt he wanted to lie next to Sophie, holding her hand like this, forever. He had never felt so close to anyone his whole life. He was sure they were soul mates - linked together in some other-worldly way.

To his disappointment, Sophie pulled her hand away from his - a little embarrassed by the closeness she felt. He was, after all, a virtual stranger. But his soul felt like one of her dearest friends.

She sat up.

Tobi reluctantly did too.

"I think I just met some of the Pleiades Council," Sophie explained.

"Who?" Tobi asked her.

"They are a group of galactic beings. Their consciousness is made up of many different galaxies. It is their turn to take guardianship of planet Earth. Most Atlantean souls are leaving the Earth plane and the Pleiades will incarnate into human bodies instead," she explained. She stopped for a moment. She wasn't sure how she knew that. Then it dawned on her that she had communicated with the star beings after all; just not with words. "The days of Amun Ra are numbered and any false deity before or after him. The Star Children will no longer want to trap themselves in a tribal way of life and they will see themselves more as a global community."

Tobi held his head. "That's a big ask," he said. "I don't think you'll be able to convince billions of humans that they've been hoodwinked by

185

religions and cultures all this time. Belief systems run deep, generation to generation, and history shows us that even after hundreds of years of destruction and oppression, the old beliefs rise again from the ashes."

"I don't think it's possible either but I suppose the Star Children have a right to try," Sophie pondered.

"People don't even know why they say Amen at the end of prayers for example," Tobi sighed. "I wonder how many of them know they are actually referring to Amun Ra, the sun god? That spell of male supremacy is reinforced every day all over the world that's for sure, but you try to tell anyone, they'll not believe you."

Tobi wanted to stay and talk about everything and anything but his head was really pounding now. "How about you come to dinner with me Friday night and we can discuss it in more detail?"

Sophie smiled. "Do you want some aspirin for your headache?" she asked. "I'm sorry I made your head hurt."

"That's okay. I'll go transcendental with you anytime, headache or no headache. I'll ride it out," Tobi said, not wanting to take any pills, thinking it might make him look like he couldn't handle pain. "I'll go home and sleep it off. Friday? It's a date then?"

Sophie wanted to say yes but was afraid she'd not be well enough to tackle an evening out. Getting ready, talking, eating, being out in noisy crowded public places; these were things she wished she could just do, but the fatigue meant they were the hardest things to do. *Maybe just one night,* she thought to herself. *If I rest all day tomorrow and all day Friday and wash my hair the day before, maybe it'll be worth the relapse that'll come after. Just one night pretending to be normal, I'd love that. One date with Tobi, even if it can't last would be so much fun. I could pretend, just for one night, that I'm just like everyone else.*

"Okay," Sophie said. "Could we go somewhere quiet though? I'm not good in noisy places."

Tobi seemed fine with that idea and didn't ask why. "I know this tiny bistro near Covent Garden. Its cosy and quiet, it'll be perfect," he reassured her.

Sophie felt both happiness and dread in equal measure. "It's a date then," she smiled.

Tobi wanted to kiss her but restrained himself. He couldn't wait for it to be Friday night.

Chapter 34

~ * ~

Thursday came and Sophie had washed her hair. As she lay on the bed to recover for half an hour, as she always had to do, Lucy went to the wardrobe to help her sister decide what to wear for her first date with Tobi. Sophie's heart sank when she tried on one of her old party dresses - she was too fat for it, which meant she was too fat for all of them. She hadn't worn them in years anyway and they were a bit out of date, except for a little classic black number which she couldn't even zip up.

"I'm at least one dress size bigger than I was," Sophie moaned.

Lucy shook her head. "When you first came back here you were too thin from pushing yourself too hard. You're not too fat, you're just bigger than these dresses, that's all."

"I've been wearing pyjamas and jogging bottoms so much lately I didn't even realise how much bigger I'd become," Sophie cried.

Lucy set her mind to work to try to find a solution. All her dresses were too big for Sophie. She thought about Minnie, but she was too short, Peony was too slim, Linnet was too tall, Adela too buxom. Who could she borrow a dress from at such short notice? The girls in the café, being much younger, didn't wear Sophie's style. *Stella? She might be the right size,* Lucy thought. *She dresses wonderfully but older than Sophie should look. Come on,* Lucy told herself, *Think!*

Lucy looked at the dresses laid out on the bed.

Sophie wiped her tears away. She felt like sh*t.

Lucy suddenly had a brainwave. She picked up her phone and rang Minnie who came to the rescue a few minutes later.

"Can you do anything?" Lucy asked Minnie urgently.

Minnie's heart went out to Sophie who was now resigned to never going on a date in her life again. She picked up the various dresses lying discarded on the bed and pondered on them. "They're all different materials except these two," she said. "This little black one and that emerald green one - I might be able to take the side seams out and put some panelling in? That'll mean it'll zip up and it'll be slimming at the same time."

"Could you? Would you?" Lucy begged her. "I'll make you as many cups of tea as you want and cook you dinner and feed you cake this evening if you'll do it."

Minnie laughed. "Of course I'll do it. It's a push but I'll have it ready for tomorrow night."

Sophie was so depressed she didn't even want to go on the date now.

"Cheer up!" Lucy told her. "You'll look stunning and you'll have a great time."

"Maybe. I don't know why I'm bothering," Sophie couldn't help saying. "He'll dump me as soon as he finds out about the Chronic Fatigue Syndrome anyway."

"No he won't!" Lucy told her firmly.

"If he does, he's not worth having anyway," Minnie said.

"If he doesn't he'll be a fool," Sophie said. "Who would take on a penniless, jobless, healthless nobody who can't even wash her own hair without needing to lie down afterwards?"

Lucy and Minnie had to agree that Sophie wasn't much of a catch in the ordinary order of things, but they didn't want Sophie to think that.

"Any man would be lucky to have you," Minnie said emphatically.

"The problem with Sophie is she doesn't want just any man," Lucy laughed. "Me, I'll take anyone who'll have me. I'm not so fussy."

Minnie giggled. "You don't have the best taste in men, that's true. From my point of view I don't want any of them. I can't seem to pick the right woman either mind you."

Sophie suddenly remembered that it was not all about her. "I'm so sorry," she said. "Here's me throwing my dummy out because I have a date and you two are broken hearted."

"It's okay," Lucy replied then, starting to well up at the thought of Jimmy. "Just because we're miserable doesn't mean we want everyone else to be miserable too!"

"Besides," Minnie said. "Living vicariously is often much more fun. You get all the excitement and don't have to put in the effort!"

"We'll just have to live together when we are older Minnie, and die old maids," Lucy laughed.

"Not old maids," Sophie smiled. "Virgin queens!"

"When you put it like that it sounds rather liberating to be single and be at the centre of your own destiny!" Minnie laughed. "Virgin queens it is!"

Minnie worked all evening in Buttons and Bows to alter Sophie's dress. She loved a challenge and she loved sewing. She was really enjoying herself, sitting at her sewing table in her darkened shop lit only by fairy lights and her bright craft lamp which shone over her sewing table.

The shop windows were starting to twinkle as dusk descended. Minnie's window is packed full of carefully folded fat quarters in wicker baskets and dozens of vibrant cotton reels neatly stacked on three tier plate stands. Antique pin cushions of all shapes and sizes along with the most unusual sewing scissors from around the world are carefully arranged in an organised jumble, and amongst this perfect chaos stands a pink vintage sewing machine decorated with gold filigree and flowers. Cute little felt creatures like mice, sheep and baby squirrels perch on the top of big bobbins which are wrapped up with antique lace, and scattered about are thimbles, jars of buttons and teacups filled with shiny beads.

Lucy had brought over some strawberries and cream shortbreads and fresh coffee. The two friends were just having a quick natter when there was a knock at the shop door.

It was Adela.

"Minnie told me Sophie had a date," she explained as she came in. "I thought she might like to borrow a handbag and some jewellery." She opened a large tote bag and produced a black Hermes clutch bag and a beautiful pink suede box which she opened to reveal a delicate diamond bracelet, ring and earring set.

Lucy could see the name embossed upon the box was De Beers.

"Wow," Minnie exclaimed. "When you said you could lend her some bits and bobs I didn't think you meant of this calibre."

"Do you think they're a bit much?" Adela asked. Since being in Little Eden she had come to realise that labels and trinkets meant nothing, even more so since Joshua's passing. What was important to her had completely changed. The quick rush of excitement on buying a new dress or handbag, a pair of designer shoes or sparkling jewels was now an empty sensation tinged with mild disgust. She looked at the jewels and sighed. "I wanted these for years and then when I finally got them they didn't seem as thrilling as the anticipation had been. I thought Sophie might get a little kick out of using them though. They ought to be worn."

Lucy tried on the bracelet and held the handbag over her arm whilst she looked at herself in the mirror. "If she doesn't, I will," she laughed. "Sophie isn't into labels, but quality is quality at the end of the day - even if it is a total rip off." Lucy realised what she'd implied. "Oh, god, sorry Adela, I didn't mean…"

Adela laughed too. "I didn't realise at the time I was being taken for a mug," she admitted. "I was young and easily fooled by the idea that something expensive was better than something cheap (she looked around the shop) or handmade with love," she added. "You're right, I did get ripped off, but if I can share them around a bit now, maybe it won't seem so depressing to think of it! I realise now, of course, that things are not the answer to emptiness or loneliness."

Lucy frowned. "I can't really imagine you ever being lonely," she said, a little bewildered that someone so beautiful could ever experience isolation.

"Before I had Josh I was always lonely," Adela admitted. "I bought things to try to fill the void. I even got into debt at one point. I don't mind admitting it now. I got hooked by the media and the sales people. They had me right where they wanted me. Aspirational magazines and TV shows - I was a sucker alright."

"Do you have lots of expensive things?" Minnie asked her.

Adela shook her head. "Not a lot. I bought a few very expensive items. I would have lent Sophie one of my Prada dresses but I don't think they would fit very well." She looked at what Minnie was creating. "I suppose you could have altered one for her though."

Minnie giggled. "I wouldn't feel confident messing with a thousand dollar dress," she said.

Adela sat down and Lucy offered her a biscuit and some coffee. "You're very generous to lend these out," Lucy said. "Sophie will be so happy. Not because they are expensive but because you are lending them to her. She still thinks you blame her for Joshua's death."

Adela nearly choked on her coffee. "What?" she exclaimed. "Why?"

"Well, she didn't save him," Lucy told her.

"Oh, poor Sophie!" Adela exclaimed. "Is she in now?" She looked over to the café and to the upper floors to see if the lights were on. "I must go and tell her she's totally wrong. Immediately!"

"Come over with me now," Lucy offered. "You can show her your things and tell her she's not to blame."

Adela didn't even finish her coffee and was out the door before Lucy could catch her up. She almost ran across the square and up the outside stairs to the café flat…

…"So you see," Adela finished telling Sophie. "You must never ever think it was your fault that Josh died. Promise me you'll never think that again?"

Sophie felt tearful, relieved and yet still more than a little to blame. "I'll try," she promised and hugged her new friend, thanking her again for the loan of the handbag and jewellery.

"Are you excited about tomorrow night?" Adela asked her, trying to lighten the mood.

Sophie's eyes were shining and she couldn't quite hide her nervous excitement. "I'm not sure," she replied. "I feel sick but I'm not sure if that's excitement or fear!"

"First dates are always such a thrill," Adela said as she put the jewels on Sophie to see what they looked like. "I've had so many. I think I was addicted to them for a while. The frisson and the shyness, the not knowing how it's going to end and all the compliments. I love the idea of being loved. That sounds very vain, doesn't it?" she asked.

Sophie smiled at her in the mirror. "No, it doesn't. Maybe being addicted to it wasn't such a good thing, but compliments are lovely - when they're genuine. It's nice to be liked isn't it? It's a long time since someone has liked me."

"You've had boyfriends where you lived before though haven't you?" Adela asked her.

Sophie nodded. "Before I became too ill, I had a few. One really serious - we nearly got married but the Chronic Fatigue Syndrome put paid to that. I became more and more housebound and socialising became less and less possible; plus, I couldn't wash his socks for him anymore!" She tried to make light of it. "I used to be quite pretty before, too."

Adela nudged her reproachfully. "You're pretty now too," she said.

Sophie stared at her for a few moments wondering what it must be like to be as beautiful as Adela and Adela guessed what she was thinking.

"You're thinking that because of the way I look relationships must be easy for me aren't you?" Adela asked her.

Sophie felt a little embarrassed. "I suppose I was, yes. I was thinking how beautiful you are and how men fight over you. I've seen you stop traffic!"

Adela blushed, "No, I've never stopped traffic."

Sophie laughed. "Don't try to deny it. That man the other week fell off his bike when he hit that lamp post outside the Deli. There was almost a four car pileup! We all saw that."

Adela had to laugh. "Okay, I admit I might have caused a few road traffic accidents over the years, but men think they have a right to whistle at me, shout at me, even grope me, just because they find me attractive. Old men, young boys, fuglies and married men - it doesn't matter who they are - they think I'm public property for some reason. I've had to develop quite a good right hook I can tell you."

Sophie suddenly felt sorry for Adela. "That's awful," she said. "I've never had any man try to grope me, thank god."

"If I had a nickel for every time my fanny's been pinched, slapped or drooled over, I'd be able to save Little Eden in a heartbeat!" Adela laughed.

"The curse of a beautiful face!" Sophie smiled. "Lancelot sees beyond your outer beauty, you know that don't you?" she added.

Adela turned away and pretended to look at some photographs on the chest of drawers.

"He's heart broken," Sophie said kindly.

Adela sighed. She still felt angry when she thought of Lancelot. "I know it's irrational but I can't help blaming him for Josh."

"Lance is no more to blame than I am though, surely?" Sophie said. "If you can forgive me, can't you forgive him?"

"The difference is, it never even crossed my mind that you were in any way to blame, so I don't need to forgive you," Adela admitted. "But Lancelot, he should have kept him safe, given him a different pony, not let him ride in the demonstration so soon. I don't know! He just should have known."

Sophie took hold of Adela's hand and sat her down on the bed. "The last person in the whole world who'd put anyone in danger is Lancelot. He's a protector. He's the kindest man you could ever meet."

"I'm just not ready yet," Adela admitted. "I need more time, that's all."

Sophie nodded. She understood.

Chapter 35
~ * ~

Sophie came into the flat as quietly as she could.
It was after midnight.

To her surprise the light was still on in the living room, and peering in, she saw Lucy, Minnie and Adela sitting on the sofas, all a little tipsy and in high spirits. An empty bottle or two of Prosecco were on the coffee table along with some half-finished bowls of crisps and dips.

Sophie smiled to herself. She knew they had been waiting up for her, wanting to find out how her date with Tobi had gone. She had stayed out longer than she had planned to and was now in hyper-fatigue (which meant that there was little chance of her sleeping that night) and she was secretly glad to have someone to talk to.

The girls all jumped up when Sophie came in. They rushed over to her, asking how it had gone.

"Where did he take you?" Lucy asked.

"Did he pay?" Minnie enquired.

"Did he kiss you?" Adela wanted to know.

"Don't miss anything out!" Lucy told her. "Start from the beginning - tell us everything."

Sophie told them all about her evening with Tobi in as much detail as she could and finished her tale by saying… "He walked me to the café door and I wasn't sure if I should kiss him or if he was going to kiss me, but then he leaned in and…it felt like the first time I had ever been kissed. That sounds silly I know, but I felt eighteen years old again! He waited till I was safely inside before he left."

"You should have asked him to come up!" Lucy declared.

"I wanted to," Sophie admitted, "But I felt as if I'd lied enough for one evening."

"What do you mean?" Minnie asked.

"Well, when he asked why I'd come back to Little Eden, I said it was to look after Aunt Lilly and when he asked why I was staying here and not going back to York, I said it was to help Lucy with the café."

"You didn't tell him about your illness then?" Adela asked.

Sophie shook her head. "I didn't want to spoil it. I'll suffer for at least a week for having gone out with him tonight but it's worth it. I needed a night like this. It's been so long since I felt special and pretty and alive. I know this is the first and the last date with him, but I can remember it as a wonderful memory for the rest of my life now."

"It makes me think of that film," Minnie said.

"Which one?" Lucy asked.

"That one, you know, the Cinderella one with Richard Chamberlin."

"The Slipper and the Rose?[23]" Sophie said.

"Yes, that's the one! There's that song they sing after the ball." Minnie sang the lilting song as she waltzed a very merry Adela around the room, 'Even though I know tonight is all there will ever be…'

"I know that one," Lucy giggled and joined in. "Rainbows raced around the room…"

Sophie laughed. "Yes! Exactly like that! Except there wasn't any dancing."

"Is he your Ace of Cups?" Minnie asked as she plonked herself down on the sofa.

Sophie sighed. "I think he might be one of them, yes. We have such a strong connection - stronger than I've felt with anyone except 'you know who'. Although soul mate relationships usually end badly in my experience so enjoying the magical beginning without having to face the reality is probably for the best anyway."

"I don't understand why you can't see him again" Adela said. "He asked you out on another date right?"

"He asked if we could do it again," Sophie admitted. "I said yes - another lie."

"I bet he'll txt her in less than half an hour!" Lucy giggled and poured them all some more bubbly, but her co-ordination had gone a bit squiffy and she spilt most of it on the table.

With that, Sophie's phone pinged and Lucy was right. Tobi had txt her from the Tube, even before he had gotten home. This was the txt:

<Thanks for a lovely time and lovely company. Lunch next Saturday? I know this amazing café in Camden I know you'll love. T>

"Reply!" Lucy urged her sister as she mopped up the drink with a tea towel. "Say you'll go."

---

23 He/She Danced with Me, Slipper and the Rose, R.M & R.B Sherman, 1976, Universal Pictures

Sophie sighed. "I won't have the energy to go out again next Saturday. Sunday is the rededication of the church and Joshua's big day. I'll have to have some energy for that."

"You could meet for an hour maybe?" Minnie suggested. Then she remembered it wasn't just about the time they would be together but the getting ready and the travelling too. "Why don't you say you'd rather go somewhere in Little Eden so you don't have to travel?" she added.

"I can't do two days of anything back to back," Sophie replied. She was getting tired of explaining herself about the CFS all the time and wanted to go to bed now.

Lucy snatched the phone out of Sophie's hand and ran into the kitchen with it, giggling to herself. She txt Tobi back, typing as quickly as she could, before Sophie could get the phone back off her:

<I'd love to but it's an important day in LE on Sunday so why don't you come and join me then instead? It'll be fun. Had a great time too. S>

Sophie looked at the txt. "You…" she began to say then found that she couldn't really be mad at her sister because she secretly did want to see Tobi again.

"You can't pass on an Ace of Cups!" Minnie told her. "They only come along once or twice in a lifetime. You'd be mad to push him away. Let him decide if he can put up with your illness or not. You never know…"

…"Yes," Adela interrupted. "He might turn out to be Mr Right who loves you for who you are. Let him get to know you."

"Then brace myself for the rejection?" Sophie frowned.

Sophie's phone pinged again.

<I'd love to join you on Sunday, looking forward to it. Sleep well, T>

"Brace yourself for a miracle more like!" Minnie laughed. "Look!"

She bent down and picked up a white feather that had appeared in the middle of the floor and none of them could work out how it had got there!

Chapter 36
~ * ~

Talking of miracles…

…Ascension Sunday dawned over Little Eden with a sweeping ribbon of gold through a pale blue sky. Some residents hoped it heralded a marvellous new beginning, not only for the town, but possibly the whole world.

Since Erik Sprott's rather ignominious departure, Iris had set about clearing the old matrix energy in the church which had been created over hundreds of years by prayers and hymns, bewitching the people and the land all around. The stone masons who had built the current sacred edifices had chipped and chiselled a thousand spells into the very fabric of the church and the Abbey, all of which now needed removing - Iris knew this could take decades. All the crucifixes had been removed, and poor Jesus, whose name had been taken in vain so many times, was given his true place as an equal amongst the saints again.

Iris had cleared the etheric energy of the Abbey complex with music, incense, aromatherapy sprays and new prayers, as well as salt which had been sprinkled all over the tiled floors and swept up daily for the week. Everyone who came in noticed a significant change in the atmosphere which they realised had been musty and rather oppressive before. Now, the vaulted roofs seemed higher and the aisles felt much wider, though of course, they could not physically be so. The buildings and the gardens were now flourishing with more delicate primroses and blousy peonies than ever before.

The restored statue of Mother Mary holding a pure white dove, which had been broken by Marcus, took her place behind the altar. She was newly painted in rich blue, ruby red and glittering gold and she seemed to exude even more compassion and serenity than she had done before.

Today was to be a rededication of the whole Abbey complex to the Holy Spirit. The vibration of the new matrix - divine feminine - was anchoring into the dragon portal. The more people who connected to it, the stronger it would become.

Ascension Day always included a procession of the Abbey Cross down Dovecote Street to St Peters Gate. Unfortunately, the event had been less well attended in recent years because Erik had made it a rather sombre and staid affair. This year's parade however brought nearly everyone out of their shops and houses to join in. The gospel song, Joyful, Joyful[24], rang through the town, and from second story windows, rose petal confetti showered down onto the parade, creating a ribbon of pink all along the street.

The day was made even more special by the fact that Joshua's ashes were going to become a relic. He was not to be buried in the church yard or scattered in the woods, as some of the residents were, he was to be given a special resting place in a stone niche by the font of St Mary's church.

A brass plaque had been especially engraved with the words:

Here lies Joshua Huggins, Star Child, who remains in spirit to help you open your heart and expand your mind. Ask for his key and your wish shall be granted...

Before everyone else arrived to hear the sermon in the church, Sophie, Tobias, Robert, Iris, Minnie and Lucy all said a little prayer as Adela placed her son into his new home. Elijah, Alice and Tambo were also there to say goodbye and hello to their friend. As soon as the enchanted urn had been placed in the alcove and the glass case closed, a familiar cool breeze was felt by all. An apparition of Joshua appeared amongst them. Elijah and Sophie could see him - the others could only feel his presence.

"Is he alright?" Adela asked Sophie. "Is my Josh alright?"

"He's saying he's happy and he's fine," Sophie told her.

Joshua shape shifted from a little boy into a bold white knight; and standing there, enrobed in fine silver chainmail and with a golden crown upon his head, looked regal and courageous.

Sophie whispered to Tobi, "Can you see him?"

Tobi shook his head and replied, "I can feel there is someone in spirit here with us but I can't see him."

She asked Robert the same thing.

Robert shook his head as well, "It's definitely Joshua, I can feel it in my heart, but I can't see him. I can see Alienor, Queen Bertha and Lilly though," he added pointing around the font to where the apparitions were standing.

Suddenly everyone turned around, thinking that the church door had opened - everyone felt sure they had heard it. To their surprise the door was still shut and no one had entered.

24 Joyful, Joyful, Hymn to Joy, Henry van Dyke, 1907

"What is it?" Robert asked her as he felt the temperature drop at least a degree.

Minnie grabbed hold of Lucy - she had goose bumps and the hairs on the back of her neck began to prickle - she didn't like it.

Sophie looked around with her third eye and saw the dreaded ectoplasm of Ramesses II had manifested into the church. *Oh crap!* She thought. *Not him again!*

Tobi squeezed her hand. "I think our old friend just arrived," he told her.

Before Sophie could be too scared however, she realised that the Pharaoh was not as he had been previously. This time he looked like a human being, not a raging beast or a marble statue. Beside him appeared twenty three more elderly men. Some were carrying wooden staffs and wearing long flowing capes; others were wrapped in wolf skins and luxurious furs. Others wore armour, and crowns upon their heads, carrying great swords in their hands. One of them wore nothing but a loin cloth and another was wearing nothing at all - he was completely naked and on his head was a crown of thorns.

Sophie tried to make out who they were. She recognised one or two of them as Abraham, Moses, King Solomon and King David. It was obvious that they were however all wizards and kings.

"What do you want?" Sophie asked them.

King Solomon spoke on behalf of them all. "We came to tell you that some of us are going to join the Star Children in the new matrix and some of us are returning home to Atlantis. Our era is over and we offer the guardianship of the Earth and of mankind to the Pleiades Council."

"How come you tried to put up a fight," she asked him. "Ramesses wasn't too happy last time I saw him."

King Solomon looked grave and spoke with a tinge of regret in his voice. "We were not all in agreement," he explained. "I have decreed that we shall leave peacefully, but there is a rogue element who are determined to fragment the sovereign template and fight to the very end."

Sophie grimaced and sighed. "Typical," she replied. "Everyone loves the idea of personal power. I don't understand it myself. Why can't everyone just agree to get along?" She looked over at Ramesses whom she realised was just toeing the line now that his power had been dispelled. The look on his face made her realise that he was not happy with the collective decision at all."

Suddenly Sophie gasped...

...morphing over the whole church was the apparition of a gigantic magical horse. It was so huge that its legs were as high as the rafters and its grand rider towered above the steeple.

Thankfully they both began to shrink down to normal size and a shining knight dismounted from his shadowy black steed.

The noble horseman knelt down before Sophie as if she were someone of consequence.

"Don't you know me?" the kneeling knight asked her.

"Should I?" Sophie answered.

The knight stood up and took off his armoured glove. Placing his hand gently upon her cheek he asked her again, "Don't you know me?"

His touch triggered something so deep inside Sophie that she nearly burst into tears.

She knew him.

She knew him with her soul.

It was King Arthur.

Chapter 37

~ * ~

"**K**ing Arthur," Sophie sighed with relief. "Of course!"
"We have been waiting millennia for you to come to us," he told her. "Now finally, it has begun."

Sophie wasn't sure what he meant. *He's been waiting for me?* She wondered. *Who does he think I am? I seem to be lots of different people at different times depending on who is communicating with me and which job I am doing. I suppose I am channelling someone he recognises.*

Unbeknown to Sophie, King Arthur saw her as a small and delicate glowing green alien being, with sparkling eyes and smooth skin. Her galactic existence was as mythological as his own. She had not returned to Earth since the fall of the Antahkarana bridge, which the Atlanteans had inadvertently destroyed when they had first attempted incarnation into human form. This etheric rainbow bridge was a link between the lower realms of the human mind to the higher dimensions. Unfortunately, without it, the vacuum in which humans found themselves became fertile ground for manmade beliefs which felt more appropriate to their animal instincts and survival. Losing the memory of their true origins led to feelings of despair and abandonment, but also to those of self-importance and absolute power.

A handsome and regal King Arthur looked over to the other kings and shamans. He drew his sword as if to challenge them and they seemed to cower before him. Then instead of attacking them, he placed his gleaming silver blade gently across Sophie's palms. As she held it before her she realised it acted like a mirror, showing her the truth like a crystal ball might show one the past or the future. Gazing into its depths, she saw the ancient wizard-king Melchizedek, wearing blue robes decorated with silver stars, holding the whole universe in his hand as if it was a child's mobile. He then crumpled up the planets as if they were nothing but paper and set it ablaze. From the ashes a mystical phoenix materialised and as it flapped its burnished wings the mobile was recreated; this time however it appeared to be made of pure crystal.

One of the Pleiades Council she had met on the pyramid platform at Giza appeared like a hologram out of the crystalline galaxy. Some of the kings didn't seem happy to witness its arrival, and a mixture of awe, loathing, reverence and jealousy filled the air. Sophie felt a strong compulsion to hand the galactic councillor the sword. In return he offered her a light saber and she couldn't help but be reminded of Obi Wan Kenobi and Yoda. The words, *Unlearn everything you have ever learnt*[25], danced through her mind.

Abraham reluctantly stepped forward and gave her his enchanted staff, which she in turn proffered to the Pleiades master. It transformed into a rainbow serpent which shimmered as it swayed before her.

King Solomon gladly offered her a shining object. It was the etheric version of the Ankh that she had used the night Joshua had died. When she in turn offered it to the galactic being, it transformed immediately into blue-white crystal, with a code of secret symbols streaming through it.

The tribal elder then extended his crown of thorns to Sophie. His reticence in letting go of it made her reluctant to touch it so she passed it as quickly as she could into the hands of the alien leader. It transmogrified into glass and shattered into millions of pieces which swirled together to create a transparent and twisted thorn tree. The rainbow serpent coiled its way around the gnarled bark and Sophie watched, mesmerised, as a vision of Adam and Eve appeared within the trunk, replicating the etheric blue-print of human DNA. Turning a deep shade of blue, their bodies merged and morphed into a superhuman hermaphrodite, sitting on a white crested ocean. This unified being, with long, black, flowing hair and a kind, wise face, held every item, the sword, the staff, the Ankh and the crown, in its multiple hands. Smiling as it was consumed by the waves, it left behind only blue sparkles dancing in the air.

Sophie was dumbstruck by what she had just witnessed.

She turned to King Arthur hoping that he might explain what has going on.

"I am the King of Kings," King Arthur told her. "I must gather together all the souls of the kings and queens who have reigned on Earth so that we can close the old DNA kingship template and allow for a new one to be created."

"A sovereign must rule with a heart and mind filled with the Holy Spirit. We must always be guided by divine compassion," Queen Bertha said. "True leadership is in service of the people, but humans have become enticed and bewitched by hierarchy and earthly power."

---

25 Star Wars, George Lucas, 1977, Lucasfilm/Disney

"A sovereign leader should never use their position for personal power," King Arthur stated. "They must remember that they are guardians of the peace and of justice. Kingship is a position of power and responsibility they should be humbled by."

"But power can corrupt even the angels sometimes," Alienor added. "True leaders are earth angels who desire Heaven on Earth."

Sophie couldn't help thinking of the lines in the Lord's Prayer - 'Thy will be done, on Earth as it is in Heaven,' and for the first time it actually made sense to her.

Utopia sounded appealing but Sophie had a feeling that it might be a long time before world leaders would rule with compassion and selflessness - maybe never. She could imagine a world where everyone lived in peace, but she couldn't imagine it ever being a reality.

The Pleiades master seemed more optimistic, however. Sophie could feel its words forming in her mind as it communicated with her telepathically. *Do not despair child of the universe.* He told her. *A new era is coming. A new matrix is being built within the DNA. We have great and wonderful plans for our guardianship. Help us to change the world by changing the keys in yourself and in the dragon lines, and by offering them to others.*

The transcendental entity then presented Sophie with what looked like a small micro-chip. She looked at it - she was not sure what to do with it.

This is the new Kingship key, the cosmic spirit told her. *Place it with Joshua. Everyone who desires to change their beliefs about community and leadership will be helped to upgrade the old codes within their DNA.*

As soon as Sophie had placed the etheric key in the niche with Josh, all the kings, wizards, knights and the galactic being, along with Joshua and Queen Bertha, disappeared into the dragon portal which had opened up in a swirl of blue watery light in the floor.

A dragon's eye was the last thing to remain - it winked and then gently closed.

The dragon portal was shut tight again.

The temperature in the room returned to normal and everyone breathed a sigh of relief. Even though they had not really been aware of what was happening, it felt as if they had missed a few minutes of real life and as if they had just woken from a strange and otherworldly trance.

"What was all that about?" Lucy asked her sister.

"Don't ask!" Sophie replied. "I can't explain it in words. It all sounds ridiculous and nutty when you really think about it. King Arthur just told me that the world will be a better place in the future but that people have to change their DNA first and let go of the old beliefs and the old men who used to rule the world have to let go of their power too."

"Well, that's okay then," Robert laughed as if he understood what she meant.

"I thought I saw Moses," Tobias admitted and looked at the others to see if they agreed with him, but no one else had.

"I thought Aunt Lilly was here," Lucy said.

"I saw Joshua," Elijah said.

"So did I," Alice rejoined.

"I felt as if I was dressed in armour and had that etheric sword in my hand," Robert admitted.

"You are all right in a way," Sophie told them. Then turning to Iris she passed on a message from King Arthur, "Iris, once you rededicate the Abbey to the Holy Spirit, the original energy of Nun will be used to create a new matrix of consciousness. Men and women will feel empowered without disempowering each other. Leaders will be elected for their compassion and their ability to unify, protect and judge with fairness. Society will be more global and less nationalistic - more inclusive and less tribal." Sophie sighed, a little unsure if she was just making the whole thing up. "Or at least that's the plan," she added.

"Well, I'd better get started then, so I should," Iris replied and looked at her watch. "It's almost time to open the doors," she said. "A new start and a clean slate, that's what we need and it's long overdue, so it is."

Chapter 38
~ * ~

So many excited people flooded into the immaculate church to hear Iris's inaugural speech that there were not enough seats to go round! They spilled out into the graveyard and into Lady Well Walk - so eager were they to find out what the new vicar would bring about.

The late morning sun scattered rainbows over the congregation in a Heavenly aura. The painted gold stars on the ceiling sparkled amongst the navy blue sky as the newly buffed candelabras twinkled in the rafters. Each highly polished wooden pew had a pretty posy of daisies and forget-me-nots tied to the end, and lush green garlands hung delicately over the archways.

The air was buzzing with excitement and anticipation.

Some members of the congregation were surprised by the presence of the Buddhist monks from the World Peace Centre. They sat together in one long pew, in their orange and maroon robes, with smiles on their faces and joy in their hearts. Iris and Dr G had both understood that the merging of the divine feminine was paramount to heal the divisions between religions.

True compassion is unconditional and holy - it is absolutely, one hundred percent, inclusive.

Dr G had given Blue the prestigious task of presenting Iris with a statue of Tara, but he forgot what he was supposed to say in English so he said it in Tibetan instead. Dr G had to translate for those who were not fluent in the ancient language! It went something like this:

"Let the new world be one in which we are all united by compassion. Let it flow through us like a river of everlasting light. With the guidance of the Holy Ones who stay in spirit to help us, may we always keep an open heart. Om Mani Padme Hum. Peace be with you."

As Iris placed the highly coloured statuette of Tara on the altar she found herself involuntarily placing her hands into prayer position and bowing her head in reverence. She couldn't stop smiling.

An exuberant Iris gave a short, humble sermon (very different from those of her husband Erik) and here is a snippet of it for you, dear readers:

"From now on, the church and Abbey of Little Eden shall be dedicated to the Holy Spirit. Everyone shall be welcome here, so they will. Faith shall replace religion. Faith in compassion; faith in humanity; and faith in ourselves. Compassion, kindness and forgiveness shall be our creed. Little Eden is a true sanctuary for all who seek to put right that which they have done wrong, and for all those who seek comfort and support. We will try our best to support each other to live life with open hearts, and when we falter or when we are lost - here in Little Eden we shall always shine the light of Love."

Sophie smiled to herself. She was overwhelmed by the beautiful, precious energy flowing through the crowded church and she could see a the bright white light of the Holy Spirit pouring from Iris's heart and into everyone else's. She said a little prayer asking Alienor and Aunt Lilly to support Iris in her work as vicar and to help her find the strength to guide everyone who came through the door seeking solace. Her prayer was answered immediately when she saw five nuns standing with Iris, ready to guide her hand, her voice and her heart and to work with her from spirit.

"We have a wonderful addition to our church," Iris explained, standing next to the niche in which Joshua's ashes lay. "Anyone who wishes to be liberated from the old spells is welcome to ask Joshua for help at any time, so you are," Iris told the congregation. "The church is always open, day or night, and our blessed boy is here for you always. He gave his life to serve us, let us willingly accept his enlightenment and through us he will live forever as an angel and a saint."

In celebration, the gospel choir sang, Happy Day[26], but in honour of the divine feminine they had changed the lyrics from 'Jesus washed my sins away' to 'Mary washed my sins away'. Even those who would never normally get to their feet, clap or dance, felt their legs involuntarily moving, their hearts opening, and found that they just couldn't help but join in. The whole church was united in song and everyone felt refreshed, recoded and remade.

At the end of the ceremony Iris invited anyone who wanted to do so to approach the altar and forgive someone towards whom they still felt anger. By the altar was a basket full of pink roses and Iris began by setting the example. First she said a prayer:

---

26 Oh Happy Day, Edwin Hawkins, 1968, Pavilion/Buddha

Forgiveness Prayer

Fill me with Forgiveness, great Mother of Mercy and of Grace.
When we are blind, we cannot see the words and actions that lead to thee.
When I and others falter, I place a sacred rose upon your altar,
And wish, that I and all others will see,
All the paths that lead to thee.[27]

Then, taking a rose from the bunch she placed it on the altar and said firmly and clearly - "I forgive Erik and Cassie and I forgive myself."

Not everyone realised that they had someone to forgive (we often have no idea how much anger and resentment lies beneath and not everyone is ready to dig) so some left for tea and cake in the church hall, some just stayed in their seat for a while in silent prayer, and some, like Sophie, went up to the altar.

Sophie tried to forgive herself for her illness.

Lucy went up to forgive Jimmy.

Robert felt he really ought to go up and forgive his mother.

Even Cedric bumbled up with Mr T, and like many of the residents, Mr T wanted to forgive Collins and Lucas for trying to destroy Little Eden.

Lucy tried to persuade Linnet to go up and forgive Marcus, but Linnet hadn't even wanted to come to the church. She had only come for Alice's sake as she was singing with the choir. She was steadfast in her fear of Marcus and mistakenly believed that her hatred of him would protect her from pain and suffering.

Lastly, Adela went up to the altar, and although she didn't say a name out loud, she made it clear whom she was forgiving, because instead of leaving her rose upon the altar, she offered it directly to Lancelot. "I'm sorry," she whispered in his ear, "I should never have blamed you, do you forgive me?"

Lancelot couldn't speak as he knew if he did he would cry. He took the rose and kissed it then gave her it back to her as a sign that he forgave her too. Before he could fully regain his composure and tell her how he felt, Adela had left the church, overwhelmed by the blissful energy she felt racing through her heart.

---

27 Forgiveness Prayer, KT King Prayers, Book One, 2015

Chapter 39

~ * ~

Most people were walking on air as they headed home. Their souls felt uplifted, their bodies were relaxed and their hearts had opened to Love. Iris was on a high which she didn't come down from for many days afterwards. She was so happy that she had stayed in Little Eden after all. She felt as if she was exactly where she was destined to be, and being a spiritual leader was most definitely her life's purpose. She felt as if she was a nun again. In this lifetime however, she no longer needed the vows of obedience, chastity or poverty. True and deep compassion bore such humble feelings within her that she wanted nothing else but to be in the service of the Light. She needed no rules or masters to keep her in check. Finally, her soul was liberated from the hundreds of past lives in which she had been subjugated by the patriarchal order. In her heart she knew that the Holy Mother had been re-awoken from behind the man-made spells.

The devotional, awe-inspiring and humble emotions the Mother inspires cannot be easily explained in words, dear readers. As many of you will know it is only by experiencing the inner connection for yourself that you can truly understand what Iris was feeling.

Tears of joy flowed as she gave thanks to the Virgin.

"What is it, Iris?" Sophie enquired when she saw that she was crying.

"I'm in Heaven," Iris replied. "They're happy tears, so they are."

Lucy, Stella and Mrs B blew out the candles and helped Iris tidy up before leaving, whilst Linnet took down some of the fresh blooms which would have wilted by the end of the day.

Sophie had an overwhelming urge to speak to Linnet before she went so she asked Tobi to meet her back at Daisy Place, where some of them had been invited back for lunch. A melancholy Linnet was carrying a large basket of flowers and was about to leave by the vestry when Sophie caught up to her.

"Wait!" Sophie called to her. "Can I have a word?"

Linnet looked surprised but nodded.

Sophie quietly shut the door for privacy. "I'm worried about you," Sophie told Linnet kindly. "I know you've been doing better with getting sober but you still seem so afraid and angry all the time. You seem as distressed about Marcus as you did when he was still alive. The Forgive…"

…before Sophie could finish her sentence Linnet interrupted her…

…"Don't start on at me about all this spiritual crap and forgiving everyone, okay!" Linnet exclaimed and slammed her basket down on the desk. "Whatever name you give it it's the same thing. It's all about trying to control people, telling them what to do and what to think, brainwashing them so they can't make their own decisions anymore. Don't tell me to forgive him - he doesn't deserve to be forgiven. Ever!"

"Forgiving someone is not for his sake," Sophie tried to explain. "It's for yours. Forgiving Marcus is so that you don't have to carry his hate, his oppression, his control and his violence around inside you for the rest of your life. Plus, and perhaps most importantly of all, it's so that you don't create more sticky karma between you. If you don't forgive him he'll come back to haunt you in the next life."

Linnet didn't want to listen. She was so full of fear and despair that holding onto the pain seemed safer than letting it go. She was ashamed of having ever been in love with Marcus so the love she had for him had transformed into hate. Most of all she was overwhelmed with guilt for not having protected Alice. Rather than admit all this about herself she covered it over with a seal of anger. She was not ready to delve inside and face her own worst fear - that she might be to blame.

If only she had told Sophie how she really felt, she would have realised that forgiveness was the key to her happiness after all, and that the shame and blame could be replaced with compassion and inner peace.

"You don't want to come back with him in the next life and the next life and the next life do you?" Sophie asked her. "You can't break free of him whilst you hate him as much as he hated you. If you can start to forgive him, and yourself, it'll let the Light back into your heart."

Linnet couldn't get her head around forgiveness just yet and she didn't want the Light to shine on her deepest wounds. "I won't be a doormat anymore," she declared. "If I forgive him - he's won. I'll be the victim again."

"But Linnet, that's not how it works," Sophie told her. "It's the opposite of what you think. Forgiving someone is walking away from them one hundred percent and being free of what they did forever."

"Are you saying what he did is right?" Linnet said bitterly. "You might be able to forgive him because he didn't hurt you! When it happens to you or your family then maybe you won't be so sanctimonious about it."

"No one is saying that Marcus was right," Sophie sighed. "And I'm not saying forgiveness is easy. In fact, in my experience, it's the hardest thing of all and takes a very long time, but once you start you're on the road to recovery."

Linnet scoffed. "You all think you know best don't you? You're all so perfect with your happy clappy crap! What you did here today - its madness - crazy! You can't take a random boy and make him a saint just like that. It makes no sense! All this about dragon portals and Star Children and a new beginning for the world - good god if you could hear yourselves! It's like some sort of cult. You're replacing one religion with another. Whatever you want to call it - Jesus, Mary, Tara, the Holy Spirit - it's all just superstitious insanity. Do you really imagine that the world can live in peace when there are people like Marcus in it? You need your heads testing."

Sophie didn't reply. She had to admit to herself that Linnet did have a point.

Linnet stormed out and slammed the door behind her.

Sophie walked up the aisle a little depressed. She knew what she believed in did seem nutty to many people. She was fully aware that it must look as if she had lost the plot to those who had never experienced the Holy Spirit. Only a few decades ago she'd have been sent to an asylum and a few hundred years before that she'd have been hanged as a witch. In Britain she was ridiculed by so called scientists and considered blasphemous by religions. Living in two realities simultaneously wasn't easy and it was becoming harder by the day. Her human mind struggled to assimilate and understand higher consciousness and she often questioned her own sanity. Her only consolation was that some people in Little Eden also believed in the spirit world and in other dimensions. She knew that she was lucky to have their support.

Catching sight of Lancelot sitting alone in the tiny St Katherine's chapel, she wondered whether to go and speak to him or not but thought she had better give him some space. As she turned to go, the same invisible force which had compelled her to speak to Linnet stopped her in her tracks once again. *Okay,* she said in her head. *I'll go and speak to him but you'd better tell me what to say,* she told her spirit guides, *As I haven't a clue how to help him.*

Sophie and Lancelot sat in silence on the comfy leather armchairs which Iris had brought into the chapel. The chapel was a truly sacred space in which the mind became still in solitary meditation once one connected to the consciousness of St Katherine. The space acted like a telephone exchange where one could ring her up and bathe in divine wisdom. Erik had installed hard wooden chairs in the enclave and a plain wooden cross was all that had adorned it, but Iris had felt the need to create a more intimate and relaxing atmosphere, and now, a small statue of an angel, surrounded by fresh flowers and a row of candles, which anyone could light at any time, graced the small altar.

Lancelot didn't know what to say. He wanted to tell Sophie how he was feeling but he was experiencing so many different emotions all at once that he wasn't sure how to articulate the jumble. When he connected with the consciousness of St Katherine his heart was quiet and it gave him a few minutes of welcome respite from the churning he felt inside.

"Adela just needs more time," Sophie told him. "Her heart is broken."

Lancelot sighed and nodded. "I know," he replied. "I just want to fix it for her."

"You know you can't do that," Sophie said gently. "She has to embrace her own healing. The problem with healing is that no one can do it for us. We can guide and support someone, be there for them (she couldn't help thinking of Linnet) but in the end each person has to battle alone between hope and despair."

Lancelot nodded reluctantly. "I can't imagine what it must feel like to lose a child. No amount of spirituality can mend that hurt, surely? I pray for her every day though."

"Prayer helps," Sophie agreed. "Keep praying. Prayer is like sending an angel to someone. Unfortunately you can't force them to accept help. Adela has a long journey ahead of her but she strikes me as the sort of person who never gives up and never gives in no matter how long it takes."

"How long will it take?" Lancelot asked, not really expecting an answer.

Sophie shrugged. "How long can you wait?"

Lancelot smiled sadly. "I can wait forever if needs be," he replied.

"Well, then," Sophie said. "Just be her friend - get to know her properly. Let her see your love for her is genuine and she may come to trust you enough to love you in return. Concentrate on healing your heart first. There's always hope."

Lancelot squeezed Sophie's hand. "And you and love?" he asked. "Tobias seems a nice chap."

"I don't know him from Adam yet," she replied. "He seems very nice but he may turn out to be quite the opposite."

Lancelot put his arm around her and laughed. "Ever the sceptic!" he said. "As you said, there's always hope!"

Sophie smiled sadly. "Somethings are beyond hope," Sophie replied. "When you are too ill to live a normal life and yet know the illness you have isn't terminal, it's hard to hold onto hope. What hope is there when the medical profession still believes CFS is all in the mind and not a biological condition? Until they do some proper research, millions of us will suffer stigma and remain abandoned by the state and by science. My hope is that the world will be a better place in the future and that's why I try to stay alive and help when I can. I suppose there is no point in wishing a happy life for myself so I wish it for others instead."

Lancelot nodded. "I hope that the Star Children will take over the world and prevent the human race from destroying itself and the planet. A world where everyone is driven by compassion instead of by survival - now that is a future worth hoping for."

"I think there are many more spells yet to clear," Sophie replied. "But we have made a start."

Lancelot put Sophie's arm through his. "At least the divine feminine is making a comeback here in Little Eden," he said.

"I hope if enough people can open their hearts to the Holy Spirit every dragon portal in the world will bubble with the Ocean of Compassion again too," Sophie replied.

"Come on, I'll take you home," Lancelot said. "Did you bring your wheelchair?"

Sophie shook her head. "Tobi doesn't know about my illness yet. I didn't want him to see me in a chair."

"You're going to have to be honest and tell Tobi about the CFS sometime," Lancelot said as he opened the door for her. "The truth will out as they say."

"I know," Sophie nodded as she stepped out into the bright sunshine. "Just not today."

Chapter 40
~ * ~

When Lancelot and Sophie arrived back at No.1 Daisy Place, they found their usual group of friends enjoying Mrs B's finger sandwiches and fresh scones, and to their surprise, they were very excited - but not about the food!

Cedric was racing around chasing his tail he was so giddy! The reason they were all buzzing was because India had just received an email from Collins' lawyers:

<info@ShaftPencillPush.com>
to Lancelot

Dear Mr Bartlett-Hart

On further instruction from Mr Collins Bartlett-Hart we are attaching a new contract regarding the financial settlement on the retirement of the aforesaid Trustee. Our client has agreed to the sum of one billion pounds sterling in place of the previous fee.

Please sign in triplicate and return two copies to our office as soon as possible, retaining one copy for your own records.

Yours sincerely,

Mandy Money
Executive Assistant to the office of Mr Boris Push

India, Minnie and Lucy were all jumping up and down with glee.
Jack was cracking open a bottle of Champagne.
Robert had to sit down in order for the momentous news to sink in.
Lancelot and Sophie hardly dare believe it at first.
India looked at Robert's dazed expression. "It means we're getting closer to paying off Collins! Aren't you happy?" she asked him. "I know we still have to work on Lucas or find Uncle Frith, but this is a massive bonus for us. Saving Little Eden might actually be possible after all."

Jack handed out glasses of Champers. "Here's to the greedy bastard who turns out to only be half as greedy as he used to be!" Jack laughed as he toasted Collins.

"Why would he do this?" Sophie asked, a little suspicious of Collins' motives.

"Maybe Collins had an epiphany too?" Stella suggested.

"It seems lots of people are waking up to the Light inside them since Josh passed away," Minnie added. "It's like a million light bulbs are going off in people's minds and hearts.

"It's Shilty's doing," Robert suddenly said.

They all looked at him in amazement.

"Why would Shilty help us when she's dumped you?" Jack asked. "No offence, old boy, but she's hardly Mother Theresa."

Robert smiled to himself. "Shilty's not so bad," he replied.

"Did she tell you about this?" India asked him. "Did you know already?"

Robert shook his head. "I didn't have a clue. She never said anything. I just know she had a hand in this, that's all. I can feel it in my bones."

"Well then," Lucy said as she raised her glass. "Here's to Shilty for seeing the Light and helping us after all."

"I didn't think she could be so selfless," Lancelot said. "I misjudged her."

"Oh, don't you worry, Shilty will get something out of this," Robert told them. "What that'll be I don't dare to guess, but she'll have her reasons."

Robert wanted to be on his own for a while and to ring Shilty to say thank you, so he offered to go and fetch more Champagne from the Deli. He didn't know what to make of this latest turn of events. Shilty had helped find a place for his mother to live and now she had somehow forced Collins to reduce his pay-off by half. As he went down Rose Walk, he couldn't help but think Shilty might be the one for him after all, but as the palpitations began to race again he started to worry more about the physical state of his heart!

Whilst Lucy prepared some strawberries to accompany the bubbly, Jack asked Sophie to join him out on the roof terrace.

"We've hardly spoken since the day of the inquest," he said as he looked out over the roof tops. "Is it going to be awkward between us now," Jack asked her, hoping that it was not.

Sophie shook her head but didn't reply. The sky was full of white fluffy vapour trails and it made her think of the angels who were looking down on them from above.

"Look, old girl, I don't know what else to say," Jack continued. "It happened and you have to forget it happened. Can't we just carry on as normal?" he begged her.

To his relief Sophie smiled saying, "I'm sorry I've been avoiding you. It's just I didn't know what to think when you told me about Marcus and (she just mouthed the next bit) the spying. I was shocked."

"And now?" Jack prompted her.

"Someone helped me get my thoughts in order about such things," Sophie admitted.

"Who?" Jack asked.

"King Arthur," Sophie replied, as if King Arthur was simply one of their friends or acquaintances.

Jack smiled in jest. "Go on, it's going to be one of those crazy stories isn't it?"

Sophie laughed. "He explained kingship to me, that's all," she told him. "I realised that there are some people who have to make the hard decisions when no one else can and to act when others are too scared to. Sometimes the law isn't the same as justice, and a true king protects the innocent in whatever way he has to."

Jack nodded. "I might not be religious or spiritual, but I know what's right and wrong, and it's not always what the law says it is."

"You did the only thing that would keep Linnet, Alice and other women safe," Sophie told him. "The law would have let Marcus have access to Alice no matter how crazy he was, and he could have gone on drugging and abusing women for the rest of his life. The law is made by men for men, things are changing slowly I know, but justice is still tipped in favour of corrupt men. I wouldn't have had the guts to do what you did, but it was the safest plan," Sophie admitted. "It was the act of a white knight."

Jack sighed. "I want you to know that I don't go around bumping people off on a regular basis, old girl. Most of my work is in intelligence not physical combat."

"I know," she said, "I'm glad you are on my side though!"

"I'm always on your side," Jack told her.

Just then, Tobi came out looking for Sophie. "Would you like a glass of Champagne?" he asked her. "Robert's just brought more in." Then he remembered. "Sorry, I forgot you don't drink. I know - a green tea instead?"

Sophie laughed. "Yes, that would be nice, thank you."

As Tobi went back inside to get her drink, Jack nudged her saying, "I knew you'd hit it off!"

Sophie poked him in the ribs. "You set us up, didn't you?"

Jack pretended to be shocked. "Moi? I'd never do such a thing," he smiled.

"You're an old romantic underneath your swagger - you don't fool me," Sophie giggled. "And you're right, we have hit it off, but I haven't told him about 'me' yet."

"What?" Jack asked her. "You mean all the hocus pocus witchy stuff?"

"Oh, he knows all about that!" Sophie replied. "In fact he's kind of into it himself - no, I mean the chronic fatigue."

"Ah!" Jack said. "You're afraid he'll run a mile when he finds out?"

Sophie nodded.

"He might surprise you, old girl," Jack suggested, and as Tobi came back outside he winked saying again, "He might surprise you."

Jack left them alone but before Sophie could pluck up the courage to start to tell Tobias about her illness they were distracted by a sudden commotion coming from inside the apartment.

They went to see what was going on.

"Come in," India urged the two of them. "I've got some more good news!"

"Wow, things are really moving fast since the Atlanteans relinquished those keys. I never expected three dimensional results this quickly!" Sophie exclaimed. "What's happened now?"

"I just received another email," India told everyone.

"From Collins?" Robert asked, hoping maybe he'd decided not to sell Little Eden at all."

"No!" India said. "From your cousin, Roger Montgomery."

"Old Roger?" Robert laughed. "What does he have to say?"

"He's offering you his estate in Lancashire to help pay off Collins and Lucas," India explained.

Robert was nonplussed. "Why? How did he even know we needed the money?"

India looked sheepish. "I might have mentioned it to a few of our relatives," she admitted.

"India!" Robert scolded her. "I specifically told you - no begging letters!"

"I know, I know!" India replied, "But I had to do something! I didn't beg exactly, I just informed them of the situation and asked if they would like to help out in any way."

"This estate?" Jack asked. "What is he suggesting you do with it exactly?"

"He says we can sell it, rent it out, turn it into a hotel, whatever we like!" India told them.

"That's amazing!" Lucy exclaimed. "Is it worth much? Have you ever seen it?"

"Roger's family live in Monaco - they have since we were kids," Lancelot explained. "They've never lived at their estate. It's near Lancaster if I remember rightly. I don't know much more about it really."

Robert agreed. "I thought they'd sold it years ago."

"I don't know anything about it either," India admitted. "Hey, how's this for an idea? What if we all have a little weekend break and take a look at it!"

"That's a great idea!" Lucy agreed.

"I don't know," Robert replied hesitantly.

"Oh, come on," Lucy told him. "Don't be a spoil sport. It might be worth a bob or two."

"I doubt it," Lancelot responded. "It's probably a ruin."

"There's land attached to it," India said. "It's called Malinwick Manor. We could look it up on-line."

The name sparked a memory for Robert. "Isn't that the house that's supposed to be haunted?" he asked Lancelot.

Lancelot thought for a moment, trying to remember if he knew anything more about it. "I think you're right," he nodded. "Aunt Elizabeth told us about it once, when we were boys, but it was just a ghost story round the fire on Halloween."

"Then we have to go!" Lucy said. "We could all do with a break and a little adventure."

"Here's to a road trip up North!" India said, raising her glass.

"Here's to more cash to save Little Eden!" Jack laughed.

"I guess we'd better find out whether there are any resident ghosts!" Lucy giggled, and looked at Sophie.

Sophie pulled a face. "I can't go," she said, but they all began to try to persuade her, they even invited Tobi in the hope she'd agree to go with them.

"You have to come," Lucy pleaded.

Reluctantly Sophie raised her cup of tea and shaking her head but with a wry smile she said, "To Malinwick Manor."

Now they all looked to Robert. He couldn't really refuse them as they all seemed to want to go. "Alright," he agreed with a wry smile. "To Malinwick Manor - whether it's haunted or not."

The End

Daisy Place
Recipes

Little Eden

Dear readers,

Well, hello again from No.1 Daisy Place. I've been asked to jot down a few more of my delicious and very easy to make recipes which are all featured in Book Two.
I hope you enjoy them, my loves,
Mrs B x

Mrs B's Mayday Cake

I make this with the children every Mayday but it is also great for St Patricks Day as it's green! I gather nettles from the woods and lemon balm from the allotments, when they are in season, and make them into a puree. I mix the leaves together and freeze them in 80g batches so that I can make this cake at any time of the year.

You'll need a 7 inch cake tin.

Bake: 180 degrees C for 35 minutes

Ingredients:
To make the puree: put 150g of washed nettle leaves and 50g lemon balm leaves into a pan with a splash of water and heat until the leaves have wilted. Put the wilted leaves into a bowl and stand it in an ice bath or pop it in the freezer (this helps keep the leaves vibrant green). When cool, squeeze out the excess liquid so that it becomes a thickish consistency (200g of leaves makes about 80g of puree).

2 or 3 eggs - weigh 2 large or 3 medium eggs in their shells and whatever they weigh use equal amounts of sugar, flour and margarine - I find you'll be using somewhere around 140g of these ingredients.

Self-raising flour
Margarine (low calorie if you have it)
Golden caster sugar
80g nettle and lemon balm puree
¾ tsp. lemon extract
½ tsp. vanilla essence

Method:
Cream together the butter and sugar with an electric mixer until light and fluffy.

Add sifted flour and mix together.

Add the cooled (or defrosted) puree, then add the lemon and vanilla and lightly mix.

Put into a cake tin and bake at 180 degrees C for 35 - 40 minutes (times may vary depending on your oven).

Cool and serve with Quark or cream cheese (you can put a few drops of lemon extract into the topping and/or add some grated lemon zest).

Mrs B's tip:
Beat the sugar and margarine together for about 5 minutes until it becomes much paler in colour and very fluffy. Don't over mix once you have added the flour. Just mix it long enough to make sure all the ingredients combine together.

Lucy's Late Night Cheesecake

There is nothing like having some cheesecake for a midnight feast - especially when you need a little pick me up! This cheesecake is a decadent and scrumptious nutty feast. You can make one big one or small ones in ramekins. I try to make a slightly lower calorie version as it is needed quite frequently in Little Eden these days! You will need a 20cm springform or loose bottom tin (or ramekins/glasses).

Chill: 2 hours in freezer

Ingredients:
200g milk chocolate covered biscuits (digestives work well and you can use 'light' digestives for fewer calories)
100g butter (softened)
20g chopped nuts (hazelnuts work well)
20g milk chocolate drops (medium to small size)
20g caster sugar
150g Quark (or cream cheese)
150g double/whipping cream

150g hazelnut spread
1tsp vanilla essence

Method:
Melt the butter.
Blitz the biscuits into crumbs.
Add the chopped nuts and chocolate drops then mix all the dry ingredients into the butter.
Pour into the tin and press down firmly (with the end of a rolling pin) to form a level base. Put in the fridge for 15 minutes to firm up.
Beat the sugar, Quark and hazelnut spread together and add the vanilla essence.
Add the cream and whip until it is the consistency of whipped cream (or you can whip the cream separately and fold into the rest).
Pour into the tin over the firm base and smooth down the top.
Place in the freezer for 2 hours, remove the tin and serve with a topping of your choice.

Mrs B's tip:
Do not leave it out at room temperature as the Quark will not hold its shape. If you are not eating it all at once put the rest back in the fridge until wanted or leave in the freezer and defrost in the fridge for an hour before serving. Cream cheese will hold its shape better than Quark.

Devlin's Salted Caramel Truffles

Perfect at any time of year and for any occasion, these are easy to make and are so luscious that they just melt in the mouth! These truffles are a wonderful Easter gift for adults and children.

Chill: minimum one hour in fridge

Ingredients:
300ml whipping cream
300g chocolate (dark, milk or white - it's your choice)
1 tbsp. butter (organic and best quality if you can)
1 tsp. vanilla essence

1tsp. salted caramel essence

Caramel pieces (to put in the middle of each truffle or small pieces of honeycomb)

Cocoa powder for dusting (and/or any other toppings of your choice)

Method:

Finely chop the chocolate (use a bar not buttons, to get the right consistency).

Heat the cream but do not let it boil then pour the hot cream over the chocolate and stir until it melts.

Add the butter and stir or whisk the mixture until it is smooth and shiny. Add the vanilla and caramel essence and mix.

Place in a lined tin or in a glass bowl and put in the fridge to cool for at least an hour.

Using a warm spoon or melon baller, scoop out small amounts from the ganache and roll into bite sized balls.

Push the caramel piece into the middle and re-roll.

Coat each truffle by rolling in cocoa powder, chopped nuts, sprinkles, freeze dried fruits, melted chocolate, edible glitter or whatever takes your fancy. Tambo and Alice like popping candy on theirs!

They will keep for a week in the fridge (try to keep them as cool as you can, at all times, or they start to melt).

Mrs B's tip:

Lightly coat your hands in coconut oil as it makes the rolling of the balls easier.

Stella's Chocolate Nutty Squares

Featured in Chapter 28, these are very addictive and oh so calorific! I cut them into very small squares and try not to eat them all myself! These yummy treats are great because you don't need to bake them - just pop them into the fridge for an hour or for half an hour in the freezer - then cut them up into squares and serve! They'll also keep for several days in an air tight container (but with Lucy, Sophie, me and the kids - they don't last long at all!). You'll need a square tin about 20cm by 20cm and some baking parchment to line it with.

Chocolate Nutty Squares

Chill: one hour in fridge or half an hour in the freezer

Ingredients:
150g butter (organic and best quality if you can)
200g milk chocolate - break into pieces and melt over a bain-marie
250g digestive biscuits (I use low calorie ones to keep the waistline a little smaller!)
150g soft brown sugar
50g coconut sugar (this makes them a little healthier but you can just use more brown sugar)
300g crunchy peanut butter (you can use crunchy almond or cashew nut butter)
2 tsp. vanilla extract
2 tsp. salted caramel essence to put into the chocolate topping (optional)

Method:
Melt the butter and peanut butter in a pan then add the first teaspoon of vanilla essence.
Blitz the biscuits in a food processor and mix in the sugar.
Combine the butter mixture with the dry ingredients and pour into the lined tin. Pat it down and compress it (you can use the end of a rolling pin to do this).
Melt most of the chocolate over a bain-marie (leave yourself 2 - 3 squares).
When the chocolate has melted, take it off the heat and add the final squares, stirring them in until they also melt - this will keep your chocolate nice and shiny.
Add the other teaspoon of vanilla extract and the salted caramel essence to the chocolate.
Pour the chocolate evenly over the peanut biscuit mixture so that it is all covered.
Put in the fridge for one hour or the freezer for half an hour.
Cut into squares and pop in an airtight container or serve.

Mrs B's tip:
For a fancy effect you could melt dark, milk and white chocolate separately and then swirl together over the top to create a marble effect!

Strawberries and Cream Shortbreads

Minnie and Lucy tuck into these delicious light crumbly shortbread biscuits in Chapter 34. These are special shortbreads as you will see, my loves, because they are made with a decadent dollop of clotted cream. In the café I serve them with fresh strawberries and some extra cream but they are also tempting all by themselves or with a coating of white chocolate. You will need a baking sheet lined with parchment paper. Take your butter out of the fridge an hour or so in advance so that it is at room temperature.

Bake: 160 degrees C for 25 minutes

Ingredients:
100g clotted cream
100g softened butter
100g caster sugar
1 tsp. vanilla essence
300g plain flour
9g freeze dried strawberry pieces (you can use more but often the packets are 9g)
150g white chocolate (optional)

Method:
Beat together the cream, butter, sugar and vanilla essence using an electric mixer until fluffy and light.
Add the sifted flour and mix until it resembles a crumble mixture.
Stir in the freeze dried strawberry pieces.
Bring it together using your hands to form a dough and roll out (about ½ inch thick) with a rolling pin (flour the bench, rolling pin and your hands to stop it sticking).
Using whatever shape or size of cutter you would like your biscuits to be, cut out and put them on the parchment paper leaving small gaps between them.
Keep reforming the dough and cutting more until you have used it all up.
Bake at 160 degrees C for 15-20 minutes until the edges are lightly golden.

Place on a cooling rack until completely cool.

Melt the white chocolate over a bain- marie.

Dip the biscuits in the chocolate or using a spoon wave the chocolate over the biscuits to create a zigzag line effect.

Pop them into an air tight container and they will last about a week.

Mrs B's tip:

When kneading the dough, do it quickly and just pull together, do not over knead or the biscuits will lose their shortness. When reforming to cut again, just pull together and press gently.

I'd love to see your bakes so pop your pictures on the Little Eden Dear Readers page on Facebook and show us what you've made!

Dear Readers

Thank you for reading Little Eden Book One and now Book Two. I hope you enjoyed them both and that you are wondering what will happen next in Book Three!

The friends still have a long way to go to raise the money needed to save the town and have just eighteen months left to raise it in. Will the mysterious Uncle Frith ever be found? Will Tobi and Sophie stay together? What lies in wait for them at Malinwick Manor? Is it haunted or not?

Please feel free to join me on social media and don't forget to come and visit the little Etsy shop. You can walk through Little Eden in pictures on Pinterest and listen to the soundtracks on my blog. All my links can be found at https://linktr.ee/ktkingbooks

If you try any of the recipes I'd love to see your bakes or read your comments on the Little Eden Dear Readers Facebook page which you are welcome to join to meet other readers and see all the latest news from Little Eden.

Please consider leaving a review on-line on Amazon as reviews help other readers find Little Eden books and they mean so much to me too.

You can also rent copies of Little Eden Books from your local library by requesting they purchase a copy and you can buy them at WHSmith, Waterstones and other retailers.

Love KT x

Dear Book Club readers,

I'm thrilled you're going to be reading Little Eden in your book club. Please get in touch and let me know where you are and a bit about yourselves. I love to hear from my dear readers! Connect with me via my link tree - https://linktr.ee/ktkingbooks.

Don't forget - you could try some of the recipes and bring your bakes along to your book club meeting. I'd love to see photos of your bakes - you can post them on the Little Eden Dear Readers Facebook Page which you are really welcome to join. There are links to all the songs mentioned in Little Eden on my blog https://ktkingbooks.wordpress.com/ so you can listen to the soundtrack as you read or bake!

Hope you enjoy the second instalment of Little Eden and that you'll look out for Book Three coming soon!

Love KT xx

Here are some question suggestions to get you started...

- ❖ How did the book make you feel when you first started reading it?
- ❖ Did you feel you got to know the town of Little Eden a little better?
- ❖ Which characters did you identify with the most this time?
- ❖ Did you feel there were plot twists and cliff-hangers? Did the switching between time-lines add to the storytelling? Which parts of the story stood out to you and why?
- ❖ Did you believe in the supernatural elements or did you think they were fictional? Have you ever had a psychic or supernatural experience of your own? Do you believe that prayer works? Have you tried meditation or prayer yourself?
- ❖ Did the characters behaviour or beliefs help you to change your opinions about anything or anyone in your life?

Printed in Poland
by Amazon Fulfillment
Poland Sp. z o.o., Wrocław